THE LAST
HOUSE OFFICER

*To Patricia Hewitt,
without whom this book would
have been simply impossible*

THE LAST HOUSE OFFICER

Gwyn
Williams

y Lolfa

First impression: 2015
© Gwyn Williams & Y Lolfa Cyf., 2015

Cover design: Tanwen Haf

ISBN: 978 1 78461 122 4

Published and printed in Wales
on paper from well-maintained forests by
Y Lolfa Cyf., Talybont, Ceredigion SY24 5HE
e-mail ylolfa@ylolfa.com
website www.ylolfa.com
tel 01970 832 304
fax 832 782

CHAPTER 1

The phone call

P HONE CALLS AFTER midnight are never good news. In fact phone calls at any time are never pleasant, thought Owen as he ran to answer the phone before the kids woke up. Even though he was half asleep – a condition that applied to Owen for much of the day anyway – he could make out that the lady on the other end of the line was talking a foreign language and, without a word, handed the phone to Padma who was by now fully awake next to him. Even though he could make out none of the conversation, he could tell by the way Padma cradled the phone and her expression of pain that he would not be getting much sleep that night, and with a long day of clinics ahead of him along with four days in a row of being on call, his stress levels began to increase.

Padma's mother had been unwell for many months with diabetic problems but over the past few weeks her condition had been more tenuous than ever due to an abscess in her leg.

'She's gone unconscious, not responding at all to Chechi!' Padma said after the end of the phone call. With tears in her eyes she said she'd told her sister to call an ambulance. Not knowing exactly the best thing to say in those circumstances, Owen tried to smile in what he assumed was a supportive manner.

'My poor mother. I need to go out there, I need to go to Malaysia to see her. Why did I put it off so long!'

Owen was quiet at this point as it was he who had discouraged her visit home earlier in the month on grounds of cost and sheer inconvenience.

'She was getting better then, she was getting better,' Owen said, more to himself than anyone else.

As they lay silently in bed the phone rang once more. More frequent talking this time and even some shouting. Owen was nervous. He had to be awake in four hours and they had been up late watching an episode of *The Apprentice* they had taped from earlier.

Suddenly Padma turned to Owen. 'I'm talking to the doctor. They want to intubate her; what about infection? Can they do it?'

Owen's mind stalled at this. 'Infection' was all he managed to force out from his mouth, against the will of his malfunctioning brain and utter disconnection with the gravity of events suddenly overpowering the bedroom, which had been so peaceful until a few minutes ago. His indecision, and indeed incomprehension, was of only momentary concern to Padma who began bellowing down the phone in Malayalam once more.

Owen felt bad that he had stopped Padma from visiting her mother now that this new hell was unfolding. As the wheels of his mind slowly started to turn he realised she should visit as soon as possible. He leant over. 'Tell them to intubate her,' he said. Perhaps she'd stay alive long enough for Padma to say her last goodbyes. As Owen donned his slippers and ambled slowly down the stairs to fire up the computer, he pushed that ugly herniating concern about his lack of sleep back into the cerebral compartment from which it was trying to escape.

As the industrial whirr of the large, and by now several years old, PC sprang into life, Padma came crashing into the room and pressed her face into his chest. They stood there in the eerie light cast by the computer's frozen start-up screen with nothing to be heard over the hoovering inferno of the hard drive save for Padma's sobs. Padma had wanted a new machine for many years but Owen's stubborn logic had dictated that it was neither cost-effective nor practical. But now that it was needed more than ever for access to the Malaysia Airlines website, the only information that was forthcoming was the 'Welcome to Windows' message on a blue background. Too tired to use this as one of her usual excuses for ridiculing her husband's thrifty nature, Padma detached herself and sat on the sofa, head in her hands.

Then the phone rang again. Both of them knew why. Padma muttered a few words and then hung up, letting out an unearthly scream of despair that caught Owen by complete surprise. Crouching under the computer desk attempting to find the source of the computer malfunction by aimlessly disconnecting then reconnecting wires at random, he abruptly stood up and almost knocked himself unconscious on the sharp edge of the wooden desk. As he rolled about on the floor clutching his occiput in agony he noticed a figure standing above him.

'I need to go home and will go whether you can find a cheap ticket or not,' it said.

Memories of Malaysia

As he lay with his back against the cool living room carpet staring at the wonky bulb in the chandelier overhead, Owen was surprised to realise that he was sad at the passing of his mother-in-law. The first time he visited her he had been dragged over for an introduction when it had become clear that he would be shoehorned into a marriage in the near future. Not wishing to upset any apple carts, or so Owen thought, he had agreed to fly to Southeast Asia only a few months into his relationship with Padma. Although they were only there for two weeks, it felt to Owen like a form of those enhanced interrogation techniques the CIA had developed at Guantanamo. Exhausted from a thirteen-hour flight and even more grumpy than usual, he was distressed to find Padma had become a completely different person just as soon as they had set foot in the arrivals hall of Kuala Lumpur International Airport. Even her accent changed. She barked orders at baggage handlers and taxi drivers in a language completely incomprehensible to Owen and seemed intent on telling him off at every available opportunity.

'Sit in the front you fool,' Padma barked as they entered their taxi. Owen fancied Padma was distressed that he seemed to utterly misjudge every social function he was meant to fulfil.

'I always sit in the back of taxis,' Owen said.

'Not in Malaysia. Only servants sit in the back.'

'You're in the back.'

The look Padma gave in response was enough to make Owen give up further reasonable discussion. Instead he tried to make conversation with the driver.

'So do you live nearby?'

'No, sir,' the driver replied. 'Ampang.' Owen was dismayed that his demonstration of worker solidarity in Malaysia had led down a blind alley at the first turn. Where was Ampang? Was it humanly possible to know less about a place than he knew about Ampang? Was Ampang even a place?

'Is it nice there?' he managed to say, without a great sense of confidence in a useful response.

'Yes.'

There it was. Owen closed his eyes, lay back in the seat and tried to sleep. When he awoke they'd reached a squat single-story terraced house in a rather dilapidated district which seemed to be hotter than the inside of a baked potato. An ineffective series of fans pushed stifling hot air around the house to no obvious effect, so far as Owen could see, and the only air conditioning unit in the house was located in one of the bedrooms. It had such an impossible task ahead of it that the only area that was even vaguely cooled by its ear-splitting rumblings amounted to about three square feet directly below it. Owen was pretty soon convinced that his Welsh blood was fundamentally incapable of surviving such overheated torment and found the only true chance of survival he had was spending every waking moment on his back on the tile floor under the fan or under the air conditioning unit at full power.

If Anita, Padma's mother, was surprised at her daughter's choice of suitor she did not show it. She was raised to accept the world as it was and to question nothing. She seemed to Owen to be fundamentally different to her headstrong daughter and although she seemed to disagree with Padma's modern ways her unquestioning acceptance of unpleasantness meant she could do little about it. After receiving her daughter and future son-in-law, she retreated into her kitchen to make chai. As she was boiling the kettle her daughter was marching around the kitchen updating her forcefully about how wonderful her new life in the United Kingdom was turning out, and how her daughter's fiancé was some top surgeon, very senior, and she was also a very senior nurse. She lived in a really fancy flat in London.

Anita silently stirred the chai and wordlessly carried the tray to one of the bedrooms. Her habit was to give the tea to the men of the house first but Owen was not in the kitchen. In fact he hadn't left the bedroom since he had arrived an hour and a half ago. There he was, sitting morosely under the air conditioner. She handed him the tea and as she did so he started speaking to her in English, a language with which she was unfamiliar. Perhaps not wishing to offend, she listened carefully with what she might have thought was polite attention and when he appeared finished, she nodded and left for the kitchen. When she returned the one-sided conversation with her daughter had turned into a tirade about how untidy and unclean her house was, with various other failings thrown in. She handed her the tea and sat down heavily in a green plastic kitchen chair.

Suddenly her daughter suggested selling the house and that was a suggestion Padma knew Anita could not keep quiet about.

'You can't sell this house,' she said.

'It's not your house, mother. Father left it to me when he died. It's better this way anyway, as you're getting old and can't manage.'

'You would put me in a nursing home? Terrible. Really terrible. A terrible daughter. Shame on you.'

'Shame on you not me,' Padma raised her voice. Although she, in all probability, had no intention of putting her in a nursing home, she seemed to resent being told that the option was closed to her. Padma always gave the impression that all options should be open to her at all times. Nobody should try and limit her options, no matter what. 'I send you money and you do nothing. You never call me.'

As she went on Anita seemed to grow weary and she became quiet once more. But although she was tired she gave the impression she was pleased her daughter was back home again. Padma was more feisty than ever and Owen reckoned Anita could never match her spirit but yes, she seemed pleased her family, her daughter, had returned. Her and her peculiar fiancé.

Annual leave

Having wasted precious moments daydreaming Owen suddenly sprang to life and ascended the stairs. As he did so he remembered reading about some study claiming that all human actions are in fact involuntary, with sophisticated cerebral processing giving the illusion of free will in the world. The article stated that our actions are decided three seconds before we become aware of our conscious decision and Owen realised that this must be true as it seemed almost inexplicable to him why he would get up from the safety of the downstairs carpet to enter his bedroom and face a difficult emotional situation with Padma, yet here he was climbing the stairs. Owen hated emotions. Not that he didn't feel them himself, more that the emotions of others set in motion complicated trains of thought that required Owen to make unfamiliar decisions. Unfamiliar decisions stressed Owen. Many things stressed Owen, in fact. Perhaps to labour a point, Owen was easily stressed.

As Padma wept in his arms and screamed like a war widow, Owen's mind inexorably drifted to the conversation he knew would face him in a few short hours with the ophthalmology department where he worked in his local hospital. What was the procedure in such circumstances? He obviously couldn't go to work. He might even kill somebody. Owen corrected himself. Ophthalmologists rarely got that sort of responsibility thrust upon them, which was precisely why Owen was an ophthalmologist. Although temporarily comforted by this thought, he suddenly imagined a patient blinded by some mistake he'd make in the morning, induced by sleep deprivation, and shuddered. As he thought again about the procedure involved in getting emergency time off work, he became stressed again as this was new to him. Suddenly he became aware that something was needed from him.

'You think that's possible?' Padma had said, looking straight at him.

Not knowing what was being asked of him and not wanting to admit his mind had been elsewhere, Owen smiled and said, 'Anything is possible, my baby,' in what he assumed was a soothing tone.

Padma smiled a weak smile. 'I was afraid you'd say no, what with the cost and all.'

Owen's spirits dropped to new lows. What had he agreed to now? Had he actually agreed to anything in fact?

'A month in India to take the ashes to Varanasi would be best this year or next?'

'A month in India,' Owen repeated softly, the hideous multifaceted implications of such a thing causing his mind to become detached from its moorings and drift a while in a soothing sea of images of funeral pyres burning in a myriad of exotic looking temples. Including, bizarrely, an image of Dame Judi Dench, the presence of which Owen couldn't really explain to himself.

After a while they both lay down silently on the bed in the dark, saying nothing but holding each other's hands, thinking to themselves. Padma about the loss of her beloved mother and how she had let her down, and Owen about the upcoming phone call, who he needed to speak to and what he'd say.

Owen reckoned Padma had regretted putting Anita in a nursing home, though she never said so. Her sister had done so upon her advice three weeks previously due to the extensive nursing requirements brought on by lack of mobility and an open discharging wound on her leg following surgery on the abscess. Her sister was unable to cope, being in her sixties herself, and Padma felt she couldn't go herself due to constraints at home. As her condition gently worsened her mother had become increasingly confused and detached from what was happening around her. In fact the only thing she knew with any certainty was that she was in a nursing home and her daughters had betrayed her. This she said with an uncanny regularity – along with the usual delirious stories of day-to-day events that included long dead relatives – every time Padma had phoned her in the final weeks of her life. Padma openly cursed herself for not being more forthright in forcing Owen to pay for a ticket home earlier and now she was paying a higher moral price. Owen ruminated that she must be thinking how she had ended up married to somebody so different to herself.

CHAPTER 2

Solitaire

ONE OF THE first times Owen had ever encountered Padma was in an outpatient clinic at a busy London teaching hospital. She was a nurse assigned to facilitate the smooth running of the orthopaedic pre-operative assessment clinic, where patients about to undergo operations at the hospitals were checked out to see if they had any underlying health problems that could complicate surgery. Padma, who in those days could see importance in everything and glamour in every clinical encounter, loved the chance to say that she was in charge and was making a real difference. Before each shift she'd iron her nurse's uniform, clip on the personal alcohol hand gel dispenser to her right pocket and slip a pocket guide to electrocardiograph interpretation into her left pocket. She would arrive about thirty minutes early to get everything in order and all the patients arranged in the correct places. If anyone important walked into her pre-op clinic Padma rather fancied they'd immediately want to recruit her for some lavish private hospital such as the one she'd worked in back home in Kuala Lumpur.

Owen of course hated this clinic. Only three months out of medical school and he had found he hated pretty much every aspect of hospital medicine. Patients were scientific specimens to be examined in a logical manner, diagnosed with an ailment and treated; or so he thought before he had started work. The bitter reality was that patients never seemed to have anything resembling textbook presentations and that diagnosis relied more on a doctor's charisma with radiology and pathology in getting tests ordered and specimens analysed than any actual knowledge of anything. When the diagnosis was then made, treating patients effectively was beyond the ability of the system in which he worked and this had sent Owen into a tailspin that took him the best part of a year to recover from. Orthopaedics he found particularly stressful. His patients would come with fractures that needed fixing; he would consult his senior colleagues to arrange the appropriate operation, prepare the patient and then watch all kinds of calamities ensue. And when the inevitable occurred and a patient was cancelled for the fifth time because of some mind-bending procedural failure, who was the monkey who had to tell the patient the bad news? The only doctor who had ever seen the actual patient. Owen.

The pre-operative assessment clinic, he felt, was an exercise in intellectual masturbation gone too far. There were endless tick boxes, flowcharts and algorithms that made what should have been a straightforward task into a bureaucratic vision of hell. Goodness knows who had thought it all up. He would arrive as close to being on time as possible – in order not to be late. But in order not to extend the torment one moment longer than was absolutely necessary, he would insist on never arriving early either. In fact staff were frequently slightly puzzled to see a young doctor earnestly reading the patient education posters in the corridor around the time of the start of clinic. Owen had found all manner of minor diversions to pass the precious few minutes between 1.20 p.m. and 1.30 p.m. in the immediate area outside the clinic. He knew for instance that the water cooler tap would remain depressed for four seconds after pressure was released and had worked out the secret of filling a cup of water to as near full as possible without spilling a drop. He knew the number of ceiling tiles in the lobby (522) and the number of wall sockets in the entire length of corridor leading up to the clinic door (thirteen). He even knew the exact length the big damp stain on the side wall extended from the ceiling towards the floor, as he had come back during one of his on-calls with a tape measure.

Unbeknown to him Padma had clocked Owen straight away during her fifth shift in pre-op. She'd met him two months' previously while doing a shift on one of the general surgical wards. A very young looking doctor – no, surgeon in fact – striding across to the reception area in a determined way, hands behind his back. Look at that, he's dropped his bleep! Having a bit of difficulty getting the battery back in. Mumbling something to the auxiliary nurse now about how the casing is damaged in some way and how he needs to get off to switchboard to get it fixed straight away. How important. How handsome.

Owen cursed again under his breath as he re-entered the clinic, now a full twenty minutes late. As he sat down heavily in his chair, the auxiliary entered and announced that only notes for three of his eight patients were available but before he had a chance to say anything else it appeared an elderly Jamaican chap was being led through his door accompanied by at least three morbidly obese female relatives.

'Who is this, nurse?' Owen said in what he assumed was an authoritative tone about three seconds before the auxiliary wordlessly closed his office door and walked away. After helping the elderly gentleman to the coffee-stained purple chair and apologising to the relatives for the absence of any other chairs anywhere in the room, bar his own, he ran off to find the auxiliary. Finding, as usual, the nursing station like the *Marie Celeste*, Owen, out of desperation rather than any real hope of finding anybody, opened the door to sister's office. There, sat in her large leather chair playing Solitaire on the new departmental computer, was Padma.

'Hello, doctor,' Padma said with a confident smile.

Caught off-guard, Owen returned the smile and forgot why he was ever there. Feeling the need to say something, even though he was totally lost for the real and pressing reason for his presence in that room, he managed to say, 'Yes, that is a good computer there. Solitaire. Excellent.'

As soon as Owen closed the door he remembered the Jamaican and grimaced. It was too late to re-enter the room. Totally socially unacceptable. After a brief fruitless search again for the auxiliary, Owen grabbed a blank piece of hospital history paper and returned to his own room to start from the very beginning.

The Sun and Doves

There were around fifteen new pre-registration house officers at the hospital, including Owen. These were junior doctors within a year of graduation. All of them were confused to varying degrees and were learning to cope in their own ways with the realities of clinical medicine. One thing bound them above all else; the Sun and Doves. This was a small pub in a side street just off the road leading to the main hospital entrance which seemed to be frequented mostly by NHS staff from the nearby hospital. The unwritten rule was that every house officer would meet here after the end of duty each day and stay there until it closed.

Owen sat opposite Alex, as he usually did. Alex was the son of a doctor and seemed to Owen to be made for the job. Alex would confidently stride the hospital corridors and make pronouncements that were delivered with such apparent inner knowledge that he made Owen feel rather uneasy at times. Alex was also tall and blond, which somehow made his pronouncements more legitimate in some people's eyes.

'Good day?' Alex said, putting his pint of Kronenbourg 1664

back on the table where it sat in a small puddle of beer – evidence of a prior spillage.

Owen grimaced, as was customary. 'Pre-op' he said, without elaborating.

'Ahh. I was in theatre today.'

Owen grimaced again, but said nothing.

'Mr Whitbread let me do some of the closure actually. Quite tricky.' Alex smiled, noticing Owen's discomfort.

Owen was annoyed at Alex for a reason he could not understand. 'What happened to that patient of yours with the wound infection?'

'Ohhh.' Alex stopped smiling. 'Bloody microbiology messed it up. I spoke with them and they told me to start him on amoxicillin. I did and guess what? Whole leg blew up. Saw him today and he looked like a Michelin man.'

Having supped some more beer, Owen felt bolstered. 'Who did you speak with, that Harvey chap?'

'Er, no. Can't remember the name.' Alex looked at the painting facing him on the wall. 'Funny how these paintings are allowed in here. They're the worst I've ever seen.'

After turning his head and pondering the picture of a man standing on a bridge for a second and finding nothing particularly wrong with it, Owen thought it would be easier to agree, as he freely conceded he knew nothing of art. As he did so Colleen sat down beside him.

'Hi, Owen,' she said.

Owen was genuinely pleased to see her. 'Hello, how are you? Shall I get you one?' he added seeing she was beer-free.

'No thanks. Reshma's bringing one over for me.'

Owen looked at Colleen's tumbling auburn hair longingly. Colleen acknowledged Alex's presence with a cursory nod, while Alex looked disdainfully at her through his beer glass. Noticing that the conversation had suddenly stopped and not really understanding why, Owen thought it would be wise to think of something to say but was unsure what would be appropriate. Before he could stop himself, his unconscious mind, lubricated just enough by Kronenbourg 1664, blurted out, 'I like that picture on the wall of the rubber duck reading that book in the library.'

Colleen smiled. 'Why?'

'Such a clever duck. Probably doing night classes. Reducing his dependency on the welfare state. I bet he's reading up to be an accountant.'

'Accountant!' Colleen snorted. 'Why accountant? Couldn't he be doing something useful to society, such as medicine?'

'Ha. Did you do anything useful today? I was in pre-op so I certainly didn't. Told a fat Londoner to lose weight and a chain-smoking Jamaican to stop smoking. Neither of them will do anything of the sort of course. I also provided an afternoon shift for a morbidly obese auxiliary nurse who did nothing to help me at all, a receptionist who didn't bother getting any notes at all practically and an Indian nurse who spent clinic playing Solitaire.'

'Come on. You got people ready for surgery. They all got blood tests?'

'Yes, I suppose.'

'Well then, what more do you want.'

'The notes would have been nice.'

Alex coughed. 'I took an active part in a total hip replacement myself. Mr Whitbread thought I was a natural.'

'A natural orthopod perhaps,' Reshma said as she sat down next to Colleen handing her a drink. 'Mr Salmon told me about your wound infection. You should speak to micro next time.'

Everyone took notice of Reshma; men in particular. Tall and almost unbelievably attractive, she stood out anywhere she went. Owen thought she was too perfect for this world and it was problematic for him whenever she came to the Sun and Doves. He found it a great trial having conversations with attractive women as the effort always drained him of far too much energy for the experience to be considered pleasant. The biggest problem was the internal monologue Owen was compelled to have with himself every time she spoke with him. This was distracting and Owen was absolutely terrified of making some awful faux pas so would speak in a very artificial way to compensate.

Colleen repeated the story of Owen's pre-op clinic. It struck Owen that Reshma came out so infrequently that this was a special effort on Colleen's part purely for Reshma's benefit. She seemed slightly irked though that Reshma had brought her half a lager rather than a full pint and Owen could not work out if this was because Colleen was considered slightly vulgar in Indian eyes for even asking for a full pint in the first place. Reshma had rather amusingly opted for some fruit juice.

As Colleen told the story, Owen was content to look at the duck picture and let his mind wander but suddenly attention was called to him rather suddenly and uncomfortably when Reshma turned to him enthusiastically and said, 'She's South Indian. She's Keralite, from Kerala, just like me. Though she was brought up in Malaysia.'

Owen panicked. What's Kerala? What was being asked of him? Should he clarify? With time ticking 'Ah, Kerala,' was all Owen could manage to say. Ah, Kerala, Owen repeated to himself, ashamed at what must be considered the amazingly inappropriate lacklustre nature of this comment. Reshma didn't seem to mind though and Owen relaxed a little. But she was still talking and he was looking at her flowing black hair. Listen, you fool, his mind was screaming at him. Her eyes caught his a few times and she smiled as Owen threw in what he hoped were approving nods of understanding into the rather one-sided conversation.

Colleen interrupted. 'Yes I'm sure all that's great but she was playing Solitaire.'

'Everybody needs a soulmate, Owen,' Reshma said directly to him. Owen melted inwardly and looked into her brown inviting eyes. 'If you like her, ask her out. You're really great, you know, and I can help if you like.'

Owen was even more baffled than usual. He watched silently as Reshma took a pen and wrote a few lines of Malayalam on the back of a paper napkin. As she did so, he recalled a conversation he'd had with a genito-urinary registrar at the same hospital when he was a medical student. He'd told him that he himself was from some place in south India, and that this was the best educated state and thus a disproportionate number of Indian doctors in Britain were from there. Must have been Kerala then.

'What does it say?' Owen asked.

'This top one says "I love you", this one says "You are beautiful" and this last one is the same as the top one but in Hindi.'

It seemed rude to ask at this stage what Malayalam was or even why she was writing down these phrases for him on the back of the napkin. He had a vague idea that Reshma assumed he fancied the clinic nurse but could not fathom why anyone would have that impression. Suddenly he felt ashamed that he was the last to realise he fancied the Keralite nurse. Did he? It would be awkward to correct Reshma at this point so he decided to go with the flow.

'Yes. I shall keep this safe and use it when I get the chance.'

'Tell me how it goes of course,' Reshma said, and grinned. She was grinning at him. How lovely. The room around her face became indistinct and for a moment he felt they were the only two people at the table. They were bonding over his apparent feelings for someone completely different but Owen felt he should appreciate the feeling of acceptance nonetheless.

Alex snorted. 'Good luck to you there, mate. I was in clinic with her last week and she kept on interrupting me, passing me the wrong forms and was generally a terrible nurse. Hey ho, she may be good in bed though, eh?' he ended conspiratorially. Not ever being comfortable with this kind of comment and not knowing the accepted ways of responding, Owen took another gulp of beer. 'I've always said you needed to get laid.' Alex went on. 'That's why you're all cynical and wrong about everything.'

'Owen's not cynical,' Reshma said. 'He sees all the beauty in the world.' For the life of him Owen could not have understood how anyone could have got that impression of him. 'You see only operations and surgery and think everything else is worthless.'

'Operations are the only thing that cures. Think about it. Everything else is just treatment.'

'What about antibiotics?' Colleen said.

'Well those too. But nothing else, and even antibiotics don't work very well compared with surgery.'

'Not if you use the wrong ones,' Colleen said.

CHAPTER 3

The Drug Chart

THERE IS NOTHING more stressful than a surgical ward round. Not so much orthopaedic ward rounds, as orthopods know so little medicine that even the most junior house officer can get by on a more or less equal basis with most consultants. That and the fact that most orthopods do so few ward rounds that they rarely see their postoperative patients once the fractured bone has been set. General surgical ward rounds on the other hand are a whole different animal. Owen's first job was as a colorectal house surgeon at the hospital and it was at that time that he first met Padma – and though he would not remember it, Padma would.

He and Alex worked for a team of three consultants who, together, accounted for most of the surgical work of the department. Since starting, he felt so completely lost that he was unsure who he was and what he was doing. His life had been reduced to getting up at half-six to copy all the patients' blood results into a big red file, complete with flow chart. He'd do a house officer ward round, together with Alex, to check everything was alright for the three 'proper' ward rounds, one for each consultant, that would follow during the course of the day. There would be no warning for each ward round. One of the consultants would bleep to say he was ready on Rose Beam ward and he and Alex would have to rush there post-haste. Each ward round would generate tasks and each task would need completing before the registrar ward round in the evening. Sometimes the ward rounds would overlap, run into each other or, depending who the consultant was, take hours to complete. All the while Owen would be getting bleeps from accident and emergency, general practitioners, other wards and from nurses demanding instant action over what Owen considered trivial things. Then there would be bleeps about why the first list of tasks had not been completed, along with a few new tasks for added fun.

Mr Silk's ward rounds were always the most stressful as he would demand speed and instant knowledge about every facet of his patient's condition. In practice such was the turnover and sheer number of patients, it was a genuinely difficult task to know which patients were under the care of each consultant. Even locating the patients was a nightmare, as without warning patients would be transferred to different parts of the ward, or even a different ward entirely. The crushing sense of doom that pervaded Owen's very being during these rounds would grow immeasurably deeper as he led Mr Silk and his retinue toward a patient that his records indicated was his but whose face and bodily features were in complete contrast.

About two months into the job Owen and Alex were leading Mr Silk on a particularly haphazard ward round of Rose Beam as the nurses had been rearranging patients all morning and the team had been on take all week so the patient numbers had ballooned hideously. Mr Silk tutted as Alex struggled to retrieve the correct blood results for a patient and Owen spilled the notes all over the bed.

'What's the urine output?'

Owen scrambled for the chart at the end of the bed – '550mls so far today,' he said in reply.

'What was it over the past hour?'

'It isn't being measured hourly but...'

'Shall I ask the nurses to measure it hourly?' Alex interrupted.

'Yes. You should already have done that.' Mr Silk was irritable and Alex seemed deflated.

Owen scribbled this command on a piece of scrappy paper in a totally illegible scrawl that he would later find himself at odds to decipher.

'What about the obs?'

'BP 140 over 95, sats 95 per cent on air and PR 110 per min,' Owen said

Mr Silk sighed as he peeled back the abdominal dressing to reveal a mucky wound with pus and blood. 'Do a wound swab and start antibiotics,' he said to no one in particular.

Alex's search for the drug chart which should have been at the end of the bed, in order to prescribe the antibiotics, was unsuccessful. He asked a nearby nurse where it was but she ignored him and moved on. Alex added this task to the list of things to do.

In the meantime as Owen led Mr Silk to the next patient across the bay it was with a growing sense of unease that he realised the notes for that patient were not in the notes tray. He apologised and half-ran to the nurses' station to see if he could locate the notes among the haphazard bundle that spilled over every work surface, acutely aware that the timer was ticking on his consultant's patience. 'Where are Mr Rafferty's notes,' he asked the ward clerk in desperation.

The overweight Jamaican rolled her chair back and glared at Owen. 'If you doctors put the notes back properly there would be no prob-lems.'

'Yes, but that doesn't help me at this moment, does it? Have you seen them or not?'

The ward clerk ignored Owen and resumed her idle staring into space. By chance Owen saw the notes under the arm of the ward pharmacist but by the time he'd returned triumphantly to the ward round, Mr Silk and Alex had already finished with that patient and were striding towards the main door to see someone on the high dependency ward. Owen thrust the notes back into the surprised arms of the pharmacist and ran after them. Just as he reached them, a short Indian nurse shouted 'Doctor' so loudly that the three colorectal surgeons stopped and stared back in astonishment at the nurse, now standing hands on hips.

'You forgot to rewrite this drug chart,' she said with a great sense of purpose. After making this announcement she raised with both hands a battered drug chart high over her head. Rewriting drug charts was so far down Owen's list of priorities that he stared back at a loss as to how to best respond to this odd situation. He rather fancied she looked like Moses holding up the Ten Commandments. Mr Silk and Alex looked expectantly at Owen. After putting the appropriate words into his cerebral Google and finding no search results detailing what to say or do in this situation, Owen shrugged and walked away down the corridor with his team.

Halo

Although Owen and Alex both conceded to themselves – but not to each other – that they were two fundamentally different personalities, they had one thing that bound them during this difficult time. Halo. There was a games console present in the doctors' mess, provided by nobody knew who, that had one functioning game and that game was Halo. Alex already had quite extensive gaming experience and was quite pleased to find this one outlet to vent his frustrations. He was irritated by the lack of surgical opportunities that had materialised so far and annoyed by his fellow house surgeon in some unfathomable way. What better way to express his feelings than by shooting aliens in the face and stealing their spacecraft?

In the beginning he was annoyed when Owen arrived in the

evening and asked to try out the two-player game. Owen would often get lost on the surface of the Halo world and was as likely to shoot Alex as the infected swarm of mutants that would attack them in the rare event that the two of them would be in the same location. During one memorable game only a week into their joint gaming bonding experience, Owen managed to get his spacecraft wedged in a computer anomaly in a cliff face that confused the console so much that Alex's player was rendered immobile but somehow immortal.

Owen was thrilled in some inner childlike way at having such easy access to modern computer games. As he grew up, his parents, who always emphasised the importance of education over entertainment, had heavily discouraged such squandering of time and money. Now that he had access to a state-of-the-art game, he felt duty bound to give it a whirl. Whenever he finished his clinical work, which was usually around 8 p.m. when he wasn't on call, he'd wander up to the mess to have a quick game of Halo before heading off to the Sun and Doves. He reckoned his time not spent in actual work was so limited it should be crammed as full of distracting activities as possible, and there were very few things more wondrous to him than the Halo universe. He'd marvel at the graphics as the Flood devoured him, relying in no small measure on Alex's superior warrior experience to kill the vast majority of the attacking swarm in order to survive to the next level.

Even though Alex was constantly amazed at the poor progress Owen made in knowing how to handle a firearm and his inability to read the signals on the screen that indicated varying hazards and rewards, he seemed to grow fond of the time they'd spend together attempting to save the universe from destruction at the hands of the Covenant. Owen also respected his colleague's skills and was happy to be a part of something new. Over the weeks they advanced together, saving their progress all the time, until it became clear that it might be possible to complete the game before their stint in the hospital came to an end.

Colleen also seemed quite surprised at the friendship that seemed to be developing between Alex and Owen. One night she entered the mess quite late to grab a bite to eat during an on-call and noticed the eerie glow of a game in progress projected on the wall facing her. She silently looked at the two house surgeons transfixed by the intergalactic war being played out of which they were such a vital part, listening to Alex instructing Owen where to fire and protecting him from attack. She greeted them both more than once but the two warriors did not respond.

As the completion of the game appeared to be in sight Owen noticed his dreams changing. Though he still had the recurring nightmare of an endless Mr Silk ward round and was plagued by thoughts of blood tests that needed to be checked and radiology requests that needed to be submitted and countersigned by a radiologist, the Halo world had started to invade his very soul. He found himself pondering who the Forerunners were and questions regarding the functioning of the Halo device itself began to assume a strangely disproportionate importance.

When the day of victory finally came, its utter success took Owen and Alex by complete surprise. Having made significant gains the previous evening, the colorectal house officers ran to the mess at every spare opportunity during the day to further their progress. At approximately 4.20 p.m., with both their bleeps incandescent with rage, Alex drove the car carrying them both along the obstacle course that stood in their way and made a huge leap over a gigantic chasm, landing safely on the other side. Owen had fallen out of the vehicle some way back but their tied destiny in the game meant that he disappeared and reappeared every so often at points relatively close to Alex, though not, sadly, in the speeding vehicle itself. As the two avatars celebrated their ultimate success and the small crowd that had gathered around the sofa shouted their approval, Owen felt genuinely happy. Alex also seemed satisfied and in an unguarded moment slapped Owen on the back and made a gorilla-like noise. Though Owen was mildly confused by this he did not let it stand in the way of an overly elaborate embrace of Colleen that under normal circumstances his overdeveloped sense of propriety would have rendered out of the question. She blushed as Owen kissed her forcefully on her left cheek and high-fived Alex.

The Date

Following his dramatic success at completing Halo, Owen danced to Rose Beam ward in a state of excitement he had not quite experienced to the same level before or since. As he passed the hospital shop, a rather shabby and overcrowded space that only seemed to stock the most obscure brands of food imaginable, he ran straight into Padma as she left the shop clutching an overpriced tube of Pringles.

'Hello there,' Owen declared in a confident tone that surprised even him. 'Pringles. I love Pringles myself, you know. You're that Indian nurse from pre-op, aren't you?'

Padma flinched. Owen would later learn that she hated being called Indian. Indians from India she considered unrefined and beneath her Malaysian sensitivities. Normally she would have excoriated someone for such a blatant insult but seeing the smiling young doctor looking down at her, possibly checking out her breasts in fact, she decided to let it go. She smiled back. 'No, I'm actually from Malaysia.'

'Malaysia,' Owen repeated with enthusiasm. 'I've been there. Very hot.'

'I'm actually a Malaysian Keralite though.' She smiled.

Owen remembered Reshma's comment and cursed the fact that he hadn't got his napkin with the Malayalam on it.

'Anyway, must dash as I've got around 36,000 bleeps to answer,' was all he could come up with.

Padma, perhaps feeling unusually moved; seized her chance. She was probably correct to do so as Owen was in a mood the likes of which she herself would never see again, so just before he turned to go she made her stand. 'Do you want to come to my place tonight for food?'

Owen did not consider the implications of this superficially innocent statement and felt invincible at that moment in time. 'Yes, that sounds just great,' he shouted back before bounding the stairs to the first floor three at a time. He had some vague sense that he knew neither her telephone number nor address, or even her name come to that. This realisation was not enough to turn him around however and he completed his trip to Rose Beam ward and started working through the extensive list of jobs the nurses had compiled in anger and irritation at not receiving instant satisfaction from their demands of the junior medical staff during their secret game of Halo. As he started rewriting a drug chart, he was bleeped by Padma, who furnished him with all the necessary details. By this stage the euphoria of victory had started to abate and Owen was nervous as to what he had agreed to and unsure what to do. He hated dates and had traditionally been very bad at them.

Just as these thoughts coursed through his brain, he was bleeped again. This time he was relieved to find it was Colleen.

'Do you want to come out to the Sea Cow tonight for food?'

'I'd love to,' Owen said, 'but it seems I've somehow ended up with a date this evening. I don't know how it happened. So no, sorry. Perhaps tomorrow.'

'Shit,' was the only other word he heard before the line went dead.

The dinner was at 7.30 that evening, only an hour-and-a-half in the future. Owen's sense of panic increased as his job list diminished and he found he completed all his tasks with only ten minutes to spare. There would be no time to shower, change or do anything fancy. Was a man required to bring flowers to the first date? He did not know, but previous date experiences had been a mixed bag at best, with flowers failing to retrieve a battle lost from the very beginning.

He remembered a date in his third year of medical school where he had arranged the dinner for a day the following week. His brain tortured his soul for every minute of the intervening six days until by the time the date occurred his speech was overly planned and topics of conversation artificial and dull. The pre-planned jokes did not amuse and his date, an attractive student from the year below, made an excuse and left before dessert. That incident had shaken Owen badly and he was very wary of repeating it. In fact he was very wary of dates, and women generally; not understanding them and thinking in some unspoken way that he was being mocked at some out-of-tune frequency. The women he preferred were those he essentially treated like men, though he wasn't overly relaxed with men either. Basically Owen was not relaxed with anyone at any point in time.

Running up the hill to her apartment, Owen sensed that Padma would not appreciate a sweaty Welshman who hadn't even bothered to wash coming to have food at her place. What if she wanted more than food? Owen was relaxed about this, for a change. The chances of a beautiful girl like her wanting anything but food with him, especially as he appeared now, was highly unlikely. In fact, he told himself, he'd go through with the date, it would be a disaster as usual, and it would be a good story to entertain his friends with at the Sun and Doves the following evening.

Reaching her door, he raised his right arm and quickly smelled his axilla. Rank. It would have to do though. He pushed her bell and within a few seconds a distinctly off-duty Padma opened the door. Her rich long black hair flowed over her shoulders and she looked so pretty Owen felt he ought to perhaps mumble an apology and leave immediately. To his surprise though she greeted him warmly and opened the door for him to enter.

CHAPTER 4

Square Plates

P ADMA WAS PLEASED to see the young doctor at her door and although he looked rather worse for wear she concluded that this was probably because he was busy saving lives at the hospital. She had spent a long time deciding the correct clothing to wear and was rather pleased her blue dress was ready and her hair looked so good. Wanting to appear cultured and intellectual, she had left open her one and only copy of the *British Medical Journal*, snaffled from the coffee table of the junior doctor's coffee room and now placed right on the table where she was sure Owen would spot it. The choice of cutlery was also of grave importance and she had spent a good eight minutes deciding if the Edmonton set looked superior to the other set whose name she did not know. Among other things Padma was confident that good middle-class types like Dr Owen would appreciate fine plates and so had taken the trouble to remove the vast collection of plates her flat cupboard held in order to remove two square plates from the very bottom. Square plates! Padma thought to herself excitedly as she washed them in the sink. He'll be so impressed!

As Owen sat down he did indeed survey the square plate and was interested. Padma excused herself and disappeared into the kitchen to finish preparing dinner but her last glimpse of Owen as she did so confirmed her belief that her choice of plate had been very wise. He seemed to be grasping the plate with both hands and examining it with what appeared to be great attention. As she was thinking happy thoughts finishing up in the kitchen, Owen lifted the plate up and turned it over to see who had designed it. He had read somewhere before that plates carried some kind of identifiable mark, though he was unsure what is was meant to look like and where it should be located. He was nervous and was amazed at how sweaty his hands had become. Having turned the plate, and being completely unable to make head or tail of the peculiar symbol underneath, he flipped the plate back over and promptly dropped it on the carpeted floor. Owen was horrified as he discovered that it had cracked exactly in half and although this further convinced him his luck on dates was unlikely to change in the near future, he managed to place both halves back on the table without obvious external sign that and damage had occurred.

As Padma returned to the table he was struck at how vulnerable she looked. How could someone so small survive in this world? She smiled shyly as she placed two potatoes on his plate, along with some unknown meat followed by some kind of liquid.

'I don't like doctors,' Padma said, 'but I like the look of you. Such nice shoulders you have!'

Owen was unsure how to respond to this but sensing that some kind of compliment was in order he said, 'Yes, and you look very...' Having regretted starting this sentence Owen then said the first thing that came into his mind, which turned out to be the wrong thing. 'Indian.'

Padma grimaced. 'I am not Indian. I am Malaysian, and I have told you this before.'

Owen was upset at this turn of events but felt he should continue with the compliments nevertheless. 'I really like your long hair. All women should have long hair you know.' Padma did not say anything and Owen started clutching at straws. 'I really like your square plates!'

Padma visibly relaxed and grinned broadly at Owen.

'Taste the food,' she said in what she assumed was a seductive manner.

Owen skewered a potato with his fork and as he bisected it with his knife, he must have used a little more force than necessary as one side of the broken plate moved a millimetre apart from its sibling. As Owen looked at his food he immediately spotted the parting of the Red Sea that was liquid escaping from his plate onto the table. 'Mmm lovely food,' Owen said and tried to push the two halves of the plate together again without arousing attention. 'Really great, just like you.' Why had he said that? That didn't even make sense; how could a person be like food?

Padma was pleased. 'Do you want any wine?' she said.

'Ach no,' Owen said a little louder than expected as he had just noticed a circular wet stain spreading on the tablecloth along with an almost total lack of liquid on his plate. And if this was not alarming enough the plate had moved so that the pattern on both halves no longer matched. He hurriedly shoved potatoes and meat from the periphery to the centre to cover up the fracture. 'So tell me, how long have you worked at the hospital?'

'About six months. You know a cardiologist asked me out a few weeks ago. I said no of course. Why go out with a doctor? I could have any doctor, I imagine, but I turned him down. He was ugly. I like you a lot.' She paused for effect, having rehearsed this line for the past two hours. 'What are you really thinking about right now, doctor?'

A distracted and somewhat stressed Owen, who had not really been paying attention, was slightly relieved by this comment. 'Wouldn't you know it? I think the plate has spontaneously broken in half.'

Dr Cabinet's Round

Owen felt the date had been a fairly typical one for him and the next day, as he did his own ward round, he'd visibly grimace as memories of the previous evening resurfaced. Thursday was a special day for him and all the other house officers as Dr Cabinet did her ward round at 2 p.m. every week on this day. The elderly care consultant would spend a few hours inspecting patients selected by all the orthopaedic house officers to see if any were eligible for transfer to her own ward. This was important, as one more patient for Dr Cabinet was one less to look after, and much time would be spent selecting potential patients and swotting up on all their details so she'd have no earthly reason to say no. Often house officers would compete against each other as they all knew that Dr Cabinet would only ever accept a maximum of around five each week.

Owen was usually very keen on getting as many of his patients transferred as was physically possible; a source of much irritation for Alex who considered it his duty to win every competition, this one included. At five minutes to two Alex met up with Owen and Colleen at the entrance to David Black ward, the biggest of three orthopaedic wards. Alex could tell Owen was distracted.

'Got your list ready?' Alex said.

'Yes,' Owen said simply, staring at a scrap of paper bearing the name of only one patient.

'Come on, mate, what's wrong?'

'He went on a date last night,' Colleen said.

'Whoa! Well done. No wonder you're tired. Who with?'

'The Indian nurse from pre-op,' Colleen answered again.

'Ha. She's a terrible nurse. Doesn't know what a Q-wave is on an ECG. Very slow with patients.' As Owen still did not respond Alex tried again. 'I'd do her though.'

Owen looked at Alex. He was unsure what response was needed here but was too tired to think of the options. He had become melancholic at the failure of the date and convinced he would never get married. He'd probably end up hurling himself off the roof of the hospital as an old man married to his loathsome job as he'd nothing else to live for. Why did he not succeed? What was he doing wrong? Should he have tried to kiss her as he left last night? She hadn't asked him for another date.

'You got your list?' Owen managed to say in an effort to move away from having to think about painful date-based thoughts.

Alex seemed momentarily confused. 'Ah yes. I think I'm going to win today. I've put every single one of my patients on my list!'

'You idiot,' Colleen said. 'If you do that you'll just annoy her again. Remember that time you took her to see that patient who'd just dislocated her new hip? She only wants to see patients she can take.' Colleen pointed towards a man in an Ilizarov frame in a bed facing them. 'See that guy. He's yours. She doesn't take anybody with visible metalwork. Take him off the list or I'll take you off the list.'

'That doesn't even make sense. I am not on my own list. Besides if that fat bitch of a medic doesn't take at least half my patients…' Alex did not finish his sentence as he could see the rolling form of Dr Cabinet push open the far door and stride menacingly towards them. As menacingly as a short plump female doctor could, anyway.

'I've got a meeting at 3.30 so we'd better be quick. You first.' Dr Cabinet jabbed a thick index finger at Colleen. 'Who do you have for me?'

Colleen led the consultant to an elderly woman sitting up in bed drinking what from a distance looked like tea. But as they got closer Owen peered at the liquid and saw that it was grey. What drinkable liquid is grey? Owen thought.

'This lady is a seventy-five year old lady, day seven post fractured NOF who...'

'Fractured NECK OF FEMUR,' Dr Cabinet bellowed. She hated acronyms. 'Continue.'

'She is recovering well. She needs a social package and we're waiting for that. Otherwise no problems.'

'Let me be the judge of that.' Dr Cabinet snatched the drug chart from the end of the bed and jabbed at it violently. 'Why is she on bendroflumethiazide? Why no angiotensin-converting enzyme inhibitors?'

Colleen hesitated. 'That's what she came in on. I think she had an MI, sorry, myocardial infarction, a year or two ago.' As she said this Owen caught the old lady's eyes. He was saddened that an elderly lady was reduced to trying to make out what everybody was saying about her, having not been addressed directly as yet and too intimidated to ask anything.

Dr Cabinet was furtively rummaging around in the notes while Colleen looked helplessly on.

'She's had a bypass and is already on Ramipril. Why is she not prescribed it?' As Colleen struggled to answer, Alex grinned broadly at Owen. 'This will not do. Get the patient worked up before my ward round. You should know that by now. You have anyone else?'

'Ah, yes.' Leading the team toward the far end of the ward, Colleen tried once more to look impressive. 'This man has been through a lot. He's eighty-two, fell down the bottom three stairs at home and fractured both his ankles two weeks ago. Had to drag himself next door to alert his neighbour as his phone wasn't working. Doing well post op but a lot of physio ahead.'

Dr Cabinet looked pleased. 'That's how people survive in this world. If you don't fight you don't win. How else can you become a senior elderly care consultant in a male-dominated London teaching hospital, eh?'

The three house officers obviously had not understood her point as they showed no reaction whatsoever. 'FIGHT,' Dr Cabinet roared. But Owen had understood. The three doctors looked on with amazement as Owen mumbled something unintelligible and ran off the ward.

As he passed the first patient on the way out she shouted at him. 'What's going on, doctor?'

'Fight,' Owen replied. 'Fight fight against the dying of the light!'

Finding Padma

As Owen jumped down the steps three at a time he cursed himself. Rage, he repeated to himself. It's rage rage against the dying of the light. Why did he keep getting it wrong? He was Welsh after all, as was Dylan Jones. No, Thomas. Pah.

He knew he had to find Padma. He'd never fought before for a girl before but knew he needed to now. It did not make any logical sense why, and the lack of logic stressed Owen. As all these thoughts churned away in his mind, he found himself looking at the sandwich section of the Friends' shop. Remembering his mission, he tore off again to orthopaedic pre-op. As he approached the door he suddenly froze. The stain on the wall outside must have been a full three inches longer. It must have been the extra rain last night. Becoming animated again, he burst through the door and ran towards sister's office. He was disappointed to see an anaemic-looking auxiliary using the computer to check her email.

'Where is Padma?'

'Who?'

'The Indian nurse from the clinic here.'

'Who's that then?'

'Padma.'

'Never heard of her. I think you got the name wrong.'

Owen closed the door. Where to now?

'Aha!' Owen shouted out loud. He had remembered Padma mentioning the night before a seminar she was attending at the education centre that day. He noticed an elderly patient sitting in a wheelchair eyeing him suspiciously. The old Jamaican had a cast on one leg with a big brown stain on one side of it. 'Are you the doctor?' he said.

'Why yes, I am,' Owen said with an unusual amount of authority that surprised him as the words he had spoken made themselves known.

'Well, why the hell don't you help me then? I have been a-sittin' here for three hours and this thing is all wet…' He lifted the leg with the cast just enough to reveal the back end of the brown stain where the colour became deeper and redder and the plaster of Paris was beginning to crumble. 'I am a patient and I know my rights, son,' he stated with a conviction that Owen found alarming.

Owen did not know what to do. As if in a scene from *Terminator*, he could see the patient sitting in his chair with the background gently flashing red and white with the words 'prime directive – find Padma' emblazoned across his visual field. All other functions were functioning sub-optimally. As his CPU tried to deal with this new task inflicted upon it, his bleep went off. This had the effect of switching Terminator-vision off and Owen quickly gathered his thoughts as he glanced at the number. David Black ward. A deep part of his unthinking brain was about to gear up to tell the patient to wait as he had an 'important bleep' to answer when a new threat entered Owen's world in the form of the patient's daughter advancing menacingly toward him from the vending machine. It had a large round face and was both tall and morbidly obese and for the first time since he came up against the homeless man who lived in a bush outside the hospital one night on the way to buy some food after a particularly busy on-call, he felt a genuine fear for his physical safety.

Although the distance from the vending machine to the wheelchair could only be measured in feet, time slowed as the threat advanced upon him. 'Boom, boom' went the echo of each footstep driven into the plastic floor as each stride brought the danger nearer. In the time-slowing moment that Owen was experiencing, he saw over the daughter's left shoulder that one of the ceiling tiles was missing. Damn, he'd have to count them all again now. By the time he had regained focus it was too late to flee.

'What is your name then, doctor? I will hold YOU accountable for this. My father has suffered like no dog should suffer. Why are you here?'

'Why am I here?' Owen repeated, almost to himself. He had often pondered this very thing.

'When you don't do anything? Who is the consultant? It can't be you as you look too young to know anything.'

Again Owen's bleep sounded. Giving up trying to formulate words appropriate to this situation – a stressful task in itself it transpired – without prior planning or fully intending to do so Owen tore off again and burst through the doors of the clinic back into the corridor. As he passed his stain on the wall he heard angry shouting behind him but he could make out few of the words. He ran out of the main entrance, past the mortuary and under the archway to the education centre. As he passed into the entrance hall his bleep sounded a third time so he stopped and answered it at the reception desk.

'Are you resuscitating this patient?' The voice was angry and its identity unknown.

'Sorry?'

'I am Dr White, consultant anaesthetist. I was asked by your consultant to see a patient he was proposing to take to theatre. I find the patient dry, anaemic and have not found any ECG. Could that be because there is no ECG?'

'My name is Owen Morgan. Are you sure you wanted me? I don't think I have a patient being taken to theatre. Who is the consultant?'

Owen could tell Dr White was very displeased at this question. 'Mr Khan. So am I talking to the right houseplant?'

Spying Padma approaching from one of the seminar rooms Owen replied simply, 'No'.

'Then who is, man!'

Padma was passing the stairs and would almost be upon him.

'Ach. I'm not sure. Not me.'

'Don't you know your own colleagues?'

'Try asking switchboard. I am afraid I'm in an emergency. Cannot talk now.'

Padma had passed him and was almost out of the main door. She hadn't seen him.

'Bye,' Owen said, and replaced the receiver.

'Padma,' Owen shouted to the crowd of which Padma was a small component somewhere in its midst. He was suddenly nervous.

'Dr Owen,' Padma said, and smiled.

'Padma,' Owen said again, more softly. Another nurse next to Padma, who was obviously a close friend of hers, eyed Padma suspiciously.

'Who is this then?' The tone was not friendly.

'This is Dr Owen. He is a good friend of mine.'

'We had dinner last night at Padma's flat,' Owen added to be helpful.

Padma winced.

'How come you have so many and I have none?' Padma's

friend said, rather cryptically, Owen thought. She turned directly to face Padma. 'I'll talk to you tonight,' she said, and walked off.

Owen watched her depart down the concrete steps. She did not look back.

'How about dinner at the Sea Cow?' Owen said.

'No. We can't be seen in public together. Come to my flat again. See you tonight, and bring chicken drumsticks if you can.'

CHAPTER 5

Venflons

D R CABINET'S ROUND was over by the time Owen returned to David Black ward. Another house officer, Aman Vaishnavi, had spied Owen and rather apologetically slunk up behind him.

'Owen,' he said.

Owen turned to face him. Owen had always felt sorry for Aman, as he seemed continuously stressed about just about everything and had never become a true member of the house officer community. In fact he could count on one hand how many times Aman had attended the morally mandatory evenings at the Sun and Doves. And a hand with one finger at that.

'Hey, Aman. How are you?' He already knew the answer to that question as his comrade had an expression of wincing pain with his left eye half-closed and his thin mouth drawn up into a pained smile that ended up looking nothing like a smile should look at all.

'Can you help me? I just can't get a Venflon in Mrs George at all. I've like tried three times. Please can you do it for me?'

Owen did not know who Mrs George was, but if it was the middle-aged angry Cockney in one of the side rooms who always swore and shouted at the staff then this was not a good development. In fact Owen had always congratulated his good fortune each time he passed that room that the patient inside it was nothing to do with him. He liked Aman though and did not want to let him down, so he tentatively agreed.

Aman's face immediately relaxed a notch and his peculiar

pseudo-smile disappeared. He'd already placed all the kit for placing an intravenous cannula, colloquially known as a Venflon, in a small cardboard tray and gently passed the tray forward with both hands to the frowning Welshman before him. Owen was touched that he'd included a packet of cotton wool balls and smiled a smile of what he considered to be genuine affection in return. Aman in return felt distinctly uneasy at Owen's look of constipatory colic.

As predicted, Aman led Owen straight to the side room housing Mrs George and practically shoved him inside before running for cover. He noticed multiple balls of cotton wool stuck at various point on both of Mrs George's arms; evidence of Aman's prior battles. He also noticed a strong body odour scent in the room and was unsure at first if this was the patient's, his own or Aman's.

'Hello,' Owen said. 'I'm Owen…'

'I don't bleedin' care! I do NOT want you to prick me again.'

'Please let me try. You need antibiotics into the vein and they're already due.'

'I can't stand doctors, you know that? Always hurting me. Look at this!' She held aloft her right arm which had around 340 small bruises on it.

'Please,' Owen repeated.

Without saying a word, the hapless Mrs George extended a flabby arm towards Owen and turned her face to the side. Owen placed the tourniquet over the upper arm and removed all the cotton balls and tape. His spirits fell as he surveyed the terrain and noticed all the scars of war. There was not a vein in sight that resembled a vein and nothing palpable either. 'Let's try the other arm, shall we?' he said.

'Crap you all are and you know it,' Mrs George cried out. 'Really you are.'

Owen placed the tourniquet on the other arm. He felt too

dispirited to reply directly and thought she probably had a valid point anyway.

After a minute of stressed silence Owen found himself reading the back cover of a book entitled *Growing your Garden the English Way* that the patient had been reading and a brainwave struck him. 'You like gardening?' Owen said. He was pleased that all those communication skills he'd been taught in medical school were finally coming in useful. By engaging with the patient, reducing her stress and finding common ground he'd succeed where Aman failed.

'Shut up and just fucking do it!' Mrs George replied, spitting globs of saliva all over him as she did so.

Owen felt, for what seemed like an hour, every patch of skin up and down her entire arm. The only candidate was a thready vein at the base of her thumb. All else was kaput. Indeed, during the time it had taken Owen to select his vein, blood-stained serous fluid had started to emanate from a multitude of previous attempts all over her arm. He cleaned the area with an alcohol swab and held the pink Venflon in his hand. No use trying the regular size green Venflon, he thought. He only had one shot at this and the chances of getting a pansy pink Venflon in were much higher than the fat green one. He held the end of the needle just over the skin. 'Sharp scratch,' he said.

'Get on with it, you fool,' she said.

Owen pushed the needle into the yellowing skin overlying the blue blood vessel trickling underneath. As the needle advanced, Owen's eyes could not hide his delight when he saw blood entering the chamber at the back end of the Venflon. This was called flashback, and was the sign of success. After withdrawing the needle, leaving the plastic Venflon in place, and taping it down as best he could, he was only slightly dismayed to discover that the patient would have to keep her thumb extended for the entire duration that the Venflon was in place so that it would work properly.

Mrs George grudgingly thanked Owen and Owen smiled in return. He then connected the antibiotics to his new Venflon, again warned her to be careful with it and left the room.

'How did it go?' Owen surmised Aman must have been hiding very near the door of the room as he was assaulted as soon as the door had closed, though he could not tell where Aman had come from.

'It's in,' Owen said. He felt a certain sense of pride at his own achievement, an unusual sensation for Owen at the best of times. He could also tell that Aman was pleased as his expression of doom slackened somewhat. Noticing Mrs George pushing a drip stand with the antibiotics attached emerging from her room into the corridor, Owen told Aman to look.

Aman immediately noticed the hugely precarious position of the Venflon placed awkwardly in her extended left thumb and his expression became one of anguish and horror again.

'You're welcome,' Owen said, and took his leave.

Chicken Drumsticks

Having remembered eating chicken drumsticks as a child, Owen trotted happily down the meat isle of the nearby Sainsbury's looking for an appropriate packet to bring to Padma. After only a minute's search, he picked up a packet of Bernard Matthews' processed breaded boneless drumsticks and headed for the counter. Men are much better shoppers than women, he mused to himself as he picked up a Mars bar as just reward for his efficient shopping experience. We just go into a shop, find what we want and run out. No time-wasting. Padma will be impressed.

Her flat was barely two minutes walk away but Owen was so buoyed by his Venflon success that he did it in one minute fifty seconds. He knew because he'd timed it on his Rolex watch, given to him as a graduation present by his proud parents a few months before. As he approached her front door, he quickly sniffed his left axilla and rang the doorbell. Why did he do that? Again, he smelled rank. What was the point in doing a clinical test only to ignore the result?

Padma swung the door open and invited him in. No kiss, no hug, not even a smile. Owen sensed an air of badness. 'No queue at Sainsbury's,' he said buoyantly, though this had no effect on Padma who still said nothing. 'I saw a dog on the way up.' Why did he say that? Was he seven years old?

'You're early,' Padma said. 'I need to take a shower. When I'm in the shower take a seat but whatever you do, don't answer the phone.'

'Why?'

'If people call and you answer,' Padma said as she twisted her right foot sternly into the linoleum floor of the hallway, 'they'll know you're here. I don't want anyone to know you're here.'

'But who might call?' Owen replied. He felt a bit upset about this. 'None of my friends know your phone number.'

'I don't care about your friends,' Padma said as she rounded the corner into the bathroom. She suddenly reappeared rather faster than Owen had anticipated as he jumped ever so slightly when she reappeared. 'Where are the chicken drumsticks?'

'Here they are,' he said as he handed her the Sainsbury's carrier bag.

Padma took them out and let the bag fall to the floor. She stood there looking at the packet incredulously, saying nothing, and Owen began to feel that something big had gone wrong.

'What's wrong? Are they not right?'

Again Padma said nothing. Owen looked over at a small African facemask hanging on the wall. When he returned his gaze, Padma still stood there holding the packet of drumsticks, gazing at it intently. She was breathing heavier now, as if a great nuclear reactor was booting up ready for a great amount of activity.

'Funny facemask that,' Owen said. A part of his brain was aware that he had stood on a landmine but was unable to stop another part from blathering out inanities.

At the end of one long breath Padma threw the drumsticks violently into the kitchen bin. 'I told you to get DRUMSTICKS,' she said. 'CHICKEN … DRUMSTICKS.'

'They are chicken drumsticks.' Owen took a small step backwards.

'No they aren't,' Padma said, softly this time. 'Why did you do it?'

'They are chicken drumsticks. Honestly they are.' Owen pulled the packet from the bin and held it in front of Padma. He pointed to the words 'chicken drumsticks' and handed her the packet back. After he had done so he noticed that some grey substance clung to its bottom, probably from the bin, and after tenaciously trying to maintain its grip on the plastic fell to the floor with a liquid thump.

'No they're not. These are some Western rubbish, which rubbish Western people eat. Chicken drumsticks are actual chicken.'

Owen said nothing. He chastised himself for missing Dr Cabinet's round in order to organise this date, only to get himself mixed up in this odd situation which he could not quite fathom.

'David would not have done this, you know.' She became animated again. 'You should know that these are rubbish. How dare you bring rubbish here. You think I eat rubbish, is that it?'

'I'd better leave,' Owen said.

Padma began to cry. 'Why did you do it?'

'I honestly don't know what you mean. Sorry. I better go.'

'No stay.' It was more an order than a plea. 'It's OK. I now know you know so little about the kitchen. I'll have to train you, that's all.'

Owen sat down. 'They are chicken drumsticks, you know,' he said more to himself than anyone else.

Padma quietly walked over to the kitchen window, opened it and threw the packet out as hard as she could.

David

Owen did not know what to do. He was in this flat with a madwoman who was now showering. Why was he still there? He dolefully looked out of the kitchen window at the plastic packet of drumsticks lying in the street. The packet glistened in the damp weather under the sodium lights. He reckoned they were about two-thirds of the way across the road but as a few cars had driven over them it was pointless thinking of retrieving them now. What a waste! He looked at the door. It would be easy to escape. It would not be polite though. Perhaps he'd wait until she'd finished showering. He went back to the window to look out at the chicken drumsticks. They'd moved along the street a few metres so perhaps another car had had direct contact.

'I'll forgive you for this.' Padma was out of the shower and had crept up behind Owen. 'I actually really like you.' As she looked up at Owen he instinctively backed up slightly but the window hindered any further backward progression. Which was probably good as her flat was on the second floor.

'You have nice strong shoulders. Good teeth. Bit of a belly but I can work on that.'

Owen said nothing. He was on new territory here. Beyond the edge of the map.

'Have a shower yourself. And remember to wash down

below.' She put specific emphasis on the last two words and smiled afterwards.

Owen was the most surprised of all when he found himself complying with these instructions. As he examined a bottle of shampoo with the water running, he noted that the product was made in Poland. Should he jump out of the window? The shampoo contained sodium. Defenestration was the Latin for throwing oneself out of a window. It pleased Owen that the word for window was the same in Welsh and Latin. And possibly French, he could not remember. The soap packet had a picture of some kind of pentagram on it. Was she a witch? No, hang on, it was a Star of David. Was she Jewish? No, he already knew she was a Hindu. Would Jewish people shower with Jewish soap anyway? Perhaps a Hindu soap would have a big Om on it. It's a gap in the market if no such soap exists already, he thought.

What could he do? Paralysed by fear he let the water wash over him but remained motionless, Polish shampoo bottle in one hand and Jewish soap in the other. His occipital lobe, containing the visual centres, told him something was in his peripheral visual field and he turned to see a grinning Padma looking at him through the clear shower door. Shit.

He turned the water off. She opened the shower door and pulled a very naked, very frightened Owen out of the shower. He trembled somewhat as she indicated that he should lie down on the bathroom floor. Although he acknowledged he was terrified he was somewhat comforted by the fact that he did not have to consciously think of anything to do. It was all being done for him. As he lay there Padma smiled as she gripped his penis with one hand and performed a sex act on him with her mouth.

Though he had never had a blowjob, or indeed any sex act, performed on him before, Owen found the whole thing hideous and as soon as it finished he smiled a wan smile. Should he thank her? He was unsure. Was it best to say nothing?

Padma threw Owen's clothes back into the bathroom and closed the door. He hurriedly put them all on but hesitated before opening the door. His right hand hovered over the door handle. Why were all his thoughts occupied by Polish soap? Finally it was opened for him and Padma led him back into the sitting room. Owen felt like he wanted to cry, but resisted the urge.

'You should know something,' she confidently stated, looking at the pot plant as she did so. 'I am engaged to a man called David. Now that I've met you I'll break it off because I think we have a future together.' Owen thought again about the packet of chicken drumsticks, glistening yellow under the streetlights with a damp haze of London rain improving the reflection of the light. Or was it refraction? Probably reflection. 'I like you a lot,' she said with a certain finality and looked directly at Owen.

'Yes,' Owen said.

'I think you like me too. Now we need to be discreet about this because he may call the flat. That's why I needed you not to answer.'

'I was wondering about that.'

'Go home. I'll deal with David.'

With some relief Owen got to his feet and headed for the door.

'And Dr Owen,' Padma called after him. 'You didn't wash down below. Disgusting Westerner.'

CHAPTER 6

The Cardiac Arrest

T HE NEXT MORNING Owen was even more bewildered than usual doing the orthopaedic ward round by himself. He had only twelve patients but Mr Nelson had been on call last night so there were another three to add to his list.

'How are you, Mr Braithwaite?' Owen said to a rather small man who had just been admitted with a fractured neck of femur.

'Bit of pain in the hip, doc.'

'That's because you've broken it. Mr Nelson is going to fix that for you later today.'

'I've broke my hip?'

'Yes.' Owen rotated Mr Braithwaite's right leg back and forth, eliciting various grunts and groans. Why had he done that? To prove to him he'd broken his hip. That was not a good thing; he'd not do that again.

'All shattered I'm afraid.' Owen then noticed the space in the drug chart for allergies was not filled in. 'Are you allergic to anything?'

'Doctors and women.'

'Hmm. Sensible. I think I'm allergic to women as well. Women; dear me.' Flashbacks of the night before had haunted Owen all morning and he had taken care not to pass by the front entrance to pre-op, choosing instead the extremely long alternative route to the ward via the chapel. In addition to this inconvenience, his progress on this alternate route had been hindered by a run-in with Mr Whitbread who insisted on telling him about the various things his patients needed doing. Owen's attempt to persuade the bearded consultant that he in fact was not his house officer, that Alex was, did not seem to register, and if it did, seemed not to concern Mr Whitbread in the slightest. As a parting insult Mr Whitbread had referred to him as Ivor. Could this be a genuine mistake or an oblique reference to a cartoon train based purely on his Welshness?

'Don't tell me you're a gay. I wouldn't be pleased if my doctor was a gay.'

'What?' Owen had lost track.

'Are you gay, doctor?'

'I'm so sorry but I am not. I am unsure why you'd ask, to be honest. Now have you signed the consent form?'

'I've not signed anything.'

'Little yellow form?'

'No yellow form. I want food.'

'Sorry, you're nil by mouth. Let me get you a little yellow form.' As he pushed the cubicle door open and headed for the nursing station to find a consent form, a rather tall Afro-Caribbean nurse approached Owen anxiously and barred his way.

'Doctor. Mrs Haswell is not DNR,' was all she said. DNR; Do Not Resuscitate.

'Mrs Haswell? I don't know Mrs Haswell. Who is Mrs Haswell? Is she DNR?'

'No doctor. She's not DNR.'

'Ohh. OK then.' As Owen tried to advance past the nurse she sidestepped, blocking his progress once more.

'Mrs Haswell needs to be DNR.'

'She is not my patient. Why are you telling me about this?'

'Because Mrs Haswell has just died.'

Owen stood upright and went blank for a second. 'You mean Mrs Haswell has just arrested? And she is for resuscitation?'

'Yes, doctor. Mrs Haswell is dead.'

'Oh my goodness. Put out a crash call, I suppose.' As he ran towards the cubicle that contained the dead Mrs Haswell, the nurse called after him.

'Are you sure doctor? A crash call?'

'YES. And bring the crash trolley!'

Mrs Haswell was not only dead but had clearly been dead for some time. What to do? It was still an arrest, technically. Owen looked at the corpse nervously. OK. Airway. Peering through the thin lips Owen was happy to see nothing inside causing an obstruction. Judging by his distance from the patient whatever Owen was looking for might well have been able to jump out of the cold unfeeling mouth and attack from some distance away. Breathing. Owen gingerly placed his left cheek an inch from the patient's mouth and looked at her chest. No movement. He felt her carotids. The thin papery skin showed no sign of underlying movement; no inner life pleading for resuscitation.

Next step, artificial respiration and chest compressions. Where was that crash trolley? The crash trolley contained a mask specifically designed to avoid the need for mouth-to-mouth resuscitation, the so-called 'kiss of life'. Having waited ten seconds without the arrival of the crash trolley, Owen pinched the patient's nose with his left hand and tilted the head back. Looking directly down at the gumless orifice, skin stretched white over the bony face, Owen gagged. He must do it. Must do it. Duty overtook his sense of utter disgust and he pressed his mouth over the cold tight skin and pushed life-giving oxygen into the lungs of Mrs Haswell. Twice. Chest compressions were much easier than this and as he looked up has was relieved to see Alex arrive.

'This… your… patient?' Owen said between chest compressions.

'Yes, man. And I saw what you did. Gross.'

'Can you get the crash trolley, or at least that mask thing. Quick! I'm reaching fifteen.'

As Alex disappeared, Owen repeated the two 'rescue breaths'; gagging heavily besides the bed for five seconds afterwards, and then continued the chest compressions.

When Alex returned he was carrying the notes rather than pushing the crash trolley.

'Here we are,' he said. 'The DNR form. I filed it in the wrong place. Sorry and all.'

'Bloody hell, Alex!' Owen said, immediately stopping what he was doing. He pushed past Alex and the notes and headed for the sink in the ward office to wash his mouth. When he entered the doctor's office he saw the tall Afro-Caribbean nurse sitting down eating from a tin of Quality Street.

'Why didn't you put out the crash call?' Owen demanded angrily.

'I told you doctor. Mrs Haswell is DNR.'

'You said she wasn't!'

'Mrs Haswell is not my patient so I can't know. Julie told me just now'

'Mrs Haswell is not my patient either! Why didn't you tell me?'

'Ah but you're the doctor and I...' the nurse unwrapped a strawberry crème and threw it into her ample mouth, 'am on my break.'

Colleen

Having stormed off the ward, Owen had long forgotten his reason for avoiding pre-op and was more than a little confused, and in fact most disappointed, to find himself face-to-face with Padma not far from the entrance. As she spoke with him, Owen looked over her shoulder and made a note that the brown stain had now reached the edge of the bin. It was also a lot fatter at the top near the ceiling.

'So do you want to come back for dinner tonight or what?'

Owen had a sense that he needed to think of some excuse, and fast.

'Look. I'm going to Westminster Cathedral tonight so can't, sorry. Perhaps t…'

'A cathedral? On a weekday evening? That's surprising.'

Owen was surprised too. 'Yes. I'll probably be a while there. I always go on a Tuesday.'

'It's Wednesday.'

'Sorry, yes. Wednesday.'

'OK. Well, what time is it, cos I'll come with you?' Owen fancied she was keener than she was last night and was completely dumbfounded by this unexpected behaviour. He had expected her to avoid him just as much as he had wanted to avoid her. And what time was mass on a Wednesday?

'Probably six-ish. That sounds a reasonable time.'

Padma furrowed her right eyebrow. 'I'll meet you at the hospital entrance at five-thirty then.' She then walked off towards the Friends' shop.

Owen was beside himself with worry when suddenly Colleen slapped him on the shoulder and gave him a hug from behind. Momentarily terrified, his nerves already badly frayed, Owen let out an involuntary 'Gaa-ah.'

'How are you, mate?' She said this with feeling and for some reason seemed really happy to see Owen.

'I'm OK. Fancy a coffee?'

As they both sat in the canteen drinking coffee from plastic cups Owen regaled Colleen with the story of the cardiac arrest and of Padma's peculiar behaviour. Colleen visibly cheered as the story of Padma and the chicken drumsticks was told and periodically snorted with laughter. Looking her square in the eyes, he asked her what he should do about Westminster Cathedral.

'I can't believe it. What an idiot you are. Why can't you just say no?'

'I can't. Too late now. Can you come too?'

'Me? Oh no! But I can do one thing for you.' She removed her Blackberry from her purse and within a minute had downloaded the mass times for Westminster Cathedral.

'Five-thirty. Just great.'

'Just call her up and cancel. Easy. She'll know you lied when you both turn up just as it's finishing anyway.'

Owen looked at his plastic cup. For no good reason he pushed his finger into the side of the empty container until the plastic suddenly gave way under the strain and a giant tear opened up along one side.

'I can't.'

'You haven't got the balls, that's why.'

'Yes. A patient today asked if I was gay as well.'

'Then go with him to Westminster Cathedral instead of Padma.'

'His hip is shattered. He can't. Not for a few weeks at least.'

'Let us both go then. Us two.'

Owen looked up from his shattered cup, and smiled. 'Yes. I'd like that.' But he worried about Padma.

Having arranged to meet at the hospital entrance at five, Owen finished off his tasks for the day and popped in to see how Mr Braithwaite was after his operation. His bed was still empty so he guessed he was still in recovery. At five, Colleen thumped him on the back as he was filling in a drug chart. Why did she do that?

'Ready?'

'Yup.' As they left David Black ward and passed the Friends' shop on the way to the entrance, Owen remarked how the logo of the stick man with the wavy lines on the corridor wall resembled some kind of endoscopic procedure. He jumped a little as Colleen let out a gigantic laugh; more than such a silly comment deserved anyhow.

At the hospital entrance the two house officers were more than a little dismayed at how rainy the weather was and Colleen said she'd quickly run back to get her umbrella that she'd left on the ward. As he waited, Owen looked at the brand new orthopaedic outpatients on the other side of the road. Feeling like an old man, Owen remembered when the place was a little primary school, back when he was in medical school. Back when he was in medical school! He'd only left a few months ago.

'Hey gorgeous,' a voice said from behind. Turning around, Owen was scared and dismayed to see it was Padma. Why oh why did he wait here of all places?

'Hello. Yes; hello.'

'Come on, I was hoping for a bit more than that after the favour I did you last night.'

Owen looked at the ground. The mosaic tiles were red and white and spelled out the name of the hospital, except where the new disabled handrail strut had cut across one of the letters. 'Yes. That was good. Thanks.' How could he make her go away?

The arrival of Colleen, busily talking as she manhandled her umbrella, caused Owen's heart rhythm to become seriously disordered as he tried to figure out if running away was a viable option or not. The two girls looked at each other.

'Hiya, Padma. I hear you're going to Westminster with Owen. I was just getting my umbrella for you.' Good old Colleen.

Padma was a bit taken aback but took the umbrella. 'Thanks, Dr Colleen. You were very efficient in clinic yesterday. Pity you could not bleed that patient.'

With that, Owen and Padma walked into the rain in search of the number 185 bus to take them to Westminster. As they negotiated a big puddle in the consultants' car park Colleen turned back into the hospital and watched them through the grimy glass of the well worn entrance door.

Westminster Cathedral

As Owen kneeled next to Padma, listening to the undulating tones of the Eucharistic Prayer he was relieved that such a moment did not call for any dialogue. This, he reasoned, was good as he hadn't the foggiest what he should say to a girl like Padma. The bus trip on the way over, thankfully, did not require Owen to say anything much as she was intent on delivering a very detailed account of the various mistakes doctors had made during pre-op that day and how she had put them right.

Sitting. standing, kneeling, standing. The eucharist itself drew nearer and during the peace, Padma made a special point of squeezing Owen's hand, looking into his eyes directly and saying 'Peace be with you', before giving him a sexy smile.

'Peace be with you too,' Owen said, smiling back.

When mass was over and the organ played, Owen and Padma remained seated while the parishioners, emanating a partially dried wet cloth smell, filed past them. They both were probably emanating some kind of wet smell as well, Owen mused.

'You know I'll remember this moment forever,' Padma said.

'Me too,' Owen said in return. It seemed appropriate somehow.

She turned to face him. 'Will you? Will you really?'

'Who is David again?'

Padma seemed annoyed. 'Why did you bring him up?'

'Are you engaged to him? If so, we cannot go out together. It wouldn't be right.'

'We aren't engaged. Not properly. I just told him I'd marry him that's all.'

'That sounds quite engaged.'

'I've got no ring.' As if to illustrate the point Padma lifted her left hand up to the level of Owen's face and wiggled her fingers.

'Still. It isn't right.'

After a moment's hesitation Padma sighed. 'I really like you. I do. I think we can be together. I think we should be together. If it doesn't work out I'll have to go back to Malaysia and…'

'What?! No, don't go back to Malaysia because of me. What about David?'

'AND,' Padma said, 'I'll come back here every year on this date to remember you.'

'I won't be dead, you know.'

'To remember our relationship. Because I like you. I have really let David down but he can cope. He will live. But for me to live, I need you.'

'Now hang on. I… like you too but relationships come and go. Don't go back to Malaysia because of me.'

'There.' Padma pointed towards a seat in one of the side chapels that line the walls of Westminster Cathedral. 'I'll sit in that seat there and remember this day.'

'Why not sit here? After all, we didn't sit over there.'

'Look. I'm just saying I'll sit there if we break up. I'll come back from Malaysia just to do it. So we shouldn't break up.'

'No,' Owen said without conviction.

Padma brightened. 'Fancy some food? Where do you want to go to eat?'

Owen turned to look at the priests at the big door talking with the half-wet post-mass Catholics. Could they smell the wetness? Perhaps it is a product of the heat and the rain, not just the rain itself. The rain was audible now in the piazza outside as some great thunderstorm let roar above the roof.

'Owen.' He turned to look, momentarily lost in thought. Padma smiled at him sweetly and kissed him forcefully on the lips. It was not unpleasant but Owen was conscious of the priests so detached himself as quickly as he could.

'I'm conscious of the priests,' he said.

'Where shall we have food, Dr Owen?'

'I remember a big floating Chinese restaurant somewhere near Canary Wharf. Shall we go there?' Perhaps Padma was not so bad after all. She seemed to like him anyway and that had to be good. A bit frightening and a bit odd, but then again weren't all women meant to be like that? Owen cursed the fact that his studies had precluded him from forming any meaningful relationships during the long years of medical school. Even as he thought this, he smiled to himself at the self-deception. There were plenty of people in meaningful relationships in medical school, just not him. It was just a big excuse really and he knew it. As Padma led him down the aisle towards the priests and the exit Owen turned to look one more time at the small wooden chair in one of the side chapels.

CHAPTER 7

The Floating Restaurant

O WEN HAD ALWAYS wondered what it felt like to have a girlfriend at one's side. He'd see other men with women by their side and would envy them without truly knowing why. So here he was travelling in the tube to Canary Wharf with a beautiful young Indian girl on his arm. An Indian who periodically squeezed his knee as well, in full view of everyone. As she silently lent her head against Owen's left cheek he caught the eye of the middle-aged Englishman on the facing seat. See what I've got? he subliminally told the Englishman. The Englishman looked away. Ha, I have won and I am the best, Owen subliminally followed up with.

Unfortunately the triumph was ruined somewhat by the fact that Owen found Padma's hair quite itchy. So much so that he had to constantly scratch his nose. By the end of the journey he'd discovered that by turning his head away from Padma's hair a small amount the itch could be controlled, although he looked very unnaturally positioned when he caught a glimpse of himself in the opposite window when the tube train was in a tunnel. The Englishman turned the page of his book. He was probably thinking that Owen was out of his depth. If he did think that, then he was right, Owen sadly concluded.

One Docklands Light Railway ride later brought the young lovers to the floating Chinese restaurant at the base of Canary Wharf. Sitting down at a table overlooking the water, Padma stared out at the grey water that surrounded the isolated cacophony of illumination in which they were seated. Turning back to face Owen, she was slightly taken aback to see that her young doctor companion had arranged his cutlery at perfect right angles and tidied up the small dish containing various condiments. Irritated, she moved the soy sauce a fraction towards the window.

'I remember when this whole building was bombed by the IRA,' Owen said.

Again Padma was irritated. Why bring up a bombing during a date? And what was the IRA?

'Yes,' he continued, unaware. 'I was home doing my A-levels I think, and a massive bomb destroyed this building.'

'I like this place. It reminds me of KLCC,' Padma said.

'What's KLCC?'

'Big shopping area in Kuala Lumpur. All big and shiny. Shops and all. Do you like shopping?'

Owen hated shopping. 'Yes. I think shopping can be fun.'

The conversation rumbled on as food was ordered, though Owen and Padma were both disappointed that the subjects covered were of very little interest to either of them. By the time food arrived, Owen was positively panicking, when suddenly he had a brainwave. Why didn't he just talk to her like he talked to Colleen and not try so hard to think of things to say? So Owen told Padma the story about the cardiac arrest – and the tension at the small table visibly diminished.

'Did you report the nurse?' she said.

'Uh. No. I suppose I should have had a word with her.'

'Nurses in this country are useless; not like back home. Back home we do all the Venflons, all the ECG and get everything ready for the doctor. Doctor is God for us nurses back home.'

Owen greeted this with approval. 'Perhaps I should work there.'

'You should. I treat all doctors here with respect though, even though house officers like you all know nothing.'

'Steady on. That's not true.'

'It is.' Padma picked up a chopstick for dramatic effect. 'I hate doing clinics with your Dr Alex. He always takes too long and messes things up.'

Owen smiled. He enjoyed hearing bad things about his colleagues. Not because they were true or because he thought so himself, but because he was so nervous about his own work that any hint of human failing in anyone else comforted him greatly. 'Tell me.'

'Yesterday I did an ECG for him. He didn't even ask for it; I did it before he had the chance. So that he knew I was an excellent nurse. Well after I gave him the ECG he lost it! "Where is the ECG?" he shouted. Wanted me to find it. You know where it was? In his textbook.'

'Yes, he does carry that huge textbook around with him, doesn't he?'

'Did he say sorry? No. Incompetent and rude Dr Alex.'

'Ha.' Owen liked this conversation now, and for the first time started feeling comfortable around Padma. 'I don't think he likes you very much anyhow, so don't worry about it.'

Padma froze, a wonton falling from her chopsticks to her plate with a wet plop. Owen did not see this or if he did, failed to recognise its significance in the way the conversation was headed.

'Yes. Before Dr Cabinet's round he was saying how you were a crap nurse.'

'What did you say in response?'

'I don't know if I said anything. Dr Cabinet's round was starting, you see.'

'You didn't say anything?' Owen was starting to become aware of an icy chill blowing across his table. Looking directly at

Padma for the first time in minutes he could sense rage boiling within her. Her breathing intensified and Owen retreated slightly in his chair.

'You worm. You didn't say anything? I'm an excellent nurse. Why didn't you tell him that?'

'Whoa now. Hang on. Doctors always say things like that. I, uh. I didn't want to make a scene. He didn't mean it. I'm sure he knows…'

'And you come out on a date with me after doing that?' Her voice was stern and slowly increasing in volume. A bespectacled gentleman from a nearby table glanced over. Owen suddenly felt the whole room looking at him and to counter this fixated his gaze at the soy sauce.

'I didn't do anything,' he whispered.

'Exactly. EXACTLY!'

'Please. You're making a scene. Please whisper. Sorry. I didn't mean to upset you. I shouldn't have brought it up.' The soy sauce was made by a company called Kikkoman. Nasty Kikkoman. He would forever associate Kikkoman with unpleasantness. Pavlov's dog and all that.

'Making a scene, am I? Do you want me to make a real scene?'

'Obviously not. Look. Let's just forget I said it. Please.'

'I can't stay here with someone who won't stand up for me when I'm being bullied.'

Padma stood up. As she did so a fair number of those seated around looked at her directly, and then at Owen.

'Sit down please, please, please.'

'You won't stand up for me. I need a man who can stand up for me.' After she finished this statement, Owen was both horrified and relieved to see her march out of the restaurant. Having sat down again he was then unsure what to do. Looking at anything other than Kikkoman soy sauce had all sorts of attendant risks. Should he stay there until the restaurant closed? Or at least until the crowd that had seen him humiliated had left and were replaced by people who were unaware of what had happened. Thankfully a waitress appeared by his side but Owen was too scared to look at her directly. Addressing the soy sauce, he asked for the bill and departed the restaurant the moment it was paid. Leaving was a challenge in itself as he could feel the glare of others, and so concentrated his gaze on the exit door. Bumping into a few chairs and nearly falling over some lady's handbag, Owen was relieved to finally push through the door and exit into the cool night. Ahh, how nice it felt to feel free again! But he wasn't free, as he spotted Padma sitting down on a nearby bench glaring at him.

Humble pie

'Why did you do that Padma? I have never felt so sad before.'

'Good. Why did you do it? Why didn't you stand up for me?' They both started walking slowly to the Docklands Light Railway station.

'I said I was sorry. I didn't mean to insult you. Alex may not have even called you crap I just…'

'What?' She stopped walking.

'I can't remember I was just saying a story. My memory is bad for these things.'

'Well it's important. Did he insult me?'

'No. Well yes, but I can't remember how exactly. But that's just Alex I shouldn't have told you and that was my fault, sorry.'

'I can't be with anyone who doesn't stand up for me.'

'OK. I'll tell him you're not crap. I'm sure he knows anyway. He thinks everyone is crap. Probably thinks I'm crap.'

'You are crap.'

Owen made a mental calculation that he had apologised

enough and no more insulting comments by Padma were justified. He didn't really want to be here with her anyway but simply walking away would have been irresponsible and unmanly. Now though, he reckoned he'd absorbed what was reasonable and was willing to leave if Padma continued.

'I reckon I've absorbed what is reasonable and I am going to leave if you continue,' he said. He expected Padma to walk off again but to his discomfort she relented and took his left arm.

'You know I like you. I just need you to be a man.'

What if he pushed her into the dock? Would anyone object? Would anyone know it was him? Hopefully she would drown. Spying a large CCTV camera on the side of a shiny new skyscraper he sighed. That plan was out of the question now.

'I am a man.'

Padma said nothing as they walked arm in uncomfortable arm towards the station. Thankfully there was not long to wait for a train, and as Owen sat down he examined a poster above the seat opposite advertising a pep-up drink. Perhaps that was what he needed. What could he do? He didn't understand this girl. He didn't understand any girl really. Why did she do that? How could he break up with her? Were they already broken up? How could you tell? What usually happened under these circumstances? He'd have to Google it.

'Come back to my place,' Padma said.

Owen froze. What fresh hell was this? He remained silent.

One tube change later brought them to the Elephant and Castle, where a bus would be able to take them both to the hospital and their respective dwellings. Still nobody spoke. On the bus, Owen was in some way pleased to see the same advert for the pep-up drink directly facing him. Perhaps he should try it.

As the bus arrived at their stop, Padma squeezed Owen's hand and led him off. In fact she led him up the small hill and into her flat. This whole time Owen remained silent although his inner cerebral flywheel was whirring so fast he thought he'd faint at several points. His hands became cold and sweaty and his pulse quickened. His cerebral computer failed to yield any search results every time he attempted to ask it how to end the terrifying situation in which he now found himself.

Padma closed her front door and started undressing, right there in the corridor in front of Owen. Owen, meanwhile, opened and closed his mouth rhythmically like a fish out of water. Padma was small and thin. Her dark brown skin shone in the bare corridor light as she beckoned Owen into her bedroom. Owen's feet remained glued to the floor; his brain having given up trying to respond to the situation in any appropriate manner. After a few seconds, Padma re-emerged and pulled Owen into her room by his tie. After a minute of undressing she pushed him back out again. 'Have a shower first.'

He did as he was told. As he showered, Owen saw the Jewish soap and almost cried with relief. A familiar face in a strange land, he said to the soap as he cradled it to his chest. A pilgrim in an unholy land.

Fifteen minutes later Owen lay on Padma's bed staring at the ceiling. So that was what it felt like. He had often wondered and now he knew. He had a vague thought that he should be more triumphant but that could be because the whole thing was so unexpected. And so terrifying. A sweaty Padma kissed him again on his lips and headed for the bathroom. As she walked through the door Owen caught her naked form against the light. How stunningly beautiful. How soft and lovely. What a nice bum she had. Really.

How lucky could one man be? Owen was content to put the awful business with the floating restaurant to one side and concentrate on the beautiful thing that had just happened. He opened the filing cabinet of his mind marked 'unclassified' and pushed the floating restaurant deep into it. He could always come back and refile that experience more appropriately later but for now he was content to lie naked on a sexy nurse's bed and think about what had occurred in the very immediate past.

Jobs

'Have you started looking for SHO jobs yet?' Alex handed Owen a cup of tea in the mess.

'What?'

'Senior house officer jobs. Have you started looking? I've applied for three already. Closing dates coming up you know. What do you want to do?'

'Oh. Pathology sounds good.'

'Pathology. Complete waste of time. Surgery is the only way forward.' Alex sat down heavily next to Owen on the sofa.

'Pathology is logical. You always know where you are. Surgery? Remember our time doing colorectal, and even more so this orthopaedic job? No.'

'Surgery is the only specialty that fixes people.'

'Remember that old ditty. Medics know everything and do nothing. Surgeons know nothing and do everything. Psychiatrists know nothing and do nothing. Pathologists know everything and do everything, though it's often too late.'

'Too late. Exactly, Owen. You should do surgery. Mr Silk always said you were a natural surgeon.'

Owen raised an eyebrow. 'I never knew that. Did he really say that?'

'Nah, but he should have done after how hard you worked for him.'

Owen sank back into the sofa again. Where was Colleen? He hadn't seen her today.

Owen was as surprised as anybody when Aman emerged

from the kitchen carrying a cup of tea. Aman never came into the mess.

'Hey, Aman. Applied for jobs yet?'

'I'm going for general practice' he said.

'GP,' Alex said. 'What a waste of time. GPs know nothing and do nothing.'

'That's psychiatrists,' Owen said.

'GP is good for me though. It's a three-year training programme and I don't want to apply for six months' jobs all the time. Every time I'd start a job I'd have to start applying for the next one straight away.'

'Why not pathology?'

'Pathology; no. I don't like dead people.'

'From what I've heard most of your patients end up dead anyway so you might as well do it formally.' As Alex said this he spat little globs of biscuit over the Playstation and surrounding area, including Owen's trousers.

Owen looked at three damp globs of biscuit near his knee. 'You had a death, have you?'

Aman looked at the floor. 'That Venflon lady. Remember?'

'Yeah.'

'She suddenly died. Pulmonary embolus probably. She's gone for PM.'

'Sure it wasn't your charm that did it?' Alex said.

'Did the Venflon last long?' Owen said.

'Although it looked weird, yes it did. It lasted right up till she died.'

'Well that's how she died.' Alex turned to Owen again. 'Death by Venflon. You could write that up.'

Owen wondered if it was possible for someone to die from a misplaced Venflon. He made a mental note to look it up on PubMed when he was next in the library.

'Very sad, actually. But do you know what the registrar said when I told him? 'Did you do a check X-ray on her knee?' Can you believe it? He just wanted to see whether the surgery had gone well for his records. Didn't really care for the patient at all.'

'Well she was a bit miserable.' Owen corrected himself. 'A lot miserable.'

'No death for you in GP land, though. And feel free to refer me all your private cases. I'll do a two-for-one hernia for you.' Alex winked like a second-hand car salesman. 'Just for you mind, Aman.'

At that moment Aman's bleep went off again and Owen caught sight of his thin colourless face losing more colour and become just a little bit thinner, if such a thing was possible. 'I have to answer that,' he said sadly to no one in particular and walked over to the phone.

'Seriously' Alex said. 'Do surgery. At least do a job in surgery and if you don't like it then do pathology. But don't just go straight into pathology.'

'That seems sensible. What jobs have you applied for?'

'Surgery, surgery, surgery. Here, in George's and in the Free.'

'I'll check to see if Cardiff applications are still open.'

'Always wanted to go home, didn't you? You come here, we train you, then you bugger off east.'

'West.'

'Same thing. You go far enough east you end up west.'

'Really.'

Alex got up. 'I'm off to theatre, ladies. Do some real work. Catch you in the Sun and Doves later.'

As Alex exited, Aman came and stood next to the seated Owen.

'I need to speak to the relatives. Apparently the son is here now and he's not happy.'

'Do you think I should do surgery?'

Aman looked directly at Owen. 'Surgery. Yes. You'd be good at surgery. What should I tell the relatives?'

'Tell them the truth. She died because of a PE.' Owen then frowned and stood up. 'Don't mention anything about Venflons.'

CHAPTER 8

Christmas

OWEN BECAME SLIGHTLY less cautious over time with Padma, although he freely acknowledged that he was out of his depth from the very beginning. So long as the sea was calm he'd continue to tread the deep water – that was Owen's philosophy. By the end of December, Owen found out that it was he who had drawn the short straw and it was he who would have to be on call over Christmas. His parents were naturally saddened that he'd be missing his first Christmas away from the family fold, but Owen now had the turbulent Padma at his side so things had the potential to be good after all. Owen had not told his parents about the existence of Padma for the simple reason that her occasional outbursts of anger were so distressing that each time they occurred he was convinced the inevitable end to their short relationship had arrived. This, in itself, was actually not too distressing a thought for Owen. Padma had also formally finished with David, which was a positive development for David, Owen thought.

'You seem distant,' Padma told Owen over the table at a South London Italian restaurant. It was Christmas Eve and the restaurant was packed full of morose Londoners. One of the benefits of Padma finishing with David was that they could now be together in public.

'Sorry. I still have jobs to apply for, actually. People tell me I should think of surgery.'

'Oh yes. Surgery would be brilliant for you. Surgeons are the best. Always know what they're doing.'

Owen pondered this. He rarely knew what he was doing with any great conviction. 'Or pathology,' he added.

Padma made a bad face.

'I've sent off applications to a few places anyway.'

'I need to meet your parents.'

Owen was in the process of swallowing a piece of ravioli but this news caused the ravioli to divert at a critical point on its journey to the oesophagus and head for the larynx. As Owen coughed violently Padma passed him a glass of water.

'I need to meet them soon. I haven't even spoken to them on the phone. Do they know I exist?'

Owen shook his head as his face turned purple and he reached for the glass of water.

'They need to see me, otherwise it will delay our plans to get married.'

At this point the water itself was also passing a critical point in its own journey southwards and was diverted into the larynx where the forlorn ravioli lay wedged up against a vocal cord. Having no alternative, Owen coughed so violently he could just about see the offending pasta soar past Padma's right ear as it headed for the door.

'I am getting older and I need to be married soon.'

Regaining his composure, Owen wiped his lips with the napkin. 'Married? Why married so soon? We've only been dating for a month and a half.'

'Well how long do you want to leave it? Six months? A year?'

'Can we not think about it another time? It's too early to even think of such things, let alone talk about them.'

Padma placed her fork, which had neatly skewered two pieces of ravioli ready for dispatch, back down on her plate. 'I am Asian. If you were not thinking of marrying me then you shouldn't have been dating an Asian girl like me, should you?'

'Hang on I didn't say we wouldn't get married at all, ever, but let's just not talk about it yet, that's all.'

'Either way, I need to meet your parents.'

Owen pondered that this was indeed the less unappealing option so agreed to set up the trip to Wales for sometime in January. Padma was satisfied at this and offered her last ravioli to Owen.

Having settled the bill, they both took the bus to Westminster Cathedral for midnight mass. They had not been there since their first proper date and as they entered Owen's eyes automatically locked onto Padma's wooden seat in the side chapel. Owen gave it what he considered a disapproving look. During the service Owen thought of his family back home attending mass at his family church without him. A pang of guilt made him close his eyes tight. Although he had been allocated to work on Christmas Day he felt sure that had he fought hard enough he might have been able to swap the shift with a non-native doctor for whom Christmas meant nothing. He had wanted to stay with Padma; that was the truth. To prove he was an adult with adult relationships. And now he had this huge marriage thing hanging over him like a sword of Damocles. How naïve and unaware had he been as he sat down to dinner earlier!

When mass ended and the crowd overflowed into the piazza afterwards Padma pulled Owen toward a nearby tavern. 'Let's have a drink before we head back,' she said.

Immediately afterwards Owen felt his mobile vibrate and was pleased to see it was a text from Colleen. He hadn't seen Colleen for a few weeks now; they had different shifts and Owen seemed to spend most nights in Padma's flat rather than the junior doctors' accommodation block.

'Colleen wishes us a Merry Christmas,' Owen said.

'I don't like her hanging around you. Why did she text you so late? It's after midnight.'

'She's just a friend. An old friend.'

'I don't like it. Tell her you've got a girlfriend now.'

'I have and she's happy. Don't worry.'

As Owen prepared to text a reply, Padma snatched his phone and turned it off. 'There. She won't be spoiling our Christmas Eve now, will she?'

The Christmas Call

Owen awoke at 7 a.m. on Christmas Day and handed Padma her present. He had spent all of ten minutes selecting what he considered a nice necklace but hadn't wrapped it. Indeed why would a person buy a whole roll of wrapping paper just to wrap one small present? Padma smiled when she opened the present and gave hers in return. It was a bottle of deodorant. Was she trying to say something? As he left the flat she gave him a peck on the cheek and Owen pondered whether married life would indeed be this pleasant. If it was then perhaps being married was not so bad. He could always get divorced quickly enough if it was not to his liking anyway.

Arriving at the hospital Owen was pleasantly surprised to find no patients waiting to be seen and indeed very few in-patients at all. An old banner had been dug out from somewhere and hung between the fan and peculiar light fitting on David Black ward. 'Merry Christmas,' it said. Well it would have said that had the end of the banner not been used to provide added strength to its connection with the light fitting. It read 'Merry Christm' instead. Owen laughed at this as he rewrote a drug chart at the nurses' station.

The mess was also deserted, except for a Pakistani anaesthetist who sat on the coffee-stained sofa watching an Asian news channel. Owen considered asking him if he wanted to partake of a game of Halo but thought better of it. His first bleep came at 3.30. One of the post-op hip fracture patients felt nauseous and wanted to vomit.

Owen would not ordinarily have reacted so quickly to such a humdrum task but with nothing else to do felt that he should do something constructive.

'How are you, Mrs Patterson?'

'A bit better now, thanks.' As she said this she retched again into a cardboard tray although nothing managed to escape her lips.

'Hmm. Let me feel your abdomen.' As Owen knelt beside her bed and palpated her wrinkly belly, he remembered his general surgery job. In some vague way he missed those days. 'You have a lot of air in there, to be honest. When did you last open your bowels?'

'Not since I've been in, doctor.'

'When was that?'

'A week.'

'Any wind?'

'No.'

'How long have you been feeling like this?'

'Oh I don't know. A few days. I haven't been able to eat anything since Tuesday.'

'Well I guess you need an X-ray to see what the problem is. I'll sort it out for you, don't worry.'

Owen picked up an X-ray card and filled it out as he wandered towards radiology. After completing the card he was amazed that it looked even more untidy than his radiology requests looked under normal circumstances. Passing though the door to radiology, he saw the plump middle-aged female radiographer sat at a chair watching the end of *It's a Wonderful Life* on a portable television in the dark. She had a small silver party hat on her head and did not look pleased to see him.

'Hello. Merry Christmas. Ho, ho, ho.' After the third 'ho'

Owen noted the frown deepen and decided his charismatic approach was falling on deaf ears so decided to come straight to the point. 'Can you please do an erect chest X-ray and supine abdominal on this lady?'

'Can it wait?'

'Not really. Perhaps it's obstruction.'

The radiographer sighed and silently took the card. After an hour of aimlessly wandering around the empty hospital waiting for the X-ray to get done he decided to go and have a good look at the stain outside pre-op. Arriving outside the door, Owen felt personally hurt that someone in estates had taken to painting over it all at some point in the past few days. The colour did not even come close to matching though, Owen noted with satisfaction, so to those who knew, the stain would always be there in spirit. As he pondered this, the bleep came to let him know the radiographer had finished and a short time later he pushed the abdominal X-ray into the lightbox on the ward. 'Very distended colon,' he told no-one in particular. And air either side of the bowel wall. That was never good. Just a glimpse told Owen all he needed to know. There was air under the diaphragm. He marched off to speak to the patient.

'I'm afraid you have air under the diaphragm,' Owen told a bewildered Mrs Patterson. He let the news sink in for dramatic effect.

'What does that mean, doctor?'

'To put it simply, your bowel has burst because it had been blocked for so long. You need an operation to fix that.'

'An operation!' Mrs Patterson placed her cardboard sick bowl back on the bedside table. 'Can't it wait until tomorrow? I've got relatives coming today. It is Christmas you know,' she said as she pointed to the banner overhead.

'No. You need an operation today. Otherwise you will die. First I need to put a needle in your vein to give you fluid and put a tube up your nose. And no more eating or drinking.' As he left to collect the appropriate instruments and to make the all-important call, he spied the banner once more. 'And Mrs Patterson; Merry Christm.'

That evening as Owen sat in the mess he contemplated the day's events. No actual orthopaedic cases, but a life saved. Mrs Patterson had gone to theatre later that day and had a perforated section of colon removed and a colostomy created. He fired up the mess computer and downloaded an application form for the only basic surgical training rotation currently advertised. It was a three-year rotation based at Old Square Hospital in the West Midlands. 'Six months of compulsory medical housejob then surgery for me!'

Telling Mam and Dad

After he finished his duty at 9 p.m. Owen called his parents from the hospital phone. He was amazed that simply putting a '9' in front of his parent's number would actually work from a London hospital but decided not to look a gift horse in the mouth. '*Nadolig llawen.* Merry Christmas, mam.'

'Merry Christmas to you too, love, but why haven't you called?'

'I am calling.'

'But it's late. It's night. Anyway *Nadolig llawen, bach.* There's a shame you can't be home.'

'I have been working, you know. It's been quite busy actually.' Owen felt guilty saying this as he remembered the fourteen cups of tea he'd had, the fact that no new patients were admitted and the fact that he'd seen almost the whole of *National Lampoon's Christmas Vacation* on the mess television.

'Yes, of course, we know. You've got such an important job. But you get well paid, mind you.'

'Well no, not really. The pay is the same whether you are on call at Christmas or not.' Owen was frequently annoyed at the fact that his parents knew so little about medical life. His father was a mechanic and his mother a shop assistant in a local Co-op. Owen had been the first person in his family to gain a medical degree, a fact that seemed to please everyone in his family but Owen. In fact Owen had been the first person in his family to have finished A-levels, let alone gone on to graduate in something.

'That's daft. I'm not sure I believe you anyway. When are you coming home?'

'Tomorrow at one. I'll be on the National Express. I'll give you a call from Neath when I arrive. Is that OK?'

'Yes. Your father will come and fetch you. Now I've kept you some turkey and we'll all have another Christmas dinner tomorrow. There's sad you couldn't be here today. We've got all your presents here safe for you.'

'Honestly I don't need presents, mam. I'm twenty-three years old.' Owen was quite glad the presents were there safe for him.

'You'll always be our boy and you'll always have some presents from us.'

'Well I hope they weren't expensive, mam, that's all. Not like last year. Remember I'm working now.' Owen hoped the presents were nice and expensive like last year. 'Did you have a nice Christmas? Did you get my present in time?'

'Lovely it was. Thank you so much for the blender. It'll come in so useful. And green! It matches the kitchen lovely, it does.'

'Well you did tell me exactly which one you wanted, mam.'

'Your father's not well though. Not well at all.'

'Oh no. How?'

'Eaten too much as per usual. Repeating on him. Idwal come here and talk to Owen. Owen. Owen's on the phone. Idwal. Owen's on the phone. Come to the phone, come on. Hang on,

Owen, your father's playing up again.' The line went quiet for a minute as Owen's father was coaxed out of his chair and directed towards the phone table in their hallway.

'I don't know why your mother insists on using this phone table. Thinks it's posh, she do. Now I have to stand in the cold hall.'

'Merry Christmas, dad. Sorry I couldn't be there.'

'*Nadolig llawen, boi.* How is work? Busy?'

'Yeah.' Owen looked at his shoes. His left shoe had a big mud stain on it. How long had he been walking around with a big mud stain on his shoe?

'Well at least you're being paid. What is it, double time, triple time?'

Owen sighed. 'Just time, dad. Just time. I'm coming back tomorrow and I'm looking forward to seeing you.'

'Well, look after yourself on the way home, son. Lots of crazy fools around.'

'I have grown up now you know. I'll be fine. You know I've got a girlfriend now and one day I'll bring her home to see you too.' Owen had planned to tell his parents at some point about Padma in order to arrange the visit home. He had almost mentioned it on three previous phone calls but the opportunity did not arise. It had not really arisen this time and he was unsure why he had just blurted it out like that.

'What? Girlfriend? I'll put your mother back on. Moira. Moira. Come back to the phone. Something to do with a girlfriend.' This time the phone was silent for barely a second as the matriarch whipped up the receiver once more.

'Girlfriend? Girlfriend? What is this girlfriend? Whose girlfriend? Your girlfriend? Who?'

'Slow down, mam. I was just telling dad I have a girlfriend now. I'll bring her back to see you one day, OK. She's nice, you'll like her.' Owen did not sound convincing.

'What's her name then?'

Owen hesitated. 'Padma.'

'Padma! Padma! What kind of name is that? It's not Welsh, is it?'

'It's Indian.'

'Indian. *O Arglwydd mawr*. Idwal she's Indian. I don't know Indian food. How can she come here?'

'She eats all kinds of food don't worry. And it won't be for a few weeks.'

'I don't even like to eat Indian food. How can I cook Indian food?'

'I just wanted you to know that's all.'

'Trust you to do something odd. Why not settle for a nice Welsh girl?'

'There are no Welsh girls in London, mam.'

'Yes,' she said sharply. 'But there are plenty of Welsh girls in Wales, see.'

'I know. Listen. I just wanted to tell you. How is Angharad?'

'You leave your sister out of this. How old is this Palma?'

'Padma. A year older than me. She's a nurse here at the hospital. Tell me more about Christmas back home.'

'Christmas is tomorrow. I've told you. Here's your sister. He's dating an older Indian woman who eats Indian food.'

'Hey, bro.'

'Hey, Angharad. *Nadolig llawen*.'

'Same to you, bro. Will be glad to see you tomorrow. Don't know exactly what you've said to mam but she's phoning someone on her mobile now.'

'Great. Anyway I'll see you all tomorrow. Say night-night to everyone, *Nadolig llawen* and all.'

'*Nos da*.' With that he replaced the handset and started the short walk back to Padma's flat. As he did so he felt as if something inside of him had just died. By telling his parents about Padma he'd broken some unspoken bond of family unity that could never truly be fixed. It was not such a good Christmas present to leave them with.

CHAPTER 9

Post Christmas Blues

O N THE WAY back to London just after New Year, Owen sat back in the coach and felt Christmas had gone well, everything considered. He'd spent Christmas Day with his girlfriend, which seemed very grown-up and responsible. The trip to Wales on Boxing Day had been more normal than he'd expected, with his family putting a special emphasis on celebrating Christmas again in the traditional way. So the best of both worlds, really. Despite this Owen had at the back of his mind a gnawing discomfort about Padma's intention to visit. Owen was frustrated that Padma wanted to see his mother and father so soon but was equally stressed with the attitude of his parents, and in particular his mother. A date had, however, been finally set for the second week of January.

He took out his mobile and prepared to ring Padma to let her know he was on the way back. As he did so, he remembered Colleen's text over Christmas, and the fact that he hadn't replied. Owen felt sure she'd understand his lack of response and dialled Padma's number. 'Hey, honey.' Owen had seen countless people on television address their partners in this manner and wondered if it was a good idea. He was not comfortable saying it but as Padma had started calling him 'babe' he felt duty bound to come up with some pet name.

'Hey, babe. When will you be back home?'

'About seven. Do you want to go out for dinner tonight? Sea Cow?'

'Nah. We'll grab a Chinese takeaway.'

Owen hated Chinese takeaways. 'Yes. That sounds good. I'll give you a call when I arrive.'

Ringing off, Owen started writing a text to Colleen. Halfway through he had second thoughts and deleted the message. Would she understand after all? Why had Padma grabbed his phone in the first place?

That evening Owen told Padma the good news about the Wales trip as they were eating Singapore fried rice in her flat.

'I'm not happy about the trip. Why are we going for a whole weekend? Why do we have to stay with your parents? Can't we stay in a hotel?'

'Stay in a hotel? Oh no, no, no. We'd never be forgiven if we did something like that.'

'I don't want to see your parents the whole time.'

'Isn't that the reason you wanted to go; to see the family?'

'I'll look up some hotels on the internet.'

'No. They're expecting us now. They are really looking forward to it.' Owen knew this last part did not sound convincing as he was picturing his mother's reaction as he said it.

Padma stayed silent. Owen noticed he had run out of wontons and took a stab at a juicy-looking one that was vulnerable on the edge of Padma's plate. Padma rather unexpectedly tried to fend off this attack with her knife but it was too late as the wonton was already in transit. The collision of knife, fork and wonton resulted in the offending wonton flying through the air in a graceful arc, coming to rest in the large plant pot next to the fireplace. Owen looked at Padma with a worried expression, but then instantly became happier.

'Look, if you don't want to go I can just cancel. Don't worry. No problem.'

Padma remained silent.

'Or *dim problem*, as we say in Wales.'

After a few minutes of silent eating, during which the tension in the room rose considerably, Padma swallowed her last mouthful of food and looked Owen straight in the eye.

'I need you to listen to me sometimes. Listen to me now. I don't like it.'

'What don't you like?'

'The trip.'

'Then I'll cancel it. No problem. *Dim…*'

'I want to stay in a hotel.'

'I don't think we can, honey bun.' Owen was confused as to why he'd used that particular moment to try out a new pet name. It was inappropriate and didn't fit anyway.

'I'm working tomorrow and I need an early night. You need to leave now.'

'But I've just got back. Don't be like this. Come on.'

'No. Please leave.' Padma looked down at her plate and refused to make eye contact with Owen.

Owen tried to kiss Padma on her cheek but at the critical moment she turned her face away. Feeling beaten, Owen obeyed and left for his own accommodation. As he negotiated his way past a drunkard who had sprawled himself on the pavement, a feeling of relief crept into Owen's soul. So the relationship had ended. But it was OK as it wasn't a real relationship anyway; a sort of practice run, he figured. Perhaps next time he'd meet a girl who wasn't so mad. Perhaps they were all mad like that, though. Owen did not have much time to consider this development as he came face to face with a jogging Alex outside the hospital.

'Welcome back, mate. Happy New Year.'

'Hey, yes. Hello Alex. I see you've taken up jogging.'

'New Year's resolution, my friend. Christmas busy?'

'I was on call, remember. Saw one of your patients, by the way. Had large bowel obstruction and went to theatre. You know, I guess that's the first patient whose life I have directly saved. Best Christmas present, I'll tell you that. Makes the job…'

'She died on New Year's Eve. Sorry, mate.'

Owen was lost for words as the enormity of this personal loss sank in. He had also made much of the episode during his recent heroic homecoming over Christmas.

'Don't worry, you probably gave her another few days of life. Another few days of unbearable agony, though. I'm off round the park. Cheer up, mate!' With that Alex tore off up the hill. As he dodged an ambulance at the entrance to A&E, Owen suddenly thought how odd it was that Alex was jogging in the dark. Wouldn't the park be closed?

Back in his room, Owen sat down in the chipped wooden chair and looked blankly at the empty wall over the bed. So Mrs Patterson had died. Well at least that horrible Welsh trip with Padma was cancelled. He'd have to tell his parents the good news.

With that thought, a text came through on his phone. It was Padma. A feeling of dread came over Owen even before he'd opened the message. It read: 'Welcome back. Have booked hotel for stay in Wales. Only one week to go, yay. Love u.'

Croeso i Gymru

The week did indeed go quickly and before he had settled back into London life properly Owen was on the train with Padma approaching Neath station, where he knew his anxious parents would be waiting to see their son with his new girlfriend. He had barely seen Padma all week and was much more nervous about this encounter than he had expected at first, if that was at all possible.

As Port Talbot Parkway came and went, Owen turned to Padma. 'Next station. Almost there.'

'It's been a long journey. Will your father take us to the hotel?' The hotel. He hadn't had the nerve to tell his parents about the hotel.

'We'll go back to the house first and then after a bite to eat, we'll talk about it.'

'There won't be beef, I hope. They do know I don't eat beef, don't they?'

'Yes, I am sure. I think I mentioned it, yes. Almost certain.' The train passed a large grey shed and Owen remembered the significance of seeing it on his many visits home during medical school. 'You know I missed home so much in medical school. I came home whenever I could and every time I passed the large grey shed, I knew I was almost there.'

'Shed?' Padma said.

'Yeah.' Owen suddenly became nervous as he realised that this time the grey shed signalled the approach of what promised to be a very awkward weekend for him. Then, right on cue, the train started to slow down as it approached Neath station.

'Come on then,' Owen said. He took the suitcase down from the baggage area and waited by the door for the train to stop. Padma sat in her seat. 'Come on, stand here.'

Finally the train stopped and Owen alighted. Padma joined him at the door. As the few passengers leaving at Neath scuttled across the platform, Owen spied his father leaning against the wall next to a vending machine. That was the position he always occupied – and the feeling of homecoming that Owen always experienced on seeing his father in the same position was undiminished, even in the sulking presence of Padma.

'Hey, dad.'

'Hello, son. Great to see you. Where is this girl of yours, then?'

Owen turned. Padma was standing in the door of the train. Owen quickly ran back and helped her off the train.

'Hello, then. I'm uh, Mr Morgan; Idwal. Great to see you. Welcome to Wales.'

'Your son almost left me on the train.'

'Oh. Well, Owen's mother is in the car. Come and say hello.'

The three crossed the bridge and exited the station in silence, nobody knowing quite the right thing to say. The family Fiesta was parked in a disabled space right next to the station entrance. Owen peered into it. It was empty. Just as Owen started thinking his mother had ran off, she pounced from somewhere beyond his peripheral vision.

'Owen baby! So lovely to see you. Welcome home, *bach.*' Turning to Padma, her joy seemed undiminished. 'Hello there, Patma. Welcome. I've heard all about you.' The two performed some kind of awkward embrace; each assuming the other was accustomed to this very Mediterranean greeting. 'Let's go home. It isn't far.'

As Idwal drove the car, his wife occupied the passenger seat but had twisted herself around in a most uncomfortable way to continue the conversation flow with the Londoners. 'Call me Moira. Or Mrs Morgan. I don't know what. Me and Idwal had a big discussion about what we should call ourselves when you're here so it's totally up to you. So long as it's decent anyways. HA.'

'Owen calls you mam so I'll call you mam too, shall I?'

'Um, yes, OK. Bit odd though, as I am not your mother, am I?'

'I'm confident she knows that, mam,' Owen said.

'Now your sister's not there, but you'll both see her tomorrow. So how was the trip? How is London?'

'The big smoke,' Idwal said. He always said this at the mention of London, although Owen never truly understood why. It seemed a kind of quirky Welsh reflex.

'You'll have to tell me all about India too. How exotic it sounds.'

'I'm actually Malaysian, mam; not Indian. It's nice to see you.

We've brought you some chocolates.' Turning to Owen, Padma asked where the chocolates were.

'In the case. We'll get them out in the house.'

'Now you'll have to go to *mamgu*'s house tomorrow of course.'

'It's a family thing,' Owen said. 'A visit to *mamgu*, dad's mother, is a compulsory part of every trip home. She'll want to know the news and all the fighters have to check into base, so to speak.'

Idwal and Moira talked at Padma the rest of the way to the house, filling her in on various details such as the recent marriages of people she knew nothing about, the deaths of people she had never heard of and some extra-marital affair that was going on involving a local county councillor.

'Scandalous, mun. Anyway we're here now.'

The car had pulled up outside an end-of-terrace house along a quiet side street and through the weak sodium light that permeated the inside of the car, Owen could tell Padma was less than impressed.

'Let me take your case, *boi*.'

'Thanks, dad,' Owen said.

Inside the house, Padma was introduced to the family dog, Rhodri, who seemed most keen to lick the newcomer and give a traditional warm hello. Padma, who was as small as the dog was big, backed up against the wall absolutely terrified and started shrieking for help. Moira and Idwal looked on utterly bemused as Owen pulled the dog off and shut it in the kitchen.

'I'm allergic to dogs,' she said.

Idwal sat down in his favourite chair. '*Duw, Duw*, allergic to dogs, eh? I knew a vegetarian once.'

'Being allergic isn't a choice, dad.'

'I'll put the kettle on and get food all served up,' Moira said, and disappeared into the kitchen.

'Sit down uh, uh…' Owen was reluctant to use the word babe in front of his father. He hurriedly searched for a viable alternative. 'Padma.'

Padma looked at Owen in a confused manner and then at the choice of seats. It was not a wholesome choice and she regretted being there. At least they wouldn't be there for long anyhow. 'We'll go straight after food to the hotel,' she said finally as she picked the chair that seemed to contain the least number of dog hairs.

'Hotel! What hotel!' Idwal was incredulous. 'We've done up the beds and everything. Your sister is staying over Aggie's place so you can have her bed, Palma. Hotel, my foot.'

'I can't stay here. I'm allergic to dog.'

'She's allergic to dog,' Owen said.

'Nonsense. A bit of dog never hurt no one never.'

Just at that moment, Moira emerged from the kitchen triumphant. 'It's ready! I spent all day preparing it. I hope you like good old-fashioned Welsh beef, Patma.'

Wales

Dinner was an interesting experience. Moira had chastised her son for not telling him his girlfriend did not eat beef, although Idwal was delighted at the result of this development; more steak for him. Moira had offered to cook Padma any other meal that she desired but the only offer she accepted was a glass of guava juice that happened to be left over in the fridge from some previous party long forgotten. She sat at the table drinking her guava juice as the household sat around her consuming great slabs of beef.

'So that's why old Billy had to have his anus washed out.' Idwal concluded his story with a dramatic hand gesture and bellowed loudly for effect.

'Language, Idwal!' Moira snapped. 'We have visitors. I do apologise, Packma. Really. But tell me, you're a nurse, yes? Nurses make such lovely wives.'

Owen almost dropped his fork here. Why would his mother even mention marriage? This was the first time she'd ever met Padma.

'What's your profession, mam?' Padma was unsure how to contribute to this bizarre conversation so decided she'd simply start over with a new one to her liking.

'Profession, *bach*? I work in the Co-op. So I guess businesswoman.'

'Which university did you go to?'

'University of Neath we both went to,' Idwal said with his mouth full of beef. Stabbing the air with his knife in the general direction of his wife, he continued, 'That's where we both met, you know.'

'Oh stop it, Idwal.'

'It's true. We met in the campus. Next to the alumnus building.'

'Oh don't listen to him. Owen here is the first person in our family to go to university. Oh proud of him, we are. Proud.'

Padma had already gathered this, as the living room next door had one entire wall devoted to Owen and his achievements. Certificates, awards ceremonies and at the very top, his graduation from medical school.

Owen leant over towards her. 'There is no university in Neath. Just so you know.'

Padma took one more sip of guava juice. It had a nasty tang that she couldn't quite figure out. 'What do you do, dad?'

'I advise the Prime Minister on…'

'Stop it, Idwal!'

'I'm a mechanic at the local garage. Keep the town running.'

'Do you have any brothers or sisters?' Moira said.

'I am one of six. I have three sisters and two brothers.'

'Six. Goodness.'

'There you go,' Idwal said. 'Catholics.'

'She's Hindu,' Owen said.

'Hindu.' Moira finished eating and dabbed her mouth with her napkin. 'What is being Hindu all about, then?'

'We worship lots of gods and we, uh, don't eat beef.'

'I thought that was Muslim,' Idwal said.

Owen sighed. 'Pork, dad. Muslims don't eat pork.'

'You're wrong, Owen *bach*,' Moira said as she cleared away the plates. 'Danny the Jew from Ponty don't eat pork. Jewish that is.'

Realising this conversation was potentially never ending, Owen thanked his parents for the food. 'We have to be off, sorry. Could you give us a lift to the Castle Hotel?'

'Stay here, *bach*. Patma, Palma, why don't you want to stay here? We've done up the bed and everything.'

'I'm allergic to dog. Thanks for the meal though, mam. I am so sorry I couldn't eat any of it.'

'She's allergic to dog,' Owen said.

'Well, come back tomorrow for lunch. I've got some lovely cottage pie ready.'

'She doesn't eat beef, mam. No beef.'

'Well cottage pie doesn't have beef, does it?'

Idwal laughed. 'No just bits of old cottages. What do you think it has in it, woman!'

'OK fine, I'll make some eggs. Now Owen, the Price house in the next street has come on sale so why don't you pop by tomorrow?'

Padma did her best to avoid looking horrified, and although she failed, Owen appreciated the effort involved. 'Owen wants to settle in London, don't you, Owen.'

'London! No he's always wanted to come home, haven't you?'

Both women looked at Owen and Owen looked cautiously from one to the other. They were both waiting for a response. Eventually he said, 'Well, I thought I'd live in London for a while and then think about coming to back to Wales.'

'London for a while. You told me you were coming home,' Moira said.

'You never told me you wanted to work in Wales,' Padma said.

'Actually I've applied for a job in the West Midlands,' Owen said. 'Surgery. I found out today that I've got an interview.'

Neither Moira or Padma said anything and Owen realised he'd succeeded in pleasing neither woman.

'Where in the Midlands?' Idwal said.

'Wednesbury.'

'Ah. You'll need the M40 from London all the way and then the M5. Leave the M6 junction nine.'

The other three stared blankly at Idwal. 'Only saying that's all.'

At that Owen and Padma made their way the short distance to the hotel.

'I'm sorry about that, Padma, really,' Owen whispered as they left the house. 'We'll get a bite to eat at the hotel. You must be starving.'

Padma wasn't really paying attention. She was trying to brush off some dog hairs that had become embedded in her trousers.

CHAPTER 10

Leaving London

A T WORK AGAIN on Monday morning, Owen concluded that the Welsh trip had been a mixed success. The whole experience had been horrible for him and he guessed for everyone else as well, but on the other hand it was over. There were only two weeks of work left before the entire group of house officers rotated from surgery to medicine and the policy of the medical school meant that also entailed decamping to a district general hospital outside London. For some this was a great tragedy, whereas for others, such as Owen, it was a breath of fresh country air after the stifling atmosphere of London. There was a feeling of transition hanging over the hospital which was felt from switchboard through to the secretaries. The workload would indeed increase for everyone once the junior doctors moved on; indeed it seemed that no sooner had they learned the ropes that they would be replaced by more doctors in need of rope-based knowledge skills. In an appreciated effort to say a proper goodbye to their surgical house officers, the medical school had arranged for them all to have lunch one day at the nearby Nando's.

'Where are you off to?' Alex asked Owen.

'Hastings. How about you?'

'Lewisham. Can't go too far away from London, after all.'

'Why? Why would anyone want to repeat what we just went through? Imagine life outside London. Some countryside, less drug addicts and less people wanting to kill you.'

Colleen sat down in a chair opposite Alex. 'You get drug addicts and murderers everywhere, Owen.'

'Not like in London you don't. I was almost assaulted the other day by the man who lives in the bush outside the dental wing. He lunged out at me while I was walking to the shop. If it weren't for the fact that he was drunk he'd have caught me too.'

'I saw him in accident and emergency,' Reshma said. 'He's actually very nice.'

'Perhaps he wanted to give you a kiss,' Alex said.

'I'm going to Lewisham too. We'll be doing medicine together. Excellent.'

'Where are you going, Colleen?' Alex said.

'Maidstone.'

'The Dr Hawthorne job?'

'Yes.'

'That's the best one. Well done indeed. Personally, I'm glad that after six months of medicine I'll never have to do anything but surgery again. They're always better when they're anaesthetised.'

Reshma scowled. 'You have no empathy or compassion. Patients tell us their inner secrets at little prompting. It is a great privilege.'

'Privilege indeed,' Owen said. 'Who wants to know the inner secrets of somebody's haemorrhoids?'

'I can see you've benefited from Alex's company,' Colleen said. 'We barely see you now as well. When was the last time you came to the Sun and Doves?'

This was true, Owen conceded. He hadn't been to the Sun and Doves for weeks now.

Aman returned from his mission to get the piri piri sauce. 'He's got his fancy Indian girl now, that's why.'

Reshma brightened. 'Wow. I am so glad. Did my Malayalam come in handy?'

'Yes, thanks,' Owen lied.

'I've got an interview for a senior house officer job for August,' Alex said.

Everyone turned to him. 'Where?' Colleen said.

'George's.' He paused to let this significant news sink in. This was no easy feat to achieve and he would not let anyone know his father was old medical school buddies with the departmental head of surgery there.

'I've got nothing yet,' Colleen said.

'Neither have I. Though I haven't applied' Reshma said.

'I'm doing GP. I'm going to apply when recruitment opens.' Everyone turned to Aman. He looked down when he realised everyone else had stopped talking. 'It's a good choice for me.'

Alex scoffed. 'How about you, Owen? When does pathology open?'

'Actually I've got an interview for surgery.'

Alex could not hide his disappointment. 'Surgery? Why did you apply for surgery?'

'I wanted to help people. Remember that lady with an obstruction? I did my application immediately after that.'

'She died,' Alex said.

'I know. It is logical though, surgery. Perhaps it'll be good for me.'

'Where are you doing it?' Alex said, concerned. Please let it not be Tommy's or Guy's, or anywhere better than George's.

'The West Midlands.'

Alex visibly relaxed. 'The Midlands. No wonder.'

As lunch ended, all the house officers said their goodbyes and were herded back to the hospital by medical school staff anxious that tasks were not being completed and patients were waiting. Owen found himself facing Colleen as they negotiated their way around the table. He looked her straight in the eyes and she looked away. He genuinely felt guilty for the way he'd treated his old friend over the past few weeks; the unanswered calls, the texts that did not receive any reply and the coffee dates missed.

'Sorry, Colleen, for the way it turned out.'

'Don't worry. You'll be a great surgeon.'

Owen was unsure about this but appreciated the comment anyway. 'I'll miss you. Come down to Hastings when you're free.'

'Yes. Perhaps I'll be able to come out to dinner with you and Padma.' By the way she said this Owen was not convinced that this was regarded by her as a good thing.

'She won't be there all the time.'

'She dominates you, you know. There won't be any Owen left when she's finished.'

'I don't know if there was any Owen there to begin with.'

'There was. And still is. I'll come down to Hastings if I get a chance. You come up to Maidstone if you can, OK?'

'Yeah. It might be difficult…'

'With Padma. Yes, I get it.'

They both looked at each other and hugged. The chances of them being alone with her outside of work for long enough without Padma being around were quite slim, Owen judged.

'Catch you for coffee before we both leave?' Owen said.

Colleen smiled. There was always hope in the world.

Old Square Hospital

With only a short time to go before his stay in London ended and his period at the coast doing medicine began, Owen travelled up to the Midlands for an interview to sort out the next part of his career after Hastings. This was a three-year basic surgical training rotation and the main advantage of this, so far as Owen could see, was that he wouldn't have to go through any job applications for a long time. He could settle down. Buy a house even. Get married? Possibly. He needed something to divert his attention.

As luck would have it his mobile rang. He reached over to the passenger seat to find it. The car swerved slightly on the M40 but few people were on the road at 11 p.m. so Owen felt comfortable taking the risk. He looked at the screen. His father.

'Hey, dad.'

'Owen. What time did you arrive?'

'I'm not there yet. Still on the M40.'

'Then you shouldn't be answering phones you foolish...' Idwal had wanted to say 'fool' but felt that using 'foolish' first had robbed his 'fool' of all legitimacy. As he struggled to find an alternative, Owen spoke.

'Sorry. I'll call when I'm there.'

'Watch the road.' With that he rang off and Owen returned his gaze to the road. It was another hour before he started seeing signs for Wednesbury and a further half-hour before he rolled into the hospital compound.

As he walked towards the security office, where he was assured his keys would be, he quickly texted Padma to let her know he'd arrived. By this point he'd forgotten about his father's call. The hospital building was a mixture of red brick Victoriana and 1960s NHS special. The perfect blend, Owen thought, as he got lost once again in a dimly-lit corridor. The hospital was of impressive size but the layout so confused that Owen spent a good part of the early hours of the morning finding the security office and then finding his room afterwards. The situation was not made any easier by the fact that portions of the hospital were being replaced and remodelled. Occasionally Owen would come across a lone porter whose approach would be heralded by increasingly loud footsteps and an attendant shadow that would loom large often before the visitor came into view. More than once, Owen found himself diverting into a side corridor to escape an approaching figure, though the exact reason for this he did not know.

Once he had located his room, Owen hung up his suit in the chipboard cupboard and unpacked his things. These consisted almost entirely of some toiletries, a change of underwear and his CV. Sitting down on the edge of the bed he looked at his watch. 2.10 a.m. Probably too late to call his father now. Feeling strangely awake, he looked again at the Rolex his parents had given him – it always gave him comfort in strange situations. A wearable comfort blanket for the junior doctor. Picking up his CV he flicked through it one more time. No time to change anything now anyway, he thought as he pushed it back into its plastic file.

Owen walked to the window and looked out over the town. It had reminded him of the industrial towns of south Wales as he drove through it earlier in his search for the hospital. There were many closed-down factories, abandoned-looking streets and even the city centre looked as it if could do with a lick of paint. The rain reminded him of home but he was comforted that he'd be only two or three hours' drive away. Looking at the road map, Owen figured the border was only around forty minutes away at its nearest point. Perhaps he could live there and commute? Looking again at the map Owen realised the futility of this. The nearest habitation on the Welsh side of the border was a village, at most, and probably populated by English at that.

Looking around the small room Owen saw there was no en suite visible. It was late and he probably should sleep. A quick shower could be obtained in the communal shower in the morning, once it had been found, but he needed to micturate in the here and now. Luckily there was a sink in the room. Owen drew the curtains, though against whom or what he did not know. A person would have to be twenty feet tall or be flying some sort of microlight to be able to catch him peeing into a sink, and frankly if such a person existed then reporting him to the hospital authorities for defiling a sink was probably the least of their concerns. He'd read somewhere that these on-call room sinks were known colloquially as NHS en suites anyway.

Secreting himself between the crisp well-worn sheets, Owen reached to turn off the light. As he did so, he noticed the wording on the bottom of the sheets. It read, 'Good Hope Hospital'. If his sheets felt homesick for nearby Birmingham then Owen felt the pillowcases probably felt worse, as these were from a Bristol hospital.

After a fitful sleep, during which he was awoken on several occasions by loud banging from the heating system and large fluctuations in temperature within the room, Owen awoke and managed to find the showers. The lack of pressure in the water system was a source of great discomfort. The only way he could get a decent flow going was to get down on all fours and shower like a dog. He was, however, gratified that there were towels provided. These came from Winchester and Eastleigh NHS Trust.

Owen breakfasted in his suit at the hospital canteen. Brushing off the crumbs afterwards, he pulled out his notes and went over the questions the interviewer might ask and how best he should answer them. After practising a few answers to himself he spied the cashier staring at him obliquely. Feeling suddenly alone and vulnerable, he pushed his crumpled notes back into his trouser pocket and got up to find the department of surgery offices, where the interviews would take place. He already felt a cramping sensation in his bowel and realised that this had more to do with the impending trial than the wet toast and crusty scrambled eggs that he'd just eaten. He hated interviews.

The Interview

Arriving a full twenty minutes early Owen found the corridor outside the interview room crammed with young doctors in ill-fitting suits. All the seats were taken so he contented himself to sit on a small coffee table next to a withered pot plant.

'Fancy putting a pot plant in a room with no windows, eh?' Owen said to a bespectacled Chinese chap who sat on a seat right next to the pot plant. The Chinese doctor looked at him blankly. After a few minutes a secretary opened the door to the interview room and called the name of the next candidate. The candidate in question was obviously Indian as the secretary had considerable difficulty in getting her tongue around the name. When no one stood up immediately, the poor secretary had to repeat the name a few times before somebody got to their feet. As this drama was unfolding Owen fished his crumpled piece of paper from his pocket and went over his answers once again. Before he'd got halfway through, the secretary called his name out and he found himself sitting on a plastic garden chair facing seven consultant surgeons behind a trestle table in an otherwise dull, windowless room. The heating seemed to be on full blast and there was a distinct smell of sweat. Sweat and fear. Owen's fear.

The surgeon in the middle, a Mr Fox, was the apparent alpha male of the group and he started the questioning. He wore a white coat, which surprised Owen. He hadn't seen a single doctor wear a white coat since starting work, his own reflection in the mirror included.

'I suppose the obvious question, Dr Morgan, is why do you want to do surgery?'

Owen smiled. This was question number one on his list and he delivered what he assumed was a perfect answer. Mr Fox smiled too; perhaps a little too much.

'That's all well and good but why do you really want to be a surgeon?'

Owen started repeating his original answer when Mr Fox held up his hand and invited a bespectacled Indian to his left to ask a question.

'Can you name a historically famous ENT surgeon?' he said.

Owen fixed his gaze on a tumbler full of water that lay on the trestle table in front of Mr Fox. What type of question was this? 'Yes,' Owen said. Oh my God! Why did he say that? He didn't know any historical ones. Only ones that were alive.

Mr Fox coughed. 'Would you care to name any?'

'Professor Gleeson from Guy's Hospital. Now he did a lot of work with...'

'He's not really historical,' the Indian ENT surgeon said. 'I was looking for Sir Morrell McKenzie.'

A Scottish accident and emergency consultant asked the next question. 'What is the job of an A&E SHO?'

'To assess and treat all acute injuries and to triage...'

'A& E isn't triage. Now an old man comes in with breathing problems that begin to stabilise but he's about to breach the four-hour limit. Do you discharge him or admit him?'

Ah, the dreaded four-hour limit. 'If he was stable I'd send him home and if he was not, I'd admit him.'

'He's in the middle. That's the point. The clock's ticking doctor.'

'Best to be on the safe side, then. Admit.'

'Take up a bed? That could cause problems.'

'I guess I'd ask a senior, I suppose.'

The Scotsman frowned. 'Difficult one, isn't it?'

Mr Fox decided to ask the next question. 'What would you prefer doing; a left hemicolectomy or a right hemicolectomy?'

Owen looked at the water once more. He guessed he

wouldn't be coming to the Midlands after all. Never mind; he didn't much like the area anyway.

'A right hemicolectomy. Because I'd get to see the liver.'

'Well the right side, yes; I agree. The reason, though, is that it is easier to do the anastomosis. How would a leaking anastomosis present itself?'

'Pain, bleeding, acute abdomen and, uh, I suppose, death.'

Mr Fox smiled. 'Death indeed. Never be a stranger to death. The good general surgeon becomes best of friends with the spectre of death.'

'Not too friendly, I hope,' Owen said.

Mr Fox's smile faded. 'A casualty SHO is trying to refer an inappropriate patient. How do you respond?'

'Politely. Tell him that the referral is not good, to go back and think again.'

'Why do you want to come to this hospital?'

Owen thought of the industrial wastelands he passed in his car last night. 'It reminds me of home. This place has a good reputation and the three-year rotation would train me well.'

'Can you be trained? Give me an example of how you were trained to do something.'

Without thinking, Owen continued on auto-pilot. 'My grandfather taught me how to gut a fish once.'

On the way back to the room Owen concluded he needed to submit more applications as he would not be coming here. The interview had faltered so badly and his mouth had dried up so completely, he was unable to produce any words by the end. If this were not bad enough he'd gestured towards Mr Fox's tumbler of water, and in trying to pour himself a glass had tipped a fair proportion over the head of department's crotch. Surgical dexterity indeed!

But the next day, to Owen's great surprise, he was called on his mobile and offered the job. He'd spend the next three years of his life in Wednesbury. He'd buy his first house. He'd get married and have two children in that godforsaken West Midlands town; something he would never have predicted that day.

CHAPTER 11

The Morning After

FIVE YEARS HAD passed and much had changed in between the job offer in the West Midlands and the sudden death of Owen's mother in law the previous night. For a start he woke up in his native Wales, where he had secured a job. Morning was breaking when Owen and Padma silently got out of bed and prepared the kids for the trip to Heathrow Airport. Neither of them had slept much in the night, Padma thinking about her dear deceased mother and Owen thinking about how he ended up in this exact situation and finding no obvious answer. He thought of such matters often and never found any obvious answer.

The plane was booked for two o'clock in the afternoon but trying to mobilise the household even for short trips was like mobilising the British Army. Owen needed to make the phone call to his department telling them he would not be in and was dreading every moment until then. The earliest he could call was 9 a.m. and the time was currently 7.55 sixty-five minutes. He made breakfast for Rhys and Ifan, his two young sons.

'Why is mammy crying, daddy?'

'Granny Malaysia isn't well, Rhys. She's very unwell.'

'Is she dead?'

Owen quickly looked around the room. Padma wasn't there, which was good. 'Uh you shouldn't really say that. Mammy will be upset.'

'But is she dead, daddy? Deady-deady dead-dead-dead?'

'Rhys! Stop it. Do you want to upset mammy?'

'Mammy took my train away.'

Owen looked at the clock. 8.05. 'Yes, she died last night. Mammy is very upset so don't you dare upset her even more.'

Ifan, who at four years old was a year and a half younger than his brother, felt duty bound to contribute. 'Is mammy going away, daddy?'

'Yes. She needs to go home. That's why we're all getting ready to take her to the airport.'

'Can I go too?'

'No. You're staying with me. Won't that be fun?' Owen wasn't enthusiastic.

'Your cooking is yuck,' Rhys said. 'I want mammy.'

Owen sighed. 8.09.

After breakfast the kids were washed and dressed as usual. Any variation in the usual routine caused huge delays and was to be avoided at all costs. Padma spent most of the time crying and packing, a sight Owen had seen a few times before, but this time, since the reason for the crying was someone other than him, he was quite surprised at how sorry he felt for her loss. After a few years of mutual antagonism, Owen did not think he'd ever feel sorry for his wife in any situation ever again, but he felt sad now. As he watched her pack clothing for the journey he saw her pick up a pair of socks and check to see if they matched. He walked over behind her and put his arms around her waist. It was the first time he'd initiated an embrace in a long time and Owen was surprised that Padma did not push him away. Instead she turned and beat his chest with her fists.

'Why did she die without waiting for me? Why, why, why?'

'She was an old woman. Her time had come. She died well.'

'Why didn't she wait for me?'

'I guess she'd waited as long as she could.'

She sobbed violently as Rhys peered cautiously around the

edge of the door frame. Owen looked at the clock again. 8.30. 'Mammy's upset, Rhys. Please go downstairs.'

'Is it because Grandma's dead?'

'RHYS. Go downstairs. Now.'

The little face disappeared and another, smaller face, took its place. 'Are you OK, mammy?'

'Come here, baby.' Padma knelt as the cherubic little figure ran towards her and embraced her tightly. Owen was released and, feeling a bit redundant, wandered into the kitchen. He opened the large Map of the Road and started plotting his trip. This was despite the fact that the journey was, on the one hand, straightforward anyway and, on the other, he'd be using the sat nav. Owen had begun to realise a few months before that he was turning into his father, but doing something so blatantly Idwal-esque as this held no fear for him anymore. 8.55. Time to give it a try.

After asking switchboard to put him through to the eye department, Owen cradled the phone to his ear as he poured himself a glass of orange juice. The phone was answered at the twenty-seventh ring, quite quickly for the eye department, Owen thought, and soon he was speaking to sister.

'I'm sorry, sister. I won't be able to come in today.'

'Really? There is a whole clinic booked. Are you unwell?'

'No. I am sorry for the trouble. I'll be in tomorrow.'

'I need a reason, Owen.'

Owen swallowed hard. He hated discussing personal things with antagonistic people while asking for favours at the same time. 'My mother-in-law died last night. I have not slept and, besides, I need to take the wife to the airport.'

Sister was put off balance a bit. He knew that he had produced one of the few trump cards that existed when calling to say you weren't coming to work. 'I am sorry to hear that.' She was sorry that she had to do a big pile of phone calls cancelling patients from the clinic, Owen imagined. 'Very sorry. I am sorry to ask, but I see you are on call tomorrow and the weekend. Will you be doing these on-calls? Locums are impossible to find at the last minute, as well you know.'

'Yes. I'll find a way. I'll get my mother to babysit. I'll sort something out.'

Sister seemed satisfied. 'Right then. I have some work to do. See you tomorrow.' Owen replaced the phone in its cradle. The call had been every bit as horrible as he thought it would but at least it was over now. A load fell from his shoulders. He just needed to sort out babysitting for the entire weekend. Some of the load reappeared again.

Padma appeared at the door and Owen instinctively gave her a big hug. He was surprised that it was an instinct and again surprised that she did not push him away.

'We better get moving.'

'I'm packed. Sure you can't come?'

'I have to work. I would come if I could.' Owen wondered if Padma knew he was not being truthful here. She did, but wanted to go through the motions anyhow.

Heathrow Airport

As they drove from south Wales to London, Owen could hear the music from *Over the Hedge*, a Disney cartoon, emanating from the portable DVD player in the back seat. Thankfully the boys were behaving and though Padma had her eyes closed in the passenger seat, he could tell that she was not sleeping. This was not difficult, as she periodically screwed her eyes tight and let out a soft moan as a trickle of tears rolled down her cheek. Owen never liked the long journey to London. Apart from the Severn Bridge closely followed by the 'Welcome to England' sign in English and Welsh, the whole journey was so featureless and boring that sleep began to beckon every time Owen passed Leigh Delamere services. He'd tried a Red Bull once, purchased at extortionate cost in the services themselves but Owen reckoned it had no effect. Padma had suggested that this was due to Owen's increasing weight; perhaps more Red Bull was needed to achieve the same effect in her husband as on a normal person.

Owen was happy that at least Padma was pretending to be asleep at present and no barbed comments would be forthcoming. Suddenly the voice from the back seat rose.

'I can't see the picture, Rhys. Move it. Move it.'

'No. Go away.'

'Boys. Be quiet. Mammy is sleeping so you have to be quiet.'

'But Rhys is stinky. He won't let me see.'

'Rhys. Let your brother see.'

'But Ifan keeps on turning the screen.'

'Ifan. Don't turn the screen.'

'Look, daddy. Ifan is trying to turn the screen again.'

Owen looked back for as long as he dared and tried his angry-looking though quiet face, in a bid to stop the argument without making Padma give up her pretend sleep and actively join in. It worked, in as much as both Rhys and Ifan scowled at their father who had now become the common enemy, while Padma remained quiet in her seat with her eyes closed.

How do single fathers ever manage? Owen had thought about this many times but had come to no satisfactory conclusion. The ever-increasing amplitude of the bumps along which his marriage had travelled of late had caused him to consider what life without Padma would actually be like. How would things work out with the children? What was the actual procedure for divorce? Would they ever speak to him again? Would she? Would he want her to? There were so many questions and so few answers that Owen often gave up thinking about such matters after a short time.

After another twenty miles *Over the Hedge* came to an end and after a brief argument about which DVD should be, next peace had returned to the car. Padma was still pretending to sleep. Should he try and wake her? Should he be supportive and say something good? If this was true then what should he say? He should have taken a few paracetamols before this journey. Finally he decided to say something profound that showed he really did care, despite everything, and he poked her in the right shoulder with his index finger and leant over. 'I liked Anita. I'm sorry she died. It'll be OK. I love you.'

Padma turned her face toward Owen and looked quizzically at him. Why did he say 'I love you'? It made no sense to Owen either. It seemed like an automatic add-on, but as Owen had not used those words for more than a year, they seemed strange and alien to him now. It was like trying to repeat old French phrases from his schooldays which he had never been able to properly pronounce and whose meaning had always been suspect and strange.

'I should have gone back a few weeks ago. You said no.'

Ah, Owen thought. The blame game. Padma was gearing up to blame Owen for her not being there for the moment of Anita's death. He had wondered when it would begin. Best to stay quiet, he thought, and thankfully this tactic worked. Padma turned her face to the window and pretended to sleep again. At least he tried, Owen concluded. That was supportive. Box ticked. Supportive husband; yes or no? Yes.

They reached the airport with little time to spare, and after Padma roused herself into action, it seemed that she might just make it. Owen certainly hoped so, as it was he who had paid for the non-refundable tickets. He knew that although Padma would think nothing of simply paying again for a later flight, the extra cost would make him weep much more emotionally over the loss than Padma had managed thus far.

As they stood outside the security paraphernalia, Padma looked Owen in the shoulder. 'Look after the boys. Please make sure they're alive when I get back. Keep them well fed. Remember to get milk and bread on the way home because we've run out and don't dump them on your parents. Take Ifan to wee-wee before he goes to bed or he'll wet himself.'

'I'll look after them. They'll have lots of fun. I hope the funeral goes well. Honestly, I am sorry. For your loss that is.' Owen did not want to admit to any liability for Padma missing out on her mother's death. From bitter experience he knew that her analytical mind would make him out to be a monster over the issue and he would have no defence.

After she kissed the boys and prepared to board the plane, something most unexpected happened. Padma turned and looked Owen directly in the eyes. 'I love you too,' she said softly, before placing her water bottle into the bin and walking into the security area. She did not look back.

Single Father

The three boys watched Padma pass through security and enter the restricted area and kept on looking for the full seven minutes that it took her to go out of view. Three orphans standing alone in the airport, Owen thought to himself. Perhaps the boys feared being left alone with their father. Owen certainly feared the extensive juggling act he'd have to complete with work and childcare duties till Padma returned in two weeks' time. He looked at them both nervously. They looked back at him and then at each other. And as if by some telepathic instinct, they both tore off in different directions through the crowds in the busy airport.

Owen opted to run after Ifan first. He was the smallest and

thus easiest to catch. Rhys was seated in a plastic helicopter by the time he was located, begging a cleaner for spare coins to make it go round. Forgetting where he was, which was unusual for Owen, he shouted so loudly that the two boys froze; bursting into tears immediately afterwards. Noticing that a few passengers had turned their heads and immediately feeling vulnerable in such a crowded place, Owen went into tunnel vision mode and tried to shut out the other people as much as possible as he manhandled his kids back to the car. The experience had shocked them so much that when Owen found out, to his dismay, that he had to wait in a long queue to pay to leave the car park Rhys and Ifan stood perfectly still.

'I want mammy,' Rhys said.

'You're yucky,' his brother added. 'Mammy wouldn't shout at us.'

'You wouldn't have run away with mammy,' Owen said.

'I want Monster Munch.'

'And I want Monster Munch too.'

Finally Owen had a way of punishing his sons for the trouble in the airport. 'No Monster Munch for naughty boys.'

As he negotiated the car through the main exit he found he was driving the wrong way. Reaching for the sat nav proved difficult as there were frequent lane changes required and no place to stop. Looking alternately at the road and in the glove compartment, Owen managed to hook the wire with his little finger and found he could ease the sat nav toward him bit by bit.

'MAMMY, MAMMY, MAMMY, MAMMY.' Ifan had other ideas. At this crucial point in the manoeuvre the sat nav fell from his grasp and rolled into the passenger footwell. It was too dangerous to get it now.

'Can you be quiet, please. Please. Just till I put this on.'

'MAMMY MAMMY,' Ifan said.

Rhys, not to be outdone, was thinking of something better to say. 'Daddy is a big poo.'

Great, Owen thought to himself. Just great. How would he cope? Why were they like this now? Why were they like this always?

'Do you want Monster Munch?'

'Yes yes yes yes yes yes yes. Please please please.'

'Well, if you can be quiet until we find the M4 then I'll get you some.'

'What's the M4?' Rhys said.

'A big motorway that will take us home.'

As silence temporarily descended, Owen regretted not being able to ask his parents to babysit. Things were not good between Padma and his parents and had not been good for a long time. Was there a specific start date, something that happened he could put his finger on and say it was all fine before that? Not really. For every incident he could think of there were other incidents preceding it that could also be called incidents. Feeling a headache develop, Owen conceded that perhaps it was all a long line of incidents that blended into each other. He had done nothing to diffuse these incidences. Or perhaps he did too much. After each battle he would emerge from the car, or from the phone, like Chamberlain back from Munich and announce peace in our time. It was never peace for long though and in the end Owen had got tired and both Padma and his parents had grown resistant to further peacekeeping efforts. Owen, of course, was regarded as the enemy by both camps and ended up more isolated than ever.

'Monster Munch,' Ifan said. To be fair, he'd been quiet until the M25 at least.

'OK. When we reach the services we'll get some.'

'Can we watch a DVD?' Where was the DVD player? Hopefully it hadn't been left in the airport. As it turned out Padma had taken it to Malaysia by accident and this loss of the DVD player when it was finally discovered seemed much more terrifying a prospect to the boys than the earlier loss of their mother had been.

'Not now. After the Monster Munch. Tell me when you see a sign for services and I'll pull in.' Owen knew full well that Ifan couldn't read, and Rhys had fallen asleep in his chair. Perhaps it would be alright. Perhaps he'd manage. Life as a single father seemed better in his head than it did in practice, as things often did. He would use this opportunity to prove himself, he decided. Prove he'd be a good single father, if push came to shove.

Owen likened himself to a cancerous cell at that exact moment in time. A cell is only cancerous once it can separate itself from its tissue of origin and successfully survive in an alien environment. There were a number of stages to go though before this could be achieved. First, it must be able to detach itself, then it must find a way of entering the blood stream. After this it has to be able to escape the bloodstream and be able to use a new-found set of skills to survive elsewhere. Owen wanted to know if he'd survive elsewhere, were he to detach himself. He had already discovered he was able to detach himself, and even swim in the bloodstream. But could he survive independently? Owen decided he did not like comparing himself to a cancerous cell so pushed the image from his mind.

Looking in the rear view mirror, Owen was pleased to see both boys were now sleeping. How did it get like this between Padma and himself? When did the rot set it? This date he knew with some degree of exactness. The date the Medical Training Application Service was launched, more popularly known by the acronym MTAS.

CHAPTER 12

MTAS

O WEN REMEMBERED THE meeting at which he first heard the words MTAS. Two years of struggle and toil at Old Square Hospital had left Owen with an MRCS (Eng) qualification, a wife, a house and a young son. Padma was also pregnant with their second child and for the first time in a while he felt that things were going in the right direction. Owen was prone to think things were going in wrong directions, so possibly this was the first time ever that he had felt that way. It felt good. He was currently working directly for Mr Fox and Mr Graham, two eminent bowel surgeons, in a senior house officer job that was widely regarded as being the most sought-after in the hospital. Yes, Owen felt at home, and that home was in Wednesbury.

After the ward round one morning, Mr Fox pulled Owen to one side. 'Have you thought about your future?'

'Of course. Once this rotation ends I will apply for a registrar's job.'

Mr Fox smiled. 'Are you still hell-bent on going back to Wales or do you want to stick around here?'

'I have to go back. I need to go back, to be honest. If I could stay here I would.'

'Well if you change your mind get in touch with me.' He winked and began to walk away. Suddenly he stopped, remembering something, and turned back abruptly. 'There is a meeting today at twelve, by the way, about the new medical recruitment system the government is bringing out. It's starting in a few months and will probably be a big balls-up as per usual for Patricia fucking Hewitt.'

Owen winced. He liked Mr Fox but was never very good at having conversations which involved swearing. Every time he'd tried to play along it had gone badly so he'd decided the best policy was simply nodding and smiling until the danger passed and the conversation passed back under the comfort threshold.

'Pass the word around; there's a good lad. I'll see you in theatre.'

'Bostin.' It meant 'OK great' in the dialect of the West Midlands and Owen always felt innately pleased with himself using the local lingo.

At twelve noon that day all the senior house officers at the hospital, many of whom Owen had first met that rainy interview day a few years before, were seated in the conference room awaiting the arrival of Mr Fox. Bang on time he marched in, white coat flowing behind him. He got straight to the point. 'The Labour government is changing the recruitment system for all medical jobs from next year onwards. It is being done in one fell swoop and will affect all jobs everywhere all at once. You are in the firing line. My advice is get your applications in before the system collapses and all applications to the West Midlands deanery will be looked upon favourably. Any questions?'

Danni, an excellent Malaysian trainee surgeon, raised her hand. 'My rotation goes right up to the end of this system. What's actually going to happen? Can't I just trust it'll all go well.'

'Yes, yes, Danni, you're doing well in the current system and if the new system will be like the old then you should have no problem. The new system will be automated to such a high degree that everything you will have done will be reduced to points on a computer algorithm. There is no room for personality, knowledge or skill beyond what the government selects to be scored in any way at all. A computer will select you for interview and will decide which part of the country it sends you to. If it sends you anywhere. You only get four choices and…'

A gasp went around the room. 'Yes, ladies and gentlemen, FOUR choices and that's it. If you get none of them you're stuffed. Up the Khyber. Down the Swanee. Did you know that that's actually a river in America? You probably knew that, David.' He winked at a tall upper gastro-intestinal surgery trainee. Owen marvelled at Mr Fox. He was like President Clinton; he really knew how to work a crowd.

An Indian trainee called Sanjeev raised his hand and in a strong north Indian accent asked his question. A few questions later Owen raised his own hand.

'Mr Fox, my rotation is due to end after this new system is meant to start. Should I stay here or hop onto the new system?'

'All contracts and all rotations here at Old Square will be honoured if any of you wish to keep those jobs. From my point of view it would be good if you did because you lot will be the last trainees we will ever get any direct say in the appointment of. But from your perspectives it would be foolish to stay. The post of house officer, senior or junior, is being abandoned. The new terminology will be 'specialty registrar'. The junior house officer has already gone of course, with these new 'foundation' doctors. Foundation.' Mr Fox shook his head in contempt. 'I suppose the only advantage if you stay on is that you can say you're the last house officer in the country.' He walked comically around the podium. 'Look at me,' he said. 'I'm the last house officer in Britain.'

The audience laughed, though with a strong current of nervousness at futures now put in sudden jeopardy by Whitehall's great plan to destroy the medical profession's ability to oppose any of its reforms.

'There is information about this on the government website. If you're wise though, you'll heed my warning and apply now for registrar jobs. In the West Midlands. I guess that rules you out then, Owen.'

Owen smiled nervously. Perhaps he should play it safe and apply for a job here and now in the West Midlands. He thought of his parents and extended family at home, waiting for a triumphant return that would never take place. On the other hand he had responsibilities. He was a father already and about to become a father again in a few months.

Mr Fox leant forward on the podium. 'Now get back to work,' he said. 'Before I fire the lot of you while I still can.'

The Pilonidal Sinus

That afternoon Owen and Mr Graham sat scrubbed up next to the heaving sterilised buttocks of an anaesthetised Greek truck driver in the day surgery unit.

'Tell me what you know about pilonidal sinuses' Mr Graham said as he drew a large ellipse around an area of indurated skin and lumpy abscesses deep in the natal cleft of the patient.

'This is where hair in the buttock area gets pushed under the skin and continues to grow. It then all gets infected and more hair gets pulled in. The pus drains from a central sinus along little channels.'

Mr Graham nodded. 'Fat, hairy truck drivers are the worst. Something to do with the rolling action of the buttocks against the seat.' The two surgeons simultaneously looked at the large set of buttocks in front of them and imagined them rolling away on a truck seat.

Owen turned to the scrub nurse. 'Diathermy.' He then passed the searing hot blade along the mark that Mr Graham had delineated, the heat coagulating the vessels as it went, reducing bleeding.

'Treatment?' Mr Graham said.

'This.'

'Yes, yes, this, but what else?'

'The Karydakis procedure.'

'Yes. He was a Greek. Greeks are hairy, so he had the practice.'

Owen was unsure what he meant by this so continued silently. He dissected the diseased tissue free and used the diathermy to cauterise two vessels which were still bleeding rather heavily. The smoke produced by the cautery stung his eyes and Mr Graham wafted it away dramatically. 'Causes cancer apparently. Don't breathe it in.'

'Bit difficult without a mask.'

'Then don't make so much of it. The scrub nurse thinks it's a barbecue. Greek buttock burger, anyone?'

After a few more minutes of burning Owen turned back to the scrub nurse. 'Nylon, please.' Owen conceded that he'd overdone it a bit with the diathermy and there was a distinct warm summer afternoon aroma in the room.

As he was trying to suture the edges of the gaping wound together, Mr Graham leant back in his chair. 'What was the mystery meeting about then, today?'

Owen passed the suture through fascia and pulled it tight before picking up the toothed forceps once more. 'Mr Fox telling us about this new MTAS system. Computerised job selection. Coming in next year.'

'Don't handle the tissue so much. Did he do his podium dance?'

Owen tied his suture and was handed some Vicryl, a dissolvable suture, for the subcutaneous tissue. 'He did, yes.'

'He said he would. The wound is looking tight. It might break open when he sits down.'

This comment caused Owen to freeze.

'No carry on. Half of mine do anyway. A lot of people just

leave it open and don't even try. He should be grateful for your efforts.'

Owen looked at the gelatinous mass in front of him and imagined sweaty hairy Greek buttocks pushing down with all their weight on the poor suture, hardly thicker than a human hair.

'Well are you sticking around or trying to go back home?'

'I think I should give it a shot at least. To go home, I mean.'

'Listen, Owen. I'm Welsh. How come I ended up in Wednesbury, you may ask? Bit of a bleeder there. Use the diathermy again. Good. The answer. It's all random. Random. Ask me where you think I would have ended up a consultant.'

'Where did you...' Owen said, before pausing to cauterise the errant vessel. '...think you'd end up?'

'Cardiff. But I'm here now. Am I glad? Yes. Does it matter where you end up? Not really.'

'I hardly see my wife with this job and never see my parents. It would be great if I could be home. Like the Jews have their Aliyah, I think all Welsh people do too.'

Mr Graham looked confused.

'In a way,' Owen added. He thought it would increase Mr Graham's understanding – though after he had said it he realised that even on a superficial level it did not achieve this aim. Perhaps he'd said it in the absence of anything else to say.

'I'll be outside,' Mr Graham said, before standing up and tearing off his gloves. He threw them dramatically across the theatre in an attempt to get them into the bin but missed by millimetres.

'Do not throw things in my theatre, Mr Graham,' the scrub nurse said.

'Yes ma'am.' Mr Graham saluted and goose-stepped out of the main door.

'And you know you can't go out that way.'

As the doors closed, Owen could hear his boss blowing a huge raspberry in the corridor. Owen liked Mr Graham. He liked Mr Fox too. He would have loved to have stayed and felt confident that he'd get on well were he given the opportunity. The schools were not so good, though, and he wanted his children, his family, to be culturally Welsh. Quite why he did want this, he did not know. *Hiraeth*, perhaps. The force that draws all Welshmen home. It hadn't drawn Mr Graham home, though. What should he do? Owen finished closing and put a large dressing on the wound.

'Finished doctor?' The scrub nurse was impatient.

'Yes. Thank you all.' Owen had been instilled with the importance of thanking everyone in theatre once the case was done but never felt comfortable doing it somehow. It made him feel awkward and he normally looked at the anaesthetic machine or some other inanimate object as he did so.

Pushing through the swing doors, Owen saw his boss had his feet up on the desk in the corridor. 'Cheer up,' he said. 'Perhaps Pat Hewitt knows what she's doing this time.' He then let out an enormous guffaw.

Old Square Mess

After clinics and theatre had finished that evening, Owen, Danni, Sanjeev and another surgical SHO called Ahmed were discussing the new MTAS situation in the hospital mess.

Sitting on a coffee-stained blue fabric chair, Ahmed was not pleased. 'We need to act on this. Go on strike, perhaps. How can we only be given four choices of where to go? What nonsense it all is with…'

'Yes,' Danni said. 'But if we apply early through the old system if might be OK for us.'

'It's OK for you perhaps but you're a year ahead of me. You

stand a chance in the old system. I'll never get a job that way. I will have to brave this new system.'

'You never know. Mr Fox did wink at the end. Perhaps we'll all be safe in this deanery. You'll never know if you don't try.'

'I haven't completed the exam, though.'

'Neither I have completed the exam,' Sanjeev said. 'I will be in the sink if this new system starts to work.'

Owen couldn't really understand how Sanjeev had ever passed the English language proficiency exam needed by all doctors from outside Europe to be able to practise in the UK, but he liked him all the same. 'Perhaps we're all panicking for nothing,' he said. 'I have faith that it might just work out well. That's what I think. The junior house officers were replaced by these foundation doctors and nothing bad took place. In fact it was a lot better organised.' Owen started to feel convinced by his own words as he spoke. 'Yes. In fact we're very lucky to be here at this time.'

'You think it will be a cakewalk?' Sanjeev said.

'Cakewalk?' Owen said.

'Cakewalk indeed. You're as dull as Patsie Hewitt if you think that.' Ahmed put his coffee cup down with such force that a good deal splashed out over his expensive blue striped shirt. 'Ach. There was never any restriction at house officer level. The main competition has always been at senior house officer to registrar level. That was where the bottleneck was and is. And always will be. If you let a computer do the selecting you're cooked.'

'But are we cooked?' Owen said. 'I want to go back to Wales. If the application system is so anonymous that nobody knows who anybody is and will select just based on points, then I stand just as good a chance as the Welsh trainees.'

'We should just apply through the old system, as Mr Fox advised,' Danni said.

'It will be actual people grading the points though,' Owen

said. 'The computer just allocates the jobs. There are still people involved.'

'We have a similar system in India but it doesn't work there so well. I think it will not be any kind of cakewalk,' Sanjeev said.

'No. What is a cakewalk exactly anyway? Where does the term come from?' Danni said.

Nobody answered. Owen leant back in his chair and as he did so it made a groaning noise. He really must start some kind of physical activity or he'd end up like Big Karim the Dental Queen, one of the Max Fax SHOs. 'Well I think it'll be just fine. We're all good trainees. Good trainees always get jobs. Just wait and see.'

Sanjeev suddenly brightened. 'You know, Owen, I have purchased a tennis bat. I would be honoured if you would play tennis with me one day.'

'Uh. I haven't played tennis for a long time and I have no racquet myself.'

'They have so much cheap things in the new sports shop in the new buildings opposite this very hospital.'

Ahmed began sipping his coffee with a look of general hostility to the whole room. Danni excused herself and went off to study. Off to study, Owen repeated to himself. Why would she do that? She'd already passed the exam. These Malaysians were a total mystery to him. They would work and study the whole time, doing nothing else, some of them. Perhaps only the Chinese ones, like Danni, he thought in retrospect. She had postponed marriage with her long-term partner to complete her surgical training. Surgical training was never complete, though. It just carried on and on until you retired. Or died. Padma's family was not like this. But then again they were not Chinese Malaysians. How confusing the state of the world was. And there Ahmed sat, glaring at everyone and no one. Perhaps the Arab response to uncertainty was anger and hostility.

Sanjeev was grinning happily and making tennis swooping motions with his right arm. A backhand, it seemed. Good to be happy at least, Owen pondered. Perhaps the Welsh response to uncertainty was just to let it happen and then complain unendingly when it did with the inner knowledge that no preventative measures were taken whatsoever. Owen glanced at his watch; the time was 6.30 p.m. If he stayed just a few minutes longer he might miss out on bathtime for Rhys. Timing was crucial. If he arrived too early he'd be made to do too much work at home, but if he arrived too late Rhys would be in bed and he would have missed out on seeing him. Padma would also be angry, and that would not do. Padma would also be angry if he was too early as Owen would refuse to complete all the new tasks invented for him after a busy day's work.

'I hope you are right, Owen,' Ahmed said. 'Mr Fox seems to think the system will fail but you seem so certain. Why? I am confused. Are you waiting for the new system to start then or applying early?'

'Oh I'll wait. The chances are better under the new system. Besides, I quite like the idea of being the last house officer. That way I'll avoid responsibility for as long as I possibly can.' Owen stood up and picked up his coat. 'Anyway gentlemen, the time has come for me to go. See you both in the morning.' Yes, Owen thought as he pushed his way out of the emergency exit towards the staff car park. He saw more of his work colleagues than his own family.

CHAPTER 13

The Young Father

'I'M HOME AT last,' Owen said as he pushed open the door to his first family home, an end-of-terrace house in a slightly run-down district of Wednesbury. He loved this house. It was so small that Padma often complained about lack of storage space but it held great symbolic value for Owen. He had found it and bought it all by himself. He had arranged the mortgage and spoken to the bank. His dear pregnant wife and son lived here and he worked in the hospital nearby. He was a provider, a man.

'We're upstairs, baby,' Padma said.

Owen jumped up the stairs two at a time and as he entered the bedroom he saw Padma drying his infant son with a large white towel. 'Oh dear, I've missed bathtime again.'

'You always miss bathtime. You're a busy surgeon, that's why.' Padma kissed Owen on the cheek.

'How are you, my little man, eh?' Owen roughed up Rhys' hair and kissed him on the cheek forcefully. Rhys laughed.

'Oi. I've just combed his hair.'

'Sorry I'm late. SO much work to do, as usual.'

'I'm proud of you. I know you've got important work to do.'

Owen thought of the greasy tea he had drunk at length with his colleagues in the mess and looked down to his feet. 'Mr Fox told us of a new recruitment system that's starting in a few months. It's a national system so hopefully we'll be able to go to Wales then, at last.'

'I have no interest in living in Wales. Can't we go back to London?'

'London? Oh no. We'd be robbed every day there. No, Wales is the key. It's always easier for Welshmen to get on in Wales than in England.'

'But you got on well here. This is England.'

'Ah, but if you think about it most people on the surgical rotation are not British. That makes Welshmen temporarily English in their eyes.'

'Whose eyes? Mr Fox's?'

'Dear me, no. The establishment.' Owen realised he had no idea where he was going with this and decided to change tack. 'It'll be better back home, that's all.'

'Will it? I prefer England.'

Owen remembered Mr Fox's suggestion to apply for one of the West Midlands surgical registrar positions when they came out in a few months. 'We could stay here actually. Mr Fox was saying how…'

'No way. No way are we staying here. Here? I hope you're joking.'

Owen grabbed his wife playfully by the waist and drew her to him. 'Then if no London, no Wednesbury and no Wales; where, my dear love, do we go?'

'Oxford. Cambridge. Malaysia.'

'Malaysia? Ha!'

'Pass me the nappy. It's in the cupboard.'

Owen started looking aimlessly in the bottom of the cupboard. 'Early morning tomorrow. Two hemicolectomies on the list and Mr Graham said I might get to do one, depending on time and everything. He's going to talk me through it.'

'Under the sheets. No. Look, stand back I'll get it.' Owen stood out of the way as Padma grabbed a nappy from one of the cupboard shelves. 'That's just great, baby. I was thinking of doing a mentorship course for nurses.'

Owen sat down uselessly on the edge of the bed and watched

Padma dressing Rhys. 'I don't know if that's a good idea. Where will you get time? I'm working all the time, you see, and we don't know any babysitters.'

'I can find babysitters.'

'But we can't trust them, can we? These babysitters can do terrible things. Much better to rely on family. Which is why we're better off in Wales.'

Padma finished dressing Rhys, and Owen quickly snatched him away and tickled him mercilessly on the bed. 'My boy, my boy, my lovely boy. You'll grow up just like daddy. Just like daddy.'

'Don't tickle him so much. He'll vomit.'

'He's enjoying it. Look at him, laughing away.'

'It's bedtime now. Stop it.' Almost as soon as she said it Rhys vomited over his pyjama suit and Owen held him away from his shirt.

Padma was incredulous. 'I told you, and now look. Find a new pyjamas from the drawer,' she said as she set to work removing the sodden pyjama suit. Padma then took Rhys to the bathroom for a wash and when she returned Owen was still hunting for the pyjamas in totally the wrong drawer. 'Let me,' she said as she retrieved a clean pair.

'I can't wait until the next baby arrives,' Owen said dreamily as Padma set up Rhys' musical bedtime mobile and got him ready for bed.

'I already have two babies, how can I cope with three?' Padma said.

'Because you love us all to bits, that is why. Now I'm going to get changed, then I'll see you downstairs.'

'Do you want to put Rhys to bed tonight?'

'I'll do it tomorrow. After tomorrow is the weekend. We'll go to Bridgnorth for the day. It'll be good.'

Owen showered, and as he did so he resolved to write

another case study for publication. Perhaps it would make the difference between getting a nice job back in Wales and ending up somewhere in England again. Life was good though, and could only get better. How lucky he was! To cap it all, good old Tony Blair had invented this new recruitment system just when he needed it the most. In the next room a weary Padma lay down next to her sleepy son and fell asleep herself, having used up all her energy with house chores and baby minding. After his shower Owen walked downstairs and realised by her absence that Padma had fallen asleep again. Excellent, he thought. Now he'd have the computer all to himself.

Bridgnorth

When Saturday dawned, Owen awoke early. Today was Bridgnorth day. The room was still in darkness and Padma was sleeping gently next to him and he kissed her on the cheek. Rhys was evidently still asleep as he was not in their bed. How very unusual, Owen thought to himself. A ray of yellow light from the sodium streetlight just outside their bedroom window illuminated the edge of an aerial picture of his grandfather's farm that hung on the far wall. Owen felt a great happiness at being able to count down the days to his eventual return home. Getting the job in the Midlands had been bittersweet; the rotation was good but every year spent away from his homeland made it less likely that he would ever return. He had tried explaining this to Padma but she had never understood.

Owen's thoughts were not allowed to develop much further, however, as Rhys ran into the room and kicked the edge of the bed accidentally. What had been a delightfully serene boudoir was now an army medical tent as Rhys screamed his lungs out. 'Mammy! Mammy!' he said. As Owen massaged Rhys's bleeding little toe, Padma roused herself almost to consciousness before drifting off to sleep again.

'How are you little man?' Owen asked his son as he carried him downstairs.

'Daddy,' Rhys said in return, and smiled.

After seating Rhys in his highchair, Owen switched on Radio Four as he made breakfast. The sun was shining, though it was cold; a perfect day for a family trip. Feeding Rhys turned out to be a bit of a struggle. For every spoonful of porridge that passed his lips, two ended up on the floor and three on his father's pyjamas. Eventually, in a moment of foolishness, Owen left the bowl within striking range and, before he had time to react, it had been batted to the floor and shattered into dozens of razor-sharp shards. Porridge had also splattered up the side of one wall and over the new rug. Rhys obviously thought this was a most wonderful spectacle as he screamed with laughter.

Owen knew bad things were afoot when he heard heavy, angry footsteps upstairs a fraction of a second after the initial impact. Before he had had a chance to reach for a towel, let alone clean up the mess, Padma had kicked the door open and stood glaring at father and son.

'I can't get any time off, can I?'

'Of course you can. This was just…'

'I have had it. Had it. I am leaving this house. You are a useless father, can't do anything. Look at this mess. Clean it up.'

'I will. Look, please go back to bed. I wanted you to sleep, have a lie-in. Please go back to bed.'

Padma advanced into the room. 'You can't clean this up…'

'Don't come any closer, there are sharp…'

Before Owen could finish, Padma placed her delicate foot on a half-inch long shard of blue china bowl which buried itself deep in her heel. She screamed so loudly that Rhys was soon adding to the chorus with his bitter crying. Owen marvelled at how a scene of beauty and tranquillity could have been transformed so quickly into a circle of hell.

'I'll get it out for you. Stand still.'

'You bastard, you utter bastard.'

'No need for language like that.'

'There is. You bastard.'

'Rhys can hear.'

'He can't understand, can he? He can only say mammy and daddy, and is good for nothing. Like you.' Rhys was still crying loudly.

Owen knew it was time to stay quiet. He loved Padma deeply but had deduced that she went through cycles of good and bad that lasted days to weeks at a trot. When she was in a good mood nothing could get her down, but more often than not Padma was in a fair to middling state of mind. Any provocation could lead to problems and Owen knew he'd suffer for around seventy-two hours from this point on. He had worked this out by averaging the time it took for Padma to recover over forty-two bad-tempered episodes. His mathematics were calculated so seriously he had even thought about trying to submit them to a journal.

The best course of action was to keep calm and carry on. Picking up a towel to clean up the mess, Padma snatched it from Owen's grasp. This was not a positive prognostic indicator.

'Please, Padma, please. We're going to Bridgnorth and...' What a fatal mistake. Never let the enemy know your weakness. Owen chastised himself for such a schoolboy error.

'We are NOT going to Bridgnorth now, are we?'

'At least let me look at your foot.'

'No. Get out. Let me finish it. Like I have to finish everything.'

Owen cheerfully removed himself to the living room. Technically, he thought to himself, he had been thrown out of the kitchen by Padma so that was one point to him on the points score. She would eventually feel guilty for this and thus it was like a unit of currency in some bizarre bank. Perhaps Owen's mess was one point for the wife though, he thought. But, ah yes, Owen had apologised, and thus neutralised that point. Suddenly Owen felt sad again. What about Bridgnorth? He was looking forward to that treat. There was an ice cream shop next to the river not far from the entrance to the funicular railway. He had conjured up visions of sitting next to the Severn with his family, eating posh ice cream all week.

After a minute, the sound in the kitchen had died down and Owen pushed open the door gently. Padma was feeding Rhys some Coco Pops.

'Hey, baby. Padma, baby. I'm sorry for the mess.'

Padma said nothing. Another bad prognostic indicator. Owen guessed he had nothing to lose now on the pressing issue of the future of the day out.

'Look, can we please go to Bridgnorth? I have been dreaming about it all week. Please?'

Still there came no response. Why were women so difficult to understand? His job was logical and straightforward and three plus seven equalled ten. With Padma three plus seven could equal eight one day and thirty two billion the next. The only thing that was certain, Owen mused, was that the answer was never ten.

Colorectal Clinic

Patients were so much simpler. Recalling the colorectal clinic he did with Mr Graham every week, Owen remembered some satisfying observations that were almost always true. Observations he had made himself.

Every Tuesday afternoon, Owen and Mr Graham would

occupy two adjoining rooms in the main outpatient area of Old Square Hospital and together they would see around twenty new patients with colorectal problems referred from local GPs. Once Owen had understood his boss's logic, he enjoyed the camaraderie of the clinic and would try hard to work in a methodical manner. Patients with warts, anal skin tags and other external lesions would be examined in a special room and those who would benefit from surgery would be listed, while those that would not were given advice and discharged.

If patients had anal problems such as haemorrhoids or fissures, they would be examined with a proctoscope pushed into their anus so that Owen could view bits of their anatomy that even their nearest and dearest might never see. Again, if a surgical solution was possible, Owen would list them, and if not, they would be given appropriate advice.

The advice for fissures, for example, was to push objects of increasingly large diameter through the anus in a bid to stretch out the sphincter muscle a bit and reduce the chance of spasm leading on to further fissure formation. He would often envisage his patients doing just this as he told them the horrifying solution to their anal dilemma. If patients were reluctant to abuse themselves in this way, Owen would smile in an understanding manner and say that yes, there was another solution. He'd then explain the surgical options, which included, among other things, taking the patient to theatre and slicing though a part of the sphincter mechanism with a knife to relieve the pressure. Normally this would cause a great deal of wincing but Owen would not stop there. The spiel had a grand finale. In the old days, Owen would tell his patient, who more often than not would by now be sitting at the edge of their chair clenching their anus, Lord's procedure would be undertaken, but this was not advised any more. What pray tell, was Lord's procedure, the patients would inevitably ask. The young surgeon would then lean forward in his chair and look the patient straight in the eyes. It involved the surgeon destroying the sphincter completely by placing all his fingers in the anus at once and separating them. Fisting someone in theatre; though Owen would never use these words. The looks of horror he'd get would amuse Owen for hours on end.

If a patient presented with altered bowel habit or other colonic or rectal symptoms, a rigid sigmoidoscopy would be performed. This was a plastic tubular device thirty centimetres long that would be gently introduced into the anus and air insufflation used to guide the device to the lower sigmoid colon. Sometimes polyps would pop into view and if so the patients could then be listed for either a sigmoidoscopy or colonoscopy at which point the polyps could be formally removed.

Sometimes the pathology could be treated there and then in the clinic. If a person was found to have haemorrhoids these could be banded in the examination room. This involved using a special suction device around whose end a tight elastic band was stretched. Once the proctoscope had been inserted into the anal canal and the haemorrhoids brought into view they could be suctioned into the tube. A trigger would then deploy the elastic band that would then constrict the haemorrhoid's base, starving it of all blood supply. This, rather amazingly, was completely painless if the band was applied above the sensory demarcation line halfway up the anal canal known as the dentate line. After a few days the dead tissue and elastic band would then fall harmlessly into the toilet bowl. A similar process was used to castrate male lambs on Owen's grandfather's farm, a fact he would also occasionally tell his patients. Such an elegant solution. That was the beauty of this line of work, Owen often thought to himself. Every problem could be broken down into its constituent parts, and solved.

There had been a bit of a learning curve, Owen conceded

that. In the early days, Mr Graham had been roused from a few pleasant chats with his long-term patients in the adjoining office by an ear-splitting scream from one of his senior house officer's haemorrhoid patients on whom the band had been applied too low. This situation was difficult to remedy, as patients would not be able to sit still for long after a misapplication so that removing the offending elastic band was a challenge. Like clay pigeon shooting, Owen said once to a less than amused middle-aged woman. He had once left a band in place due to this difficulty and found out the next morning that his patient had been admitted overnight as the extreme anal pain had caused urinary retention.

Learning through these mistakes made him a better surgeon in the end, Owen thought. He even fancied that he was forging ahead in being able to diagnose patients in the waiting room before he had even heard their histories, let alone examine them. Once he stood at the door and told Mr Graham what he thought each patient's diagnosis was, simply by how they looked. The middle-aged woman in tinted glasses had irritable bowel syndrome. This was a polite way of saying that nothing was wrong, of course. The young woman in a power suit had an anal fissure and the overweight chap in a sweatshirt had haemorrhoids. Two elderly women who stood rather than sat had altered bowel habit and the elderly man who was as thin as a rake had some kind of neoplastic growth. Mr Graham scoffed at his fellow countryman's spot diagnoses but after the clinic had ended had conceded that there had been a grain of truth in the colorectal waiting room diagnosis algorithm Owen had invented.

Owen thought it best not to try and publish these observations. He still stung internally whenever he recalled the occasion he'd sent for publication to the BMJ criteria for diagnosing a disease he believed he had been the first person to recognise. A disease widespread in the Wednesbury area, but which, it seemed, had not been formally described, in which Punjabi women of a certain age would present with all-over body pain of no obvious aetiology. He had christened his new disease Middle Aged Asian Lady Pain Syndrome, and had even come up with the acronym MALPS for short. The editor had written back suggesting the whole thing smacked of racism and possibly sexism too and although Owen was offended at such an accusation Mr Fox thought the whole thing was hilarious beyond words.

Owen thrived in a world of logic and thus enjoyed his work now more than at any time in his career, especially more than those dark London days. The love and support of Padma in a good mood more than compensated for his illogical home life and now there was a chance to go home to work, courtesy of MTAS and the lovely Patricia Hewitt.

CHAPTER 14

MTAS applications

B Y THE TIME applications for the new Medical Training Application System were about to close every senior house officer at Old Square, and probably every senior house officer in the country, had written and re-written the answers to the various application form questions at least fifteen hundred times. These ranged from asking about leadership skills, strengths and weaknesses, and activities outside medicine that were relevant. They had all come to the conclusion that this was a more horribly random process than they had feared, with the lunatics at the Department of Health well and truly in charge of the asylum. Doctors with PhDs were horrified to learn that this three-year postgraduate qualification gave them the same number of points as a doctor who could describe how hill walking in Cumbria enhanced their leadership qualities. The space for published papers was so small that only the best few could be entered and the number of points was capped anyway.

Danni and Sanjeev were particularly scared, as a mastery of the English language was pivotal to success, rather than surgical or clinical excellence or other more measurable qualities. Owen, on the other hand, was more delighted than ever, as this increased addition of randomness might just give him the edge over a more surgically competent trainee with more experience and a steadier hand than his. Ahmed was the ultimate winner though, as he had heeded Mr Fox's advice and had successfully applied for a position before the new system started. Not Owen though, as Owen was going home.

'What did you write in the "outside medicine" box?' Owen asked Danni in the corridor outside the main surgical wards.

'Nothing. I don't know what to write. I only do medicine. I live for my work. This is a disgrace.'

Owen smiled. A disgrace indeed. Yes he, Owen, would triumph when the hard-working, constantly-studying Danni would falter. Ahh, New Labour.

'Why Owen, what did you write about?'

'I said that helping my grandfather deliver lambs as a child taught me empathy, compassion and clinical obstetric skill.'

'What?! Empathy with a sheep. Is it even true?'

'No, not really. Who can they ask, though? It's all fiction anyway. They are asking you for fiction, Danni. Now go forth and write!'

'I am a doctor. I can't write fiction. I won't. I'll simply put the truth down, that I study and that is why I am good.'

Owen smiled inwardly again. Poor Danni. She just didn't understand the mindset of the humanities-qualified buffoons who had devised the system. If you played the game on their terms then you'd be home and dry, he told himself.

While obtaining a Diet Coke from a vending machine in the main hospital corridor, Sanjeev came up behind him appearing, to all intents and purposes, in need of voiding. Hopping from one leg to the other he looked at Owen like a wounded puppy. 'Please help me, my friend. I just can't do the questions. I can't.'

'What are you stuck on?' Owen was not pleased, as the bottle had become wedged in the corner of the vending machine, refusing to drop to where it could be accessed.

'I need to say a mistake I have made.'

'Just say something good in a bad way.' Hitting the front of the machine did not release the entrapped bottle of Coke. 'Put down that you once were about to consent a lady for a procedure but you realised in time it was for a different operation than that on the list. You found out because you double-checked and you told theatre, your boss and the Prime Minister about it so there would be no confusion; something like that.' The bottle still refused to fall. Owen pushed another 80p into the slot to select a bottle of Dr Pepper from a higher level. Perhaps the impact of that falling bottle would dislodge the first.

'I have written about the time I missed a chest infection in an old lady and she died.'

Owen looked Sanjeev in the face for the first time. 'Good God, man, don't put that down. Put down the consent thing.' Owen smiled as a double clunk from the machine told him that his plan had indeed worked.

'But that is not true. What about the question about skills outside medicine?'

Owen handed Sanjeev the bottle of Dr Pepper as they headed for the mess. 'You always talk about tennis. Sorry I never had time to play, by the way. Put down you love tennis and this gives you hand-eye co-ordination.'

'OK, I see what you get at. I see.'

Owen paused. 'Why, what had you put down already?'

'I am very good at astronomy. I love astronomy.'

'Nah. Scrub that and put down a team sport. There's probably a point for that.'

Sanjeev was crestfallen. 'I can't put astronomy in?'

'There is simply no room, Sanjeev. You only have two hundred words for each answer. Each answer needs to be like gold. Gold, I tell you.'

Mr Fox advanced on the pair from the nearby Greggs bakery brandishing a pasty in his left hand in a modified 'black power' salute. 'Remember to apply in good time, boys. Deadline is midnight tonight.' With that he was gone.

'We have until midnight,' Owen said to Sanjeev. 'Use every

minute to get it right. Don't send it now. I'll be in the library tonight if you care to join me.'

With Mr Fox's words still in his mind, that very night Owen was sitting in the hospital library with nine other junior doctors modifying bits and pieces of the all-important future-deciding online application. By 10 p.m. Owen considered himself finished. Clicking 'submit' however did not bring the relief he had expected. Instead a message appeared in white on his computer screen; 'No nodes,' it said. Owen tried again, and again there were 'no nodes'.

Panic gripped him like never before. Time slowed and his visual field constricted to a tunnel such that the only bit he could see now was large lettering telling him there were no nodes. Owen instantly remembered his year two secondary school mathematics exam. This was an exam in which he had panicked at a question on the second page and fear had shut down his mental processes to such an extent he could not answer any other question and even spelt his name wrongly on the back of the exam sheet. Fear flooded over him again as he pushed his chair back and stared blankly ahead, his heart racing.

'You OK there?' The voice was David's.

'No,' Owen managed to squeeze out. 'There are no nodes.'

'No nodes?'

'I can't submit it. No nodes.'

Other people heard this and panic spread around the room in much the same way as it infects crowds at football matches or causes stampedes at rallies.

'Oh no,' someone said. 'I can't submit too. No nodes!'

'No nodes!'

As Owen sat looking at his computer screen he entered a transcendental paradise where his computer was held up by clouds as the walls of the library and surrounding hospital fell away revealing blue clouds and a bright yellow sun. 'How does my dog smell,' a booming voice called out over the vast expanse ahead of him, 'when it has no nodes?'

'I've done it. It's gone through!' David had succeeded.

The bastard, Owen thought, but the shout was enough to free him from his dream world. Owen tried again. No nodes.

Around the room it seemed some were managing to push the application through and others were not getting any nodes. What on earth were nodes anyway? Why had the government not anticipated this? Did they expect everyone to apply in stages throughout the two-week period in bizarre non-typical behaviour for humans? In a scene that, oddly, Owen remembered forever more, he leant forward as if in slow motion and pressed the button on his computer one last time. This time it was different. A success message came on screen and Owen joined the jubilant faction in the library and could at last be sympathetic with the proportion who still had no nodes. The time was 10.50 p.m.

By the time midnight arrived there was only one person left who had not had any nodes. There were ten house officers cheering the hapless obstetrician on, when at 11.30 he made the ballsy decision to redo one of his answers. Despite the warnings from his colleagues, he tried resubmitting his application at ten to midnight and got multiple no nodes messages a few times. Once it looked like the application had gone through but it turned out the system had crashed. A few more attempts to submit eventually brought out a new message. This one read 'your application has timed out'. It was too late. Like the supporters of a successful rugby team after a match, the other doctors respectfully departed the room leaving the only loser alone, weeping into the keyboard of the computer under the strip fluorescent lighting of the staff library. Outside he could hear the whoops and hollering of the others.

Seniority Calls

Owen was indeed feeling happy. He had been released from a two-week trial of tinkering with answers he had crafted well before the process had even started. Comparisons had to be made with others and inside knowledge, true or made up, would circulate detailing the scoring methods of those who would be analysing the forms. Now there was nothing he could do about his answers and his time outside work, which was limited before the application process had even begun, was now his family's once more. At least until the results would become known in a few weeks' time. Padma was supportive on and off and Owen was keen to reward her. Not with a trip to Bridgnorth, as this place had now become synonymous with marital discord, but with a shopping trip perhaps. If Owen spent a day doing something he truly despised then perhaps Padma would feel good towards him again, at least for a while. That is how Owen thought about the situation, anyway.

The day after the application had gone through Owen had two main thoughts; planning his family day out and finding out if anyone else had failed to submit in time.

'Sanjeev,' Owen called out when he spied his friend coming out of the theatre changing rooms around mid-morning. 'I didn't see you in the library last night. Did you get the application through OK?'

'Oh yes, thank you so much. Yes.'

'What time?'

'About 5 p.m.'

'Did you have any nodal trouble?'

Sanjeev looked confused so Owen guessed there had not been any. 'There was an axillary abscess but I have incised it now.' This time both Owen and Sanjeev were confused.

'Someone is kicking off on the ward so I have to see them

now. I'll catch you later.' With that Owen continued his way to the ward, where he had been called by a desperate nurse as one of Mr Graham's patients was delirious and lashing out at the staff.

As he entered the ward, a nurse grabbed him by the am and launched him into a cubicle where three foundation doctors were attempting to hold a flailing patient down to get an intravenous line in. They were clearly failing.

'What's happened here?' he asked.

Mike, one of the foundation doctors, answered. 'This is Mr Edward Parsons, a forty-six-year-old man who initially presented two years ago with blood-streaked…'

'No. What operation did he have and when?'

'Uh. A hemicolectomy, a few days ago. He was eating and drinking and getting ready to go home. He was fine immediately afterwards as well with…'

'What are the obs?'

Sister, who had been hiding behind the open door, stepped forward and Owen had an immediate sense of foreboding. On reflex he took a half-step backward.

'This man's blood pressure is 110 over 60 and his pulse rate is 130 systolic. Sats 90 per cent on three litres.' Sister waved her left arm over the chaos that was occurring in the cubicle. 'Look at this. Sort this out immediately or I will inform Mr Graham.'

Owen assessed the situation. Expectant staff and a flailing, clearly delirious patient who needed oxygen, intravenous fluids and some blood tests. Everybody looked to him, though he did not know what to do. 'First things first. Let's put some oxygen on, get a line in and take some bloods.'

A nurse tried to place a mask over the patient's head but after a second it was removed and Owen caught sight of it out of the corner of his eye launching past Mike's head. 'OK. The Venflon then.'

The foundation doctors held the patient's arm down against the bed as Owen palpated for a vein. He'd need to be quick as his junior doctors were struggling and the patient had started to shout loudly, rocking the bed back and forth as he did so. Grabbing a green Venflon, Owen pushed it into the vein and was overjoyed to see the sign of success, the all-important flashback. Perhaps he knew what he was doing after all.

'Hold him still. I need to tape it down.' After securing the Venflon, Owen took some bloods and flushed saline through it. Job done. He felt a little proud. He had succeeded where others had failed. For a change. Yes, perhaps Owen was becoming senior after all. A general surgical registrar in the making.

Feeling buoyed, he continued to act like a surgeon in a play. 'Right,' he said to the whole room. 'We need theatre prepared because this is probably a leak. Mike, listen to his chest to see if there is adequate air entry. Sister, please inform Mr Graham. Sister…'

Sister had departed some time before to do just that and at that moment reappeared with the boss. Mr Graham nodded his head sagely and asked Owen the score. He gave what he considered a succinct, useful answer; gesturing to the patient at the end in a dramatic manner emphasising the need for theatre.

Mike at that point let go of the patient to listen to his chest as he had been instructed. Owen saw Mr Graham's right eyebrow flinch and his gaze moving to the patient. It only took a second for Owen to rotate his own head to see what he was looking at when he caught site of Mr Parson's huge fist on a direct collision course with his own face. It was too late to take any aversive action and before he knew anything else he was on the cubicle floor, the Venflon ripped out and the patient's blood dribbling all over him.

'I can see you've got it all in hand there, Owen,' Mr Graham said. 'See you in theatre. Carry on.' With that he was gone.

As Owen picked himself up, various nurses and doctors asked him if he was alright but he shrugged in what he hoped was a brave manner. He had to reassure the troops that he was in full control. 'Oh it's fine,' he said. 'Yes. Happens all the time really.'

'Patients punching you?' asked the nurse quizzically.

'Oh yes.' Owen's attempt at displaying experience and seniority had not really gone according to plan.

Selection

For the next few weeks Owen only really had one thing on his mind as he nursed his bruised chin, went to work and tried to enjoy his home life as best he could. The MTAS selection process. Would he get all four interviews and would he get Wales specifically? Padma would ask him about his day and she'd have to repeat herself a few times as he was retreating to his MTAS dream world so often now. Even when he attended the second ultrasound scan for his wife's pregnancy he was thinking of MTAS.

Indeed her belly was growing and Owen projected the new child would be born six weeks before his contract at Old Square came to an end. Hopefully he'd know where he would be going before then. So much uncertainty was worrying for Owen, a self-confessed man of logic.

'You OK, hun?' Padma asked walking home after the scan. 'You seem distant.'

'I guess I'm always distant.' Why had he said that? That made no sense and wasn't even true. 'Sorry. I'm thinking of this job thing all the time.'

Padma stiffened. 'What about the baby?'

'Well, of course, also about the baby. The baby is the main

thing. I wouldn't be doing anything if it wasn't for the baby.' Owen considered he'd gone far enough down this line now. 'I just need the job secured for us, for the baby, that's all.'

'You spent so long doing that form if you don't get your interviews I will choke you to death.'

'Sorry about that. They needed to be perfect.'

'Towards the end you spent hours just moving commas about. I saw it.'

'It has to be perfect. Some people didn't even get the application in on time because of this whole business. I saw it in the library, remember?'

'I remember. That fool.'

'The system crashed, Padma; he was no fool.' Owen knew he was a fool. He had told him so for changing his answer at the last minute. An answer that would now never be read.

'I'll be glad when this is over. The strain you're putting me and the baby through.'

'It'll be better then, in Wales, I promise.'

When selection day finally arrived in early March, the ward computers were buzzing with activity. Interview offers were to appear throughout the day and nervous tension found many SHOs checking and rechecking the MTAS website every few minutes or so. It was like waiting for A-level results. Clinic delays lengthened and ward work went undone as every junior doctor in the land sucked the life out of the internet to see what their futures held. When Owen first checked the website there was only one interview offered. He was not unduly concerned though as that deanery was Wales, his first choice, and surely more offers would come. David and Danni on the other hand had no interview at all while Sanjeev had three.

'How the hell did you do it?' Owen asked him.

'That I cannot know. I changed my answers like you said and it worked.'

'But I had even better answers than that so how come I only have one?'

If Sanjeev looked hurt then David was angry. 'That's it then. I have no interviews. I'll have to wait until the summer and reapply in round two. What a disgrace.'

'It's still morning. Wait till five tonight and if you have no offers at that point I suppose it's safe to panic then.'

'Owen that's balls. No more offers will come.'

'Trust me. The MTAS people said to wait till the end of the day.'

'You are too trusting of MTAS. That's your problem.'

'Just you wait,' Owen said as he detached himself from the computer to do some actual work.'

As it turned out David was correct. Nobody received any more interviews that day and a sense of gloom fell over the junior staff as the day progressed. Despite this Owen was selfishly actually quite pleased that so many of his colleagues had not been shortlisted for interviews. The more people attending interviews the less the chance for him.

By the time evening fell, Owen loaded MTAS onto the home computer and was staring hypnotised at the screen displaying the one and only interview that he had secured. His other deanery applications had obviously been binned, but with such cracking answers Owen did not know why. At least it was Wales.

The next day the national news media was awash with the MTAS scandal as it became clear that a large slice of the junior doctor population would be denied any interview in round one. To Owen's extreme dismay, a Department of Health under pressure then announced that everybody would get their first choice interview after all. Suddenly the attractive competition ratio that had kept Owen laughing and giggling to himself all night blew away with the morning wind. It was a free-for-all now, and Owen never won in a free-for-all. It was difficult getting served at a busy bar and this situation was much worse. Danni and David relaxed somewhat as a surgical career became possible for them once more and it seemed that Sanjeev was the only person who remained overwhelmingly optimistic throughout.

As Owen prepared to go home one day, he met Ahmed in the theatre changing room. He was grinning broadly.

'I told you to apply. You didn't listen. Now look where you are. You should have listened to Ahmed.'

'I should have listened to Ahmed.' Owen sat down on the bench to put his shoes on. 'I'm in a situation, you know. Padma's a few months gone now and if I don't get a job with this one interview, I'm done for. A house, a mortgage and a child with one on the way. What do I do?'

'You should have applied like me. Mr Fox practically begged you. You wanted to go home to your Wales and look where that got you, eh. Welshman.'

'How are you getting on anyway as a registrar? Is it as good as you expected?' Please let it not be as good as he expected. Have some mercy on a man down on his luck.

'It is excellent. I did the right thing.'

Brilliant, Owen thought. 'Any tips for the interview?'

'Yes. You should have applied for the West Midlands.'

Owen gritted his teeth. 'In the absence of a time machine, do you have any tips?'

Ahmed grinned again. 'Become a Muslim, and then once you have done that, start praying, brother.'

'Cheers. Thanks for all the help.' As Ahmed departed, Owen threw his theatre shoe against the door as hard as he could.

CHAPTER 15

The Visit to Wales

THERE HAD NOT been a visit to the Morgan home in Neath for quite a few months. While this had been welcomed by Padma, she had never actually vetoed a trip and it was Owen who bore the moral responsibility of this oversight. Stress levels were increasing incrementally in Wednesbury as the deadlines, for both application and pregnancy, loomed ever larger. The phone calls from Wales over the same time period were getting ever angrier and Owen felt that any continuance might lead to insurmountable problems just when he needed stability the most. A weekend had been planned weeks ahead and finally the time had arrived to go home. Owen was not on call on the Friday they were due to travel but Mr Fox had specifically requested his assistance for a difficult laparotomy in such a way that Owen felt unable to turn him down. By the time he left theatre it was well past nine and the journey itself was anything up to two-and-a-half hours.

Arriving back home, Owen was all ready to get into apology mode, had even rehearsed his lines, but was pleasantly surprised to see Padma smiling at him, all packed and ready to go. 'Sorry I'm late. Emergency.' Owen felt a bit silly every time he said something like this. He was not the main surgeon and had spent most of his time holding a retractor. In no way was any clinical victory due to him. Indeed Owen was mildly peeved one day to find he was late in theatre but Mr Fox had started without him, using a metal clamp attached to a tripod-like structure to hold back the bowel in his stead. 'Just set up the robotic Owen,' he had said. 'It has better communication skills than you too.'

'Don't worry darling. You're a surgeon and I'm a surgeon's wife. I understand. I'm in the medical profession, you know.'

Owen looked at his wife suspiciously for a second, decided it was best not to look a gift horse in the mouth and kissed her on the cheek. 'Let's get going. Where is Rhys?'

'Sleeping. Carry him to the car, please.'

As he cradled his young son in his arms a feeling washed over him that he was missing out on all the growing up bits that were meant to be good. His father had told him about the *Cat's in the Cradle*, though more in a bid to get him to visit his old man than anything to do with Rhys. His son might grow up just like him. What a hideous thought! Owen paused at the car door. Idwal had never been like that though. He had always been there when he was growing up. What did Harry Chapin know anyway? Owen kissed the sleeping Rhys and strapped him in the car seat.

The going was better than expected on the M5, but then again they were four hours late due to the operation. Padma was asleep beside him in the passenger seat and Rhys was actually snoring. Adenoids perhaps, Owen thought.

Arriving well after midnight, he had hardly had time to stop the engine and wake up Padma when his father materialised by his window.

'Morning, *boi*.'

'Hey, dad. Sorry to keep you up so late. Where is mam?'

'Getting food ready.'

'Food. Oh dear.'

Padma awoke with a start, her body realising before her brain that the car had come to a halt. 'Darling, are we in Swanage yet?'

'No, Neath. We're there, get up.'

Padma became suddenly aware of her geographical location and her eyes focused on a smiling Idwal. 'Oh. Dad. Hello.'

'Hello, Padma. Come in all of you. There is the little one!' He unbuckled Rhys and carried him to the house. 'It's been a long time since I saw you, it has. Too long.'

'Don't talk to him, dad,' Padma said. 'He's sleeping.'

'He'll forget all about us, *bach*, he really will. You know we've hardly seen him this year. His mother, sorry grandmother, has been apocalyptic about the whole thing.'

'That's a bit strong,' Owen said.

An aproned Moira appeared at the door her eyes full of sleep. 'I've got food for you all. Lamb cawl. Your favourite, Owen.'

'Yippee,' Padma said without meaning. Moira cast her an evil glance.

After putting Rhys to bed, Moira and Idwal sat around the kitchen table watching Padma and Owen eat cawl.

'How is work then?' That inevitable question would always arise from his mother, followed by a driving question from his father.

'Fine thanks, mam. We cut out a foot of bowel today from a man who had been stabbed in his belly by an angry wife. That's why we're late. Sorry about that.'

Idwal grimaced. 'The things you see. You know I've never seen a man's bowel.'

'You're a mechanic,' Padma said flatly.

Idwal felt a bit put out by this comment but let it pass. 'I'd love to see bowel, I would. See what it feels like and...'

'You be quiet about bowel and guts at the table,' Moira said. Her tone mellowed considerably as she turned to Owen. 'Why did she stab him, *bach*? Was it an affair he was having?' She topped up his glass of Coke.

'I don't know, to be honest,' he said. In the background he heard his father complaining that he hadn't used the word guts, just bowel.

Before he could take a sip of Coke, Padma removed the glass from Owen's side and tipped it down the sink. 'Don't drink Coke before bed. It'll rot your guts.'

Idwal was triumphant. 'See. She said it that time, not me.'

Owen nodded to his mother to indicate his gratitude for not responding to multiple provocations. He was tired and would communicate better in the morning. Finishing off the cawl, he got up, thanked his parents for staying up late and made for the door. With one gigantic burp, Idwal seemed to indicate a satisfactory conclusion of affairs and they all headed for bed.

While alone in the confines of his own dog-cleansed room, specially cleaned by Moira the evening before so Padma could sleep in the house, Owen switched his infernal mobile phone on and found out he had a voice message. Who could this be? He locked himself in the bathroom and pretended to do a number two as he checked it. Could it be Colleen? He hoped it was. He hadn't talked to her in a long time as it was an unspoken agreement that Padma hated to hear anything about her, and perhaps inexplicably, Owen felt somehow adulterous talking to Colleen at all. These feelings were not lessened by the fact that all communication had to be under the radar and he had even told Colleen not to call him at home. Perhaps the biggest surprise of all was his old friend's understanding acceptance of these humiliating terms.

But no, Owen's heart sank as it turned out the message was from Sanjeev. Owen had told him he was going home and his colleague and friend had inexplicably decided to accept a long-forgotten offer to visit him in Wales. In fact he would be there in the morning, though thankfully he wouldn't be staying overnight. Telling Padma this news now seemed almost offensive, so Owen decided to do what he always did in these circumstances and leave it for some other time.

Sanjeev's Visit

As a grinning Sanjeev sat at his parent's kitchen table, Moira busied herself making sandwiches for him, happily telling him about her new Spanish classes while Sanjeev gave encouraging respectful answers in a heavily stilted Indian accent. Idwal was playing in the front room with Rhys while Padma was glaring at Sanjeev with open hostility across the table. Thankfully either Sanjeev was completely oblivious to this, or was so unusually well-mannered that he did not acknowledge her unspoken threats.

'Well, how marvellous to have an Indian doctor in the house. Our doctor, he is Indian, Sandeep.'

'It's Sanjeev, mam.'

'Oh, I do apologise.'

'Please do not have the need for any apology. It is my humble pleasure to be here in my good friend Owen's house.'

'Terrible that war in Afghanistan, isn't it. Are your family alright?'

'Mam. Afghanistan is a comple…'

'Do not worry, Mrs Morgan. I am Indian and my family are all well. I am most grateful for your concern though.'

'Different country, mam,' Padma said. Then, turning to Sanjeev, 'Why are you down here again?'

'I wanted to visit Cardiff then I thought, oh my goodness, Owen has his mother and father in Wales. How impolite it would be not to see them.'

Moira squirmed with delight and handed the grinning Sanjeev his third sandwich in a row. 'Are you married, Sandveej?'

'Oh no, Mrs Morgan. I will get married later, when I am settled.'

'Will it be an arranged marriage, *bach*?'

He smiled. 'No, but there is not really such a thing anymore. Assisted is a more geographically correct term.'

While Moira and Sanjeev talked, Padma sat down next to Owen and pinched his inner thigh forcefully.

'Why did you do that?' he whispered.

'I have had enough of this. I never get you out of work and now this. We're in Wales and a fat Indian is ruining all the time I do get with you.'

Owen lowered his voice a little. 'I could hardly send him away now, could I? I didn't know he was coming till he turned up at the door.'

'I bet you did. I wanted to go to Dan-yr-Ogof caves anyway, not sit here all day long.'

Without proper usage of his cerebral filtration systems, Owen stood dramatically and said, 'We're off to the caves. Anyone want to come?'

'Why yes, of course, I will love to see the caves,' Sanjeev said enthusiastically. While Owen appreciated the enthusiasm, Padma had just run out of the room and he felt duty bound to follow her to see what the matter was. He found her face down on the bed in the spare room.

'You OK?' Owen knew she was not but could not think of anything more poetic to say.

'Of course,' she said, still face down in the pillow. 'I am so happy about Sanjeev, the caves and that you didn't do anything to stop it all going wrong.'

'What could I do?'

Padma abruptly sat up and looked straight at Owen. She was cross now. Owen was sad that the face-down phase had ended so suddenly, now that the following phase was probably going to be 'angry Padma'.

'Throw him out. Tell him to leave.'

'I can't, it's not nice.'

'I can do it if you want. Do you want to see me do it?'

There came a knock at the door at that instant. It was Idwal and Rhys. 'Hello there. Rhys has had a bit of an accident and been sick on himself. Probably he needs a bit of cleaning up; I know I do.'

Owen opened the door to see a vomit-covered Rhys in his grandfather's vomit-covered arms. 'Sick he was.'

'I can see that, dad.' Owen was unsure where to pick up Rhys as he was pretty much covered in vomity slime. There was a bare patch on his left leg and around the neck but Owen could not easily think of a way of carrying him using just these two areas that would not contravene some health and safety legislation. Padma lost patience during these vital seconds of thought and roughly snatched her son away from his grandfather.

'I'll do it. Just like I do everything. You Morgan men just make Rhys vomit all the time. And not just Rhys,' she said as the bathroom door slammed and the bathwater started running.

With Padma's departure, the mood lifted quite considerably and Idwal slapped Owen on the shoulder. 'Come and have some tea, eh?'

'Best change the old shirt first, dad.'

'Ach yes. How's that friend of yours doing downstairs? Has your mother stopped making sandwiches yet?'

'No. She's still at it, and he's still eating them.'

'Good for him. See you downstairs.' As Idwal tore off his shirt he noticed a rather large splodge of vomit on his trousers as well. After a moment's consideration, he considered the splodge did not constitute a bar to his continued wearing of the trousers and he used the shirt to wipe off as much as he could. He was glad his son was home for the weekend though the exchange on the landing was the most he'd spoken to him directly since he'd been back. Such busy lives, with the cat in the cradle and all, he thought to himself as he pulled a fresh shirt from the drawer. There were so many things he'd planned on asking him. As he pulled the shirt over his head the familiar clamping pain gripped his chest once more and he sat heavily on the bed. These pains never lasted more than two minutes and, sure to goodness, they subsided in the normal manner. This was indeed one of the things he'd wanted to talk to Owen about, but he guessed it would have to wait till another time.

Self Harm

The journey back in the car the following day was not pleasant. Padma had refused to go to the caves the day before but in retrospect Owen felt that taking Sanjeev alone had been a miscalculation. His wife had been surly and unco-operative ever since and had hardly spoken a word to him all day.

'Look. I said I was sorry. He was a guest. What could I do?'

Padma turned her face to the window and remained silent.

'We'll go to the caves another time, without Sanjeev.'

Still nothing.

'Look. We're passing Brecon now. You've never been to Brecon before have you? We'll go one day.'

So it continued. If Owen had been wise he would have stopped talking once it was clear that Padma had her heart set on the silent treatment for a few days. Owen wasn't wise, and every time he spoke Padma's ire would be raised notch by notch – until critical mass was achieved outside the OK Diner on the outskirts of the small market town of Leominster.

'You're always saying we should go to this OK Diner. Do you want to go there now?'

Padma turned and looked directly at Owen for the first time that day. Owen immediately realised the danger he was in and slowed down the car accordingly.

'Owen, you pathetic excuse for a husband, I have had enough.

Enough of you and your farmer family in that beat-up, pathetic house in Neath. I will never go to Wales again. Get a job in London or I will divorce you.'

'Wow. That was a bit strong. Just asking if you wanted to go to the OK Diner that's all. That was all very hurtful if…'

'I don't care. I don't love you and I want a divorce.'

Owen stared at the road ahead and it was his turn now not to say anything. Padma had been rude in the past, rude and certainly hurtful, but nothing like this. Divorce? She surely didn't mean that, but saying it all the same was morally wrong. Unfortunately for Owen he had not heard the last of it either.

'You are really pathetic too. You know. Pathetic. Like that Sanjeev you're friends with. Always trying to be nice to everyone and ending up pissing everyone off. I am your wife. Do you know how much time you spent with me in Wales?'

Even if Owen had wanted to answer this question, his mood was depressed now and he felt unable to muster the troops to even think of a suitable response.

'An hour. When I didn't go to the caves, you don't go to the caves. When I don't like the guest, you remove them for me. Polite, impolite, I don't care. I hate Sanjeev. I hate him. You should have got rid of him.'

Her voice had risen now and Rhys had started to cry in the back seat. A small cry at first but as her diatribe continued so the volume rose.

'I know you always go on about this job application thing and the stress of work and all. I don't give a fuck. I really don't. I hate you.' Rhys's cry was loud now so that he was beginning to drown out his mother's words, if such a thing were possible. She turned around in her seat to face her infant son. 'BE QUIET, RHYS. NOW.'

Predictably, after a moment of stunned silence on Rhys's part, the screaming and shouting reached new levels. Owen was shaking at this sudden negative turn of events and pulled over to the side of the road.

'Why would you be so mean to all of us? Don't shout at Rhys, he…'

'SHUT UP. Shut up. I'll leave you and Rhys and go back to Malaysia, is that what you want?'

At that moment in time that option did in fact sound good but on the other hand who would babysit Rhys when he was in work? His parents were too far away and he worked such long hours that he'd have to get a live-in nanny to do the work. That would be expensive.

'Why are we not driving? Drive you pathetic lump. Drive! I don't want to be stuck here in this car with you any longer than I need to be.'

Owen opened Rhys's door and tried to comfort his son but it was to no avail. He was inconsolable, but so was his father, and both Morgan boys cried all over each other in a lay-by on the road from Leominster to Kidderminster.

'Drive! I can't drive, so you drive. Drive now. You keep me jobless in the house and don't teach me to drive. When I learn to drive I'll leave you. Leave you all and then where would you be?'

Happy perhaps, Owen thought to himself as he gave up trying to stop his son from crying and got back into the driver's seat himself. He held his hand up and was surprised to see how much it was shaking. Perhaps Padma was right. Perhaps he was pathetic. Perhaps the correct thing to do now would be to punch her in the face. Men in the old days did that. They'd certainly do it under this level of provocation. What was the protocol though? Owen felt confused at these thoughts and held his head in his hands.

'What now? Drive. Drive. DRIVE. DRIVE.'

Owen punched the steering wheel in frustration, hurting his

little finger, which began to bleed slightly. What was the point in that?

'Yes, show Rhys what a father should be like. Violent and angry. Yes. Yes. Show him. Do it again.'

'I think I'm hurt,' Owen said to himself more than anyone else.

'Excellent. Do it again, then.'

How lovely it would be to strangle her to death, to push her out of the moving car or to hit her bloody face repeatedly until she stopped breathing, he thought. These thoughts were recognised as evil and Owen was above evil. His resistance was the proof of his victory over evil. Yes, it made sense now. Padma was the evil one.

'Padma,' he said. 'Stop being evil.'

'Evil am I? I can show you evil. Do you want me to show you evil?'

Owen was frightened that if she did he would be unable to contain his own evil and so, on some basis, recognised the need for a de-escalation before real harm was done. He started the car and drove on, trying to imagine nothing had happened at all. Nothing to see here, officer.

With the new movement of the car, Padma fell silent and a sort of uneasy peace descended. Owen felt his little finger. It would be bruised and that might affect his operating tomorrow, damn it.

CHAPTER 16

The Interview

A WEEK OR two of silent treatment from Padma eventually brought out her good side again and Owen guessed he'd be in for a peaceful spell for at least a week. His finger did bruise in the end but had thankfully not affected his operating skill. Perhaps that was due to an overall lack of skill in the first place, Owen pondered. An interview date for the Welsh deanery was given for two weeks in the future and preparations were made, the portfolio beefed up and questions practised in the mess with colleagues till late in the night. This was his chance, his one-and-only chance to go back home, and he intended to give it the best shot possible. The other bonus was that it resulted in spending long hours away from Padma, a situation which benefited them both.

Sanjeev was a particularly helpful interview practice companion, as he himself had been lucky to end up with more interviews than anybody else. The interview date in March was circled in red on the calendar and when that morning finally arrived, Owen got dressed in his one-and-only suit and placed his portfolio on the passenger seat in a determined fashion. Should he give Padma the chance to wish him luck before he left? She was still in the kitchen and although he'd said he was leaving, this had garnered no response. He went back into the house anyway, kissed Rhys on the top of his head and tried to hug Padma. Surprisingly she responded positively, kissed Owen on the cheek and wished him the best of luck. Now that surely should be a good sign.

It took only two hours for him to reach Cardiff. The interviews were taking place in a large city centre hotel that was teeming with doctors in suits walking in various directions with vast bundles of paper. One of the drawbacks of MTAS was that a whole new dimension of paperwork was needed and for this interview alone Owen carried a thick file with him that he would never see again. Armies of clerks and secretaries were at hand to relieve doctors of various forms and a long queue at a single photocopier in the business centre on the second floor suggested not everyone had their house in order.

'Dr Morgan?'

'Yes.'

'Two photocopies of your medical school certificate please. Thank you. Do you have the original?'

'I do.' After a minute's fumbling in his file, he handed the clerk his certificate.

'Great. I can tick my box now. Please stand in that line there to have your competencies checked.'

After spending ten minutes in a long line of suited doctors, Owen was almost at the front when there seemed to be a hold-up. The Asian doctor in from of him evidently did not have some key document and for them the adventure was over. Trial by paperwork.

'Dr Morgan?'

'Mr Morgan actually. Owen.'

The clerk lost her smile. 'Paperwork.'

Owen handed her the file and she spent a few minutes putting ticks in boxes and papers in various folders.

'Passport.'

Owen handed her a photocopy of his passport. The clerk smiled. 'I need to see the actual passport or you cannot continue with the process.'

Owen fished around in his trouser pocket and handed it over.

The clerk's smile disappeared. She ticked a box on her form and stuck a big sticker on Owen's suit. It said '244' next to a big green dot.

'Next.'

Owen moved on. Where to go now? Aimlessly wandering around the massive hotel lobby through crowds, he asked countless official-looking people but none of them knew anything. Wandering back to the surly clerk who had given him the number, she spied him before he could ask a thing and pointed impatiently towards the stairs to the floor above. 'Up there. Up there, I said.'

Upstairs Owen found a smaller lobby area in which legions in identical suits had occupied every available seat and those standing were moving in slow currents between the tables, perhaps to use up the time. Presenting himself to a small trestle table, he was relieved of yet more forms and led to a hotel room in which the bed had been removed and thirteen candidates like him stood morosely looking at their portfolios. Each had glum acceptance of bad news in their eyes before they had even started. Perhaps the sheer numbers had robbed them of hope.

'Which interview are you here for?' Owen asked a bearded Muslim chap he happened to find himself next to.

'Obstetrics.'

'Oh. I'm here for general surgery. Good luck.'

'Same to you.' The silence of the room and the tension it contained precluded further conversation so Owen was content to sit on the window sill and look at the University of Wales building on the other side of the road. The sun was shining for a change. Just as Owen was thinking how nice it would be to get it all over and done with, he sensed a sudden alertness in the room and turned to see what new development was taking place.

A clerk stood at the door brandishing a clipboard and pen. 'Green 230 to 235.'

As those convicts went off to be hanged, fresh inmates were pushed through the door by yet another clerk. All of these had red dots, Owen noticed.

'I see you have a red dot,' he said to one of the new recruits.

The doctor in question eyed Owen suspiciously but remained silent.

After another few minutes of anxious silence, Owen and a few others were summoned by another clerk and taken to a suite of rooms upstairs. Each was handed a single piece of acetate, a piece of paper and a felt tip pen. The piece of paper informed them that in the next room there would be a clinical paper. They were to read it and then summarise its findings on the acetate using the pen for presentation to the interviewers in an adjoining room.

'Bit like an SAS mission,' Owen said to the candidate next to him.

The clerk heard this and turned around sharply. 'Those found talking will be removed from this process.' The other candidate looked at Owen sternly. A minute later a bell rang and it was time to begin.

The Trial

The clinical paper was about the use of painkillers in general practice, a subject about which Owen knew very little. Evidently the other candidates felt likewise as he could hear much muttering and nervous coughing in the room. After reading the paper, Owen started his summary on the acetate but realised after his first line that the lettering was too big. All attempts to rub off the felt tip pen were futile so Owen decided, with time running out, that the only real option open to him was to make the summary as brief as possible and at least keep all the letters the same size. If he made the lettering smaller as he progressed down the page then on top of the fact that he'd look like an idiot, the acetate would look like Willy Wonka's peculiar consent form from the film and that would simply never do.

'Stop writing everyone.' The clerk was back. She practically pulled a Chinese doctor from her seat as she herded all of them towards the door. Looking at Owen, she said, 'Green 244, you're in this room.'

For once Owen was starting to feel genuine frustration and anger rising above his fear and Owen looked at the clerk with annoyance. 'I am not a number. I am a free man,' he said, immediately regretting it. He suspected it had just slipped out from some cerebral file and reasoned that his levels of nervousness were such that several filing cabinets of information were now open in his mind and whole secretaries were running around clutching bits of paper banging into each other. Paper was flying all over his skull base and the entire cranial office was in considerable disarray.

The clerk looked quizzically at Owen. 'When time is up you move to the next room until all three rooms have been visited,' she said. 'If anyone does not visit all three rooms they will be removed from this process.'

Hopefully the others won't visit the other three rooms, Owen thought, which would give him a fighting chance at least.

The bell sounded and before Owen realised what was happening, he was standing in another hotel room where three weary consultants sat behind a table. There was an overhead projector to his right.

'Green 244. Please present your paper.'

Owen placed the acetate on the projector in thirteen different ways, none of which displayed his page the right way up on the projector screen. Why use an acetate anyway? Everything was PowerPoint these days.

After finally getting it right, he then stumbled through the presentation, his voice getting ever tighter as his mouth became drier than the Mohave Desert.

'Do you want some water, uh, Dr Morgan?' a female consultant asked.

Owen had taken a sip of water but before he'd said much more he found himself in another room faced with three new consultants who were looking through his portfolio. What had just happened? Had he suffered a kind of absence seizure and forgotten what had taken place? Probably not as he wouldn't be in this room now, they'd have simply removed him from the process.

'Have you done any research?' the thin bespectacled surgeon asked.

'Why yes, I looked at postoperative anastomotic wound leak rates as you can see…'

'That is audit. I asked about research. Re-search. Where you test for a hypothesis.'

'Oh. Yes, I have done that as well actually. If you look in there you'll see I did a sleep apnoea project as a medical student. I looked at oxytocin and vaso…'

'Yes, yes.' The consultant ticked a box. 'Any publications?'

'I have a list. Here it is.'

'Do you have any hobbies?'

'Astronomy.' Why did he say astronomy? That was Sanjeev's hobby.

The consultants stopped and looked at each other. 'Any lesson, uh, astronomy, has taught you about medicine?'

'Sorry, yes. I understand. I like rugby and that's a team sport and working in a team is what we need to be a good surgeon. Sorry.'

The consultant ticked a few more boxes and again Owen was whisked to the third and final room, though this time a second or two of conscious memory of waiting outside a hotel door told him he hadn't passed out in the intervening minutes. Three new consultants were seated before him though these new ones did not introduce themselves.

'One of your patients suffered a burst abdomen following a laparotomy that you were responsible for closing, Mr Morgan. How do you manage this situation?'

Owen panicked. He had no recollection of this at all. Even if it did happen he certainly wouldn't have put in his portfolio. Perhaps it did happen and the events were so horrifying he'd blocked them out.

'I don't recall that at all. I'm…'

'No.' The consultant who had asked him was impatient now. 'This is the scenario room. I tell you a hypothetical situation and you tell me what you'd do.'

'OK. What was the situation again?'

After precious seconds had been wasted repeating the question, Owen dived head first into telling them what needed to be done but in no logical order whatsoever.

'And what do you tell your consultant?'

'All of what I just said.'

'And what else?'

'Uh, sorry, I guess. My suture must have come undone. Something like that.'

Owen was unsure if this was what was required but he did not think it was, as the consultant made no tick in any box.

The consultant to his left asked him what he'd do if his consultant turned up to work drunk.

'He'd never do that,' was his reply.

'This is a hypothetical situation, what would you do?'

Owen did not know. 'I would say "Are you drunk?" and see what he says'

'He says he isn't, but he smells of alcohol.'

'I'd say "You smell of alcohol" in all probability.' Owen paused to try and gather his racing thoughts. 'Probably best he doesn't operate.'

'Probably?'

'Definitely.'

'He still wants to. What do you do?'

'Stop him. Tell him not to, or I'd report him.' Owen was beginning to understand what they wanted here. 'I'd tell him about GMC guidelines.' Tick. 'And inform my senior.' No tick.

'Which senior?'

'Another consultant?' No tick. 'The head of department?' Tick. 'Management possibly?' Tick 'The CEO of the hospital?'

No tick. 'That will be enough, Mr Morgan.'

The third consultant spoke for the first time. 'You'll hear from us in a few months.'

As Owen left the room he shook his head. Few months? He needed to know soon. He only had a few months before his contract ended and a new baby entered the world.

The Waiting Game

When he arrived back, Padma had opened the front door before he'd had a chance to get out of the car and embraced him as he did so. Owen decided to give up trying to read his wife and just be thankful for every good day he got with her.

'How did it go? Any luck? When do you find out? Tonight or tomorrow?'

'Oh. It went alright, if you know what I mean.'

'Alright? That means you did badly. How bad?'

'Alright. It was alright. The whole thing was a bit of a farce really.'

They both entered the house and Padma set about making some tea for her returning surgeon husband.

'I don't know when I'll find out, that's the thing. They said a few months.'

'Then I guess that means no job.'

Owen sighed. He hadn't figured that perhaps that comment meant no job for him. What was he to do? He couldn't apply for more as MTAS had sucked all the training posts into the vast black hole at its core and the only other work that was advertised were miserable staff grade positions. A Caucasian staff grade. Who would ever have seen such a sight?

Padma brought the tea through to the living room where Owen had opened up the MTAS website on the home computer. 'England has a second round of training posts going on. If I don't get the Welsh job I'll have to apply for England. For some reason there isn't a second round in Wales.'

Padma brightened. 'Great. Put London down. We'll be a lot better off down there.'

Owen's mood fell to a new low. 'I need to go home. We need to go home. To Wales. I want Rhys to speak Welsh and have the education I did.'

'You don't speak Welsh though.'

'I know a few words,' Owen said. 'I can teach them to Rhys.'

'Do it in London.'

'I might have to.' The prospect was so depressing Owen could not bear to think of it for long. 'I'll apply everywhere in England and take the first job that comes up.'

'Daddy.' It was Rhys. He'd walked unsteadily up to his father's chair and gripped his leg. 'Daddy,' he said again.

Owen picked him up and sat him on his knee. 'Well done Rhys. Well done. Say 'da iawn'. Da. Iawn.'

'Daddy.' Rhys started to struggle in a bid to regain the floor but Owen held on.

'Da. Iawn.'

Rhys started to cry. 'Mammy,' he said then so Owen placed him back on the floor and turned to Padma.

'You see. I can't do it here. It needs to be back home. We can send him to a Welsh school.'

'There is a Welsh school in London. I looked it up.'

'But it won't be the same. Besides the London one is private and we don't have money to waste on that sort of thing.'

Padma picked Rhys up and he vomited a little on her blouse.

'See,' Owen said. 'It's not just me he does that to.'

'You boys. You both give me trouble. I only hope this one's a girl.'

Owen looked at her growing abdomen. He hoped he'd be able to sort his employment problems out before he or she entered the world. What if he didn't? He'd name it Pryderi perhaps, meaning 'worry', like in the *Mabinogi*. He was unsure if he'd remembered that correctly and knew that this line of thought was useless anyway so he let his mind go blank. When it had rebooted, worrying thoughts about the future continued to feature.

Padma took Rhys upstairs to clean up the fresh batch of vomit but what would Owen do if he ended up with no job? Should he apply for a different specialty? If he did that, all the work he'd done in surgery, completing the exam and doing all the courses, would have been a complete waste of time. An expensive waste of time. Padma would never let him live down the £1,400 he'd wasted on a box set of study files for the exam he'd bought early in his career that did nothing but direct him to books which were not part of the deal and had to be purchased separately. The bloody STEP course indeed! If he did anything other than surgery all this would have been a waste of time. June the 10th was when the results would be out, almost the same due date that had been given to Padma.

The stress caused him to feel a slight twinge in his chest so he lay down on the floor. June the 10th was indeed a few months away. He knew that every day from this until then he'd be thinking about the result. And the pregnancy. Probably both in an alternating fashion he decided, for if he thought about them both at once it might result in a cerebrovascular event.

CHAPTER 17

Labour Pains

THE WAIT WAS indeed long and when the week of destiny arrived, circled in red on the calendar, it seemed as if Owen would have his result before the baby arrived. The tenth was on Thursday, and on Wednesday evening he and Mr Graham sat in the café at the foot of the new cardiothoracic unit at Old Square Hospital.

'How's wifey?' he asked.

'Fit to burst. It'll be a relief to get it all over with.' He knew he was lying before the words were even out of his mouth. It would be a disaster. He'd have more responsibility than ever and he was flailing around in the dark as it was.

'I bet. You've only got a few more weeks left here now.'

'Tell me about it. I have no idea where I'll be next. None.'

'Why didn't you apply here like we told you?'

'I should have done. Ahmed went on at me about that. How is he getting on as a registrar?' Please let it be terrible. Please say he was too young, it was too early for him and he did some major mistake. Please, please, please.

'Really well, actually. He did his first laparascopic cholecystectomy yesterday.'

Damn. 'That is excellent news. I am so glad for him.'

Mr Graham smiled. 'Look, you'll get a job, but it might be anywhere. You need to be flexible and go to where the work is. My reference will set you up nicely. Trust me now, you'll get a job.' Owen didn't trust him. 'By the way are you still OK doing that extra colorectal clinic with me tomorrow afternoon?'

'Oh yes.' What colorectal clinic? He'd forgotten all about this, if ever he knew about it in the first place.

'Good. Best get back to the ward round, eh?'

'Thanks for the coffee.'

That evening Owen sat again at the computer staring at the blank screen. No job announced yet. It was a day early anyway, but then again he'd done this daily since the interview.

A very swollen bellied Padma came up beside him and handed him a cup of tea – part of the ritual that had developed around the goddess MTAS.

'How are you, baby? Any babies yet?'

'Not yet. Perhaps on the weekend.'

'Yes. If you could keep it in beyond tomorrow that would be good. I wouldn't want the addition to find his father unemployed.'

'I'll do my best. No curry and no sex then for me.'

'You had curry today.'

'No sex, then.'

'Chance would be a fine thing. Where's Rhys?'

'I've put him in bed. You've hardly seen him these past months. He can't say 'daddy' anymore, you do know that, don't you.'

Owen sipped his tea. 'The cat's in the cradle, eh?'

'What?'

'Never mind. Let's get to bed.'

The minute Owen had got off to sleep alongside Padma's expansive form, she shook him awake again violently.

'What's wrong? Where is Rhys?' Owen was unusually disorientated.

Padma had switched the light on now and was kneeling at the side of the bed in obvious discomfort. It was half past midnight.

'Is it coming?'

'Of course it's coming. Why do you think I'm in pain here on the floor, you idiot?'

Owen slapped himself in the face. 'Right. But I've got colorectal clinic tomorrow.'

'What the hell do you want me to do then, hang upside down till it's convenient for you to have another child?'

'Sorry, yes. I'll get dressed.' He got out of bed and hurriedly pulled a mismatched set of old clothes from the drawer. 'No need for anger now, is there? I'll get Rhys.'

'NO! Don't wake him yet. Wait till I'm ready.' With that she groaned heavily and her face became red.

'Don't have the baby here. I haven't done obstetrics since medical school. Shouldn't you call the midwife or something to let them know we're coming in?'

'NOT YET, Owen, I'll do it later.'

'OK. Please, no shouting.'

'It's difficult with a moron like you.'

Owen glared at Padma. He felt the feelings of violence rise in him again, as so many times before. But he had controlled them so far and wasn't going to give into them now.

'Stop staring and get the bag ready. Start the car. Do something. DO SOMETHING.'

'OK, OK,' Owen said as he ran around the room doing very little of practical value at all.

Padma hauled herself to her feet and opened the bedroom cupboard. 'The bag is in here. Take it to the car. Bring me the house phone.'

Owen worked well under orders in such circumstances and after he'd handed Padma the house phone she dialled the midwife to let her know she was coming in. Owen lifted a sleepy Rhys out of bed and carried him through the house randomly, one moment looking for his shoes, the next switching the kettle on for a cup of tea. When Padma saw that Rhys was in the process of waking up in her husband's arms, she screamed all manner of obscenities at him.

'Not in front of Rhys. Calm down. Let's go to the hospital.'

'Is my bag in the car at least?'

'Of course.' As Owen strapped Rhys into his seat, he made a cute gurgling noise before vomiting a little on his hand. Checking to make sure Padma hadn't seen this, he wiped off most of it with a tissue and then launched himself into the driving seat.

'This time,' Padma said, recalling the journey to hospital for Rhys's birth, 'don't go over the speed bumps. Go the other way.'

'Of course,' Owen said automatically as he drove his wife to hospital the way of the speed bumps.

D-Day

After six hours of labour Padma finally gave birth to her second son at ten to seven in the morning. Owen had gone through various phases of carrying the dazed and confused Rhys around the abandoned hospital corridors he knew so well and sitting exhausted by his wife's side as the midwives played with his son in their coffee room. After the birth Owen telephoned his parents to tell them the good news.

'Mam. Padma has...'

'Oh she has, has she, *bach*.' She seemed positively chirpy at this time of the morning. Was it a wrong number? Owen wondered. 'Boy or girl?'

'Boy. All healthy.'

Moira turned her head away from the receiver but Owen could still clearly hear her shouting. 'Idwal. Idwal. Padma's given birth. She's given birth. Yes. A boy. I don't know, I'll ask. Any name yet?'

'Ifan.'

'It's Evan, it is Idwal.'

'Ifan, Ifan. Mam, are you coming up today at all to see the baby?'

'Yes, of course I am. Padma's staying in the hospital though, yes?'

'Yes, but I need to be in clinic this afternoon and I have no one to look after Rhys.'

'You can't go to work. Get your paternity leave. Stand up for your rights.'

'I promised, mam. Please. I need to sleep too.'

'Hello Owen, this is your father. Well done there, *boi*.'

'It wasn't much to do with me, to be honest. Not really.'

'Now whatever anyone says, you stay home today, right?'

'Please, dad, tell mam to come up if she can.'

'Now I am working, I am, otherwise I'd have loved to have come up. Here's your mother.'

'Owen I will be on my way, I will. I am looking forward to seeing you, Rhys and Evan.'

No mention of Padma. Such a shame things had broken down somewhat since the cave incident, Owen thought. After bidding his mother goodbye, Owen returned to the delivery suite to find his wife had been moved through to the ward already.

'Thought I'd lost you,' he said as he leant back against the chair and gave Rhys a yellow plastic duck to play with.

'I'm not leaving that easily. How does he look?'

Owen stood and gazed at the shrivelled baby in the cot where a large white NHS blanket covered him from the neck down. He was evidently dreaming of milk, Owen thought – his lips were moving rhythmically as he breathed. 'He looks brilliant.' Odd way to describe a baby. He chastised himself for having not chosen a better word.

'Come here,' she said. She was smiling, so Owen guessed it was safe to approach. As he put his arms around her, Rhys was bundled up too in a three-way hug. 'Does he look white or Indian?'

'White now, of course. Not much sun in there,' he said jabbing at Padma's deflated belly.

'Good. Keep him white.'

'He is what he is, baby. Half-Indian, half-Welsh. We'll love him any way he turns out.'

'I know that. I just wanted a white baby this time.'

'Now's not the time to be racial, Padma. Just enjoy the fact that he's healthy and here.' Why did skin colour matter so much to these Asians?

'Have you told your family yet?'

'Oh yes. Mam is on the way up.'

Padma didn't seem pleased. 'Why so soon? Tell her to come up on the weekend.'

'I need to get some sleep before the clinic this afternoon.'

'What clinic?' She was definitely not pleased now.

'Mr Graham asked me do the colorectal clinic today. Just three hours that's all. Then no more work for a fortnight.'

Padma was too tired to fight but Owen suspected she'd store this betrayal in her memory banks for use at a later date instead. 'You do what you want to do.'

'Get some sleep yourself. You've been working all night.'

With that Ifan started to stir. 'Hand him here, Owen, I think he needs some milk.' Owen gently lifted his newborn son out of the cot and as he did so he could feel his heart racing away in his fragile chest. So gentle, so fragile, Owen thought. With that, Ifan opened his eyes and stared directly as his father. This would have been a moment any father would remember forever, but Owen recalled from medical school that the eyes of a newborn only have visual acuities equivalent to hand movement recognition and so he could have been Mother Theresa for all Ifan knew. Why did medical school have to rob every such moment of all its depth and meaning? Perhaps it was just he who was himself robbed of all depth and meaning, he pondered.

'Hand him here. Stop staring at him.'

Owen did as he was told and then picked Rhys up, tickling his belly as he did so. 'You have a brother now, yes you do. Yes you do. Tickle, tickle, tickle.' Rhys grinned at his father before vomiting all over him.

Mr Graham's Colorectal Clinic

As Owen pushed open the clinic door that afternoon, he found Mr Graham behind his usual chair with his feet on the desk. 'Heard your wife gave birth overnight. Congratulations.'

'Thanks.'

'Didn't expect you here, in all honesty.'

'My mother's looking after Rhys.'

'Rhys?'

'My son.'

'Oh. Don't worry there is still plenty of work to do. We didn't cancel any patients. How did you get on with this MTAS crap?'

MTAS. He hadn't checked. Mr Graham could see his surprise so offered his own computer for the all-important checking, getting up out of the seat for him.

Owen gratefully accepted the invitation and finally summoning enough courage to log on he saw that his screen was exactly as it had been all those other times he had checked over the past few weeks.

'Well?'

'No offer of a job, but I'm not rejected either. It's the same as before.'

'Sorry. It must be stressful for you.' Mr Graham stood close to Owen and he realised this was his cue to get out of the chair. 'Best get on with the clinic. Well done on the baby again.'

Owen sat down at his own desk in his own office, his head spinning uncontrollably. The walls were tipping this way and that and he felt like vomiting himself.

'Are you OK there?' a nurse said to him as she distorted in the heatwave effect that had appeared in the room.

'Yes.' He realised he did not sound convincing. 'Can I have some water, please?'

'I'll get it later. Do you want the first patient in now?'

Owen put his head on the table to try and stop the spinning. He did not reply but although the nurse disappeared, he noted neither patient nor water appeared in the room. What could he do? No job. Why? Why no news? His interview was months ago, surely they'd know by now. Perhaps the best way to know was to phone them up. But if he did that, what if the news was bad? Perhaps he should start seeing patients first; a bit of logic would be useful.

The first patient was a young man with an anal tag. Owen was very pleased about this as the amount of thinking required was really quite minimal. The second patient had haemorrhoids, but thankfully did not want them treated in the clinic by Owen. Normally he would do his best to encourage treatment with bands in the clinic, but he conceded that the patient was probably wise not to trust an unshaven, unfocussed doctor who seemed about to fall asleep, with a weapon aimed directly up their anus. After the third patient, a case of altered bowel habit for which Owen organised a colonoscopy, he decided to call the Welsh deanery in Cardiff. Finally he got though to a Ms Wales, who claimed to be responsible for managing the system.

'Oh, the Wales deanery has exited the MTAS system so we're doing ours differently now. The website will no longer be used by us.'

'But do I have a job or not? Will you email me later today, is that what you'll do?'

'No. We'll email you a choice of jobs once we know if you're selected.'

'Oh no! When will you know that?'

'I don't know. I cannot tell you.'

'But I need to know. My wife gave birth today and I have no job in six weeks. When roughly will I know if I've got a job or not?'

'Any time before October.'

'October! October! But…'

'We have to wait for people to accept or decline jobs, you see.'

'Well do you know where I am on the list? Is it likely to be soon or at the end?'

'I do know but I am not at liberty to tell you that information, I'm afraid.'

Owen, at a total loss for words, replaced the receiver and did his level best not to start crying. After a fight lasting around four minutes, he stifled the emotion and called in the next patient.

Four more patients were seen before Owen had another thought. What about round two in England? Should he apply or not? If he didn't, he risked ending up with no job at all, but if he did and he was offered a job before the wretched Welsh deanery had completed their job allocation then he could be prevented from going home. He decided to email Ms Wales these questions, stifling the urge to call her lots of four-letter words for being so unhelpful.

The last two patients were a little more complex, but Owen had by this time detached himself from all emotion so he was probably more clinically accurate than ever before. In fact, Owen had detached himself from his very body and felt like he was watching the consultations from a small kitchen chair sat somewhere in his own cranial cavity. He even fancied he made out the inside of his skull around the rather blinkered and distorted view of the patient he was getting from his unorthodox vantage point.

'Well. Clinic has finished. Thanks for the help today, Owen. I appreciate it. Now I gather you probably want to go back to the wife and kids.'

Owen could sense Mr Graham was in the room but could not seem to locate him. This was possibly because his gaze was frozen on the cross-sectional model of an anus that sat on top of his desk.

'Any idea when you'll be back from paternity leave?'

'Two weeks, I guess,' Owen said to the anus.

'Right, then. If you want to come back sooner then we'd be pleased to have you, otherwise, see you in two weeks.'

'Bye.' Owen sat frozen in his chair as the nurse tidied up the notes and whisked away the instruments. He was only stirred from his paralysis when a cleaner asked him to move his legs so she could vacuum under the chair.

'I ought to be getting back,' he said to the cleaner. 'My wife gave birth last night.'

'Well done, mate,' the cleaner replied. 'No wonder you look like shit.'

CHAPTER 18

Paternity Leave

I F HORMONALLY PREGNANT Padma had been challenging for Owen, then post partum Padma was off the page. He was grateful for his mother's help in the beginning but a cold war was developing between her and Padma and after three days she was dispatched back to Wales and her son was left defenceless.

Only two weeks, Owen told himself. He didn't fancy work much at the moment either, as any thoughts about his job reminded him of its imminent end and lack of further employment. So he toiled day and night trying to look after Rhys, going to and fro to Mothercare to get supplies and getting up all hours of the night to deal with Ifan. Padma would do this too, of course, and the fact that she'd chosen to breastfeed gave Owen immediate comfort as he himself lacked the appropriate glands to be useful in that department.

This was the case until a friend brought a curious battery-operated milk extractor for her and from that moment on a supply of milk existed in the fridge that Owen could utilise in case Ifan needed any. But how would he know if he needed any? Owen had developed a treatment algorithm that could diagnose most of Ifan's needs as and when they arose. If there was crying, first check the nappy. If it was dirty it would be changed, if not he would try milk. If milk did not work then sleep was the answer and appropriate song-based sleep-inducing tricks would be tried in a bid to comfort his son. Occasionally he would get glimpses of the MTAS whirlwind that surrounded his house tearing off the occasional roof tile and cracking the occasional window, but he would put such thoughts out of his mind as best he could by concentrating on the lesser horror of being a new father again.

Various friends and relatives came visiting and that was always nice as chocolates were invariably the gift of choice. The chocolates never stayed around for long though since devouring these unexpected surprises was the one thing that kept Owen sane. His father came up one day although he didn't stay for long; his sister did not come at all. The relationship between Angharad and Padma had been particularly bad since Padma took umbrage at being excluded from a photograph at Angharad's wedding a year ago.

Owen was preparing milk when he heard a shout from upstairs.

'Coming,' he replied.

'Where are you? Rhys is up here. Why is Rhys up here?'

'He wanted to see the baby.' Owen screwed the cap on the milk bottle and carried it upstairs.

'I am trying to sleep. Get him downstairs. Now.'

'I've got the milk for Ifan here.' Owen handed Padma the bottle.

'Thanks. Any news on the job?'

A sharp pain tore through Owen's head. 'No. I think the computer hates me. I never get any emails from Wales.'

Padma sighed. 'You need to look at England. If Wales won't have you then you have to apply in England. Look at your family here, we all need you and you are the only one working.'

Only one working indeed, Owen thought. Not for very much longer. 'I know I need to start looking.'

'Please take Rhys down with you.'

Owen carried his son down the stairs as Padma fed her newborn in the warm sticky bed.

The doorbell rang just as Owen reached the foot of the stairs. It was the midwife.

'Hello there, Dr Morgan. How is she? Is she in?'

'She's upstairs, please feel free to go up. Do you want any tea?'

'I never say no to tea. Four sugars please.' With that she disappeared upstairs.

Four sugars, thought Owen, as he boiled the kettle. No wonder she was the size of a Mini. 'It's a wonder her arse can get up the stairs, eh?' he said to Rhys, who uncomprehendingly smiled back.

As he waited for the kettle to boil, he saw the breast pump on the kitchen worktop. He held it in his right hand and pressed the switch, laughing at the sudden jump Rhys made when the whirring noise started up. There was still a little breast milk left over in the pump. What does breast milk taste like? Owen wondered as he unscrewed the bottle. He had some sense that this was in some way wrong but decided to proceed nevertheless. Gingerly he held the bottle up to his lips and poured a small amount into his open mouth, or it would have been a small amount had Rhys not slapped his arm at that moment causing the bottle to empty into Owen's startled mouth.

The taste was unusual and unpleasant and Owen spent the next minute coughing and spluttering over the sink, for a fair amount had got into his trachea as well. 'Well, that's science for you,' he told Rhys. 'You have to experiment, otherwise you just don't know.' Rhys, uninterested, wandered away to play with the Thomas the Tank Engine on the mat and Owen carried the tea upstairs. He found the two women exchanging pleasantries with the midwife balanced precariously on the edge of the bed to Padma's side.

'Tea.'

'Thanks, love. Well, isn't she doing well, eh?' The midwife gestured back towards Padma with her thumb, being too round herself to easily accomplish a more delicate indication of whom she was talking about.

'Yes. Of course.'

'Baby is also doing well. The weight has dropped a little but it's what you expect with these little mites, eh?'

Little mites? Owen shuddered at such floss. 'Yes. Good. Well, I'll be downstairs if you need me.'

'Any problems that you have, Dr Morgan?'

Owen was taken aback by this and turned abruptly to face his cherubic questioner. 'No. No problems. Thanks for asking, though.'

'No problem, my love.'

Ach. Owen descended the stairs once more and decided to grab the bull by the horns. He switched the computer on and as the whirring monster came to life for the first time in a week, Rhys came over to see what was taking place and the two boys watched the screen fire up in equal measures of awe and trepidation.

Round Two

There was still no word from the Welsh deanery. With weariness, Owen called up the lovely Ms Wales who, it appeared, was on holiday. How could someone go on holiday in the middle of this crisis? An even less useful version of her seemed to be fielding all the calls in her absence and although she was polite she seemed to be so ill-informed about everything that she might as well have been plucked randomly off the street and pushed in front of a bank of ringing phones. Perhaps she had been, Owen thought after he hung up.

'There is nothing to do but apply again in England,' he said to Rhys, who was attempting to reach the big button that would have switched the computer off. 'Or perhaps Australia.' That didn't seem too crazy actually, but the headache of moving a young family halfway round the world soon put paid to that idea, since he was having a migraine as it was.

Scrolling through the surgical jobs that were available in England, all of which were on a one-year contract or less, he chose a few that sounded good and started applying for them. These applications were relatively easy as he copied the answers he'd previously spent so much time drafting for MTAS and pasted them into multiple forms at once. By the time the midwife came downstairs, he'd already applied for three jobs in round two.

'Bye there,' she called as she opened the door, though she had closed it before Owen could articulate a reply.

Applying for jobs was so easy that an hour passed and Owen found he had applied for all the surgical jobs in the country, of which, admittedly, there were not that many.

Rhys finally managed to reach the big round button and the computer started its shutdown sequences. Owen picked up his squirming boy, who was obviously delighted at having finally achieved his aim, and sat him on his lap.

'When are you going to talk, little boy?'

'Daddy,' he said.

'Well, I'm glad you're saying that again. It was all mammy before, now wasn't it?' Owen rubbed Rhys's nose against his own. 'Do you want to go to Australia? Australia? Or to Wales?'

'Daddy.'

'Going to daddy is also an option.'

Owen put his son on his knee and bumped him up and down in the fashion of a carousel horse. After a few minutes of uncontrollable laughter, he lost his grip and fell to the floor. Laughing leads to crying, as his father always said. His father.

He hadn't called in a while. He gently rocked Rhys back and forth in his arms as he called Neath.

'Hello, 891 261.'

'Hello, mam. It's Owen.'

'How are things, *bach*? How's the little one?'

'Lost some weight, the midwife said, but doing well otherwise.'

'You feed him well, get the milk down him.'

'Padma's breastfeeding so it's a bit difficult that.'

There was a sharp intake of air. 'Breastfeeding, my foot. You were brought up on powdered milk and look how you turned out.'

Owen resisted telling his mother about the current 'breast is best' teachings but the pause caused by his internal debate gave Moira space to advance her cause.

'No, you were never at my teat.'

'Stop talking now! Yuck. Thanks for coming up to babysit anyway.'

'You should not have gone to work that day, oh no. Your Uncle Harry would have turned in his grave if he'd have known. People died to get workers' rights, you...'

'Yes, yes. Is dad alright?'

'Feeling a bit under the weather, he is. Idwal. Idwal. Sorry Owen, he's gone as deaf as a post.' Owen heard his mother walk away from the phone and then Idwal's subsequent lumbering approach.

'Hello, *boi*.'

'You don't sound yourself, dad, is everything alright?'

'Yes. Bit of a pain in the chest that's all. Too much bread and butter pudding earlier. How's the baby?'

'Good, thanks. Sleeping upstairs with his mother. Hopefully we'll be able to bring him home to Wales to see all of you in your native environment before too long.'

'Great news.' Idwal held the phone to one side as he sneezed an almighty sneeze at the other end of the line. 'Sorry, *boi*. Come down anytime. Angharad been up yet?'

'Not yet. I'm sure she's just busy.'

'I'll tell her to get her arse in gear. Too busy. Family is family and there is not anything more important.'

'She's a vet. Vets work long hours.'

'Yeah, well. You're up in the Midlands and she's in London so the family have all spread out anyway.'

He sounded sad. 'I am trying to come home. I came for an interview, remember, but they haven't given me a job so far.'

'Bloody Welsh. They won't even employ their own people. Oh yes, foreigners, bring them in. Bring them all in, but no Welsh. No it's…'

'You've been listening to mam too much. You're related to a foreigner now and your grandchildren are half foreign.'

'They're Welsh, they are. Land of my fathers it is, not mothers.'

Owen could hear his mother in the background. 'It's Jews are the land of their mothers.'

Owen was unsure of the validity or relevance of this last point so he bid his parents a happy farewell and hung up the phone. Hopefully things would work out. There was no ultimate way of knowing but he thought it wouldn't do any harm to start praying again. Praying for deliverance through this difficult time.

Durham

Paternity leave ended a week later, though it felt like a year, and Owen was back in work again getting a well-deserved break. As if this piece of news was not good enough, the first email he opened on his first day back was from a hospital in Durham inviting him for interview. The post was only for one year and although this was undoubtedly good news, the nature of the great gamble that was MTAS was even more apparent to Owen. Wales had not deemed it necessary to let him know the results of the interview he had attended many months before, but it was in Wales he most wanted to live and work. On the other hand, the interview in Durham was for a good job and this would most certainly be better than nothing. Owen was not a natural gambler and these decisions put more pressure on his already strained constitution such that he developed an altered bowel habit and considered asking one of his colleagues to have a quick look up his rectum after one of the bowel clinics. Many years later he was thankful he had not acted on this particular impulse.

As the interview date with Durham approached, there was still no word from Wales so he decided to give the delightful Ms Wales another phone call.

'Hello,' he said. 'Any news on the interview results? I have another interview you...'

'Mr Morgan. I have already explained to you that we have not decided. You will be informed in due course.'

'When, though?'

'In. Due. Course.'

'A week? Two weeks? I just want a rough estimate. I need to make important decisions here and as...'

'It depends how quickly other people get back to me. I really can't tell.'

With that the line went dead. As the days passed, more and more of Owen's colleagues were securing posts and his nervousness was increasing accordingly. The game of musical jobs was continuing and Owen was still without a seat.

By the time the interview in Durham took place in early July, there were less than four weeks left till P45 day and tension was high among all the trainees in Old Square Hospital left without a job. The drive to Durham was pleasant and reminded him somewhat of the time he first attended the interview in Wednesbury. How times were sweeter then, he thought. How young and hopeful life seemed. Unmarried and childless, about to embark on a career, on life. Now he had a wife, children and a house, but no obvious career yet. His father did not call him on this trip to give advice on the best route. In fact, Owen had not even informed him that he was making the trip. Times had indeed changed.

The interviews were packed with worried surgical trainees. Owen noticed their professional cases and well-planned portfolios and looked again at his own battered laptop case and lever arch file. There were only three jobs and a worrying number of attendees. Besides, he thought, if Durham was anything like Wales even if he was successful he wouldn't find out about it till after the 2020 Olympics.

After the interviews ended, a secretary herded the interviewees into a special room while the panel convened.

'I think they're deciding right now,' an Indian interviewee in a suit told Owen.

'Really?' He had not expected this. 'I don't think they'll be that quick. Trust me, they wouldn't decide right now. They've only just interviewed the last one. No way they're announcing the results.'

The secretary who had herded everyone into the room cleared her throat loudly. 'Would everyone please stay here for another few minutes. They're deciding right now and will announce the results shortly.'

The Indian looked smugly at Owen and moved off to speak to someone else. Owen sat on the floor and placed his head in his hands. Switching his phone on, he got a message from Padma asking him to get nappies, milk and various other items from Sainsbury's on the way home. Great. What to do about this job?

If he were offered it, he would be a fool to turn it down – but what about Wales? Phoning Ms Wales instantly seemed a waste of time and he reasoned the only time he would ever contact her again would be to find out her address so that a hired killer could be sent in the right direction.

As Owen was pondering these murderous thoughts, one of the consultants from the interview panel returned with a crumpled-up piece of paper. 'Hello everyone,' he said, and the room instantly went quiet. 'Could Mr Abdel Haqq, Salim Jalil and Owen Morgan please come through to the other room. Everyone else, you have been unsuccessful. Sorry.' A low gushing noise went around the room at this point, the sound of hopes breaking on rocks and souls in anguish and despair. 'I ask you all to wait here for a further few minutes, however.'

With mixed feelings, Owen was led through to another room where the panel sat on top of, rather than behind, the table at which he had been interviewed earlier.

Mr Sandford, a tall Scottish upper gastro-intestinal consultant, congratulated the three of them. Immediately after doing this, he unexpectedly stepped towards them and lowered his voice. 'Gentlemen. These are troubled times and we have a department to run here. You are all offered a job but I ask you to decide right now whether you want to accept it or not. If you turn it down, I'll ask the next person down the list, still seated in the room opposite, if they want it. I imagine, however, you would not be here if you were planning on turning down a job offer.'

'Can we have until tomorrow?' Abdel Haqq said. Owen could tell it was him as he hadn't yet removed his cheap name sticker from his expensive suit. 'I need to check another job…'

'You CANNOT have any more time than now. Decide now, or I will get the next candidate.'

Owen felt weak. He had no option but to accept, but felt he

was betraying his country, his parents and his future all at the same time. Abdel Haqq also heeded the warning and fell into line as all three accepted their future.

Mr Sandford smiled but he clearly was not finished. 'I want your word of honour gentlemen that now that you have accepted this job you will not pull out.' After this he solemnly shook the hands of the three newly appointed Fixed Term Specialty Registrars, as they were now termed, and turned to the secretary. 'You can let the sheep out now, there's a good girl.'

CHAPTER 19

Hiraeth

THE NEXT DAY Owen was holding a retractor for Mr Fox in main theatre while his boss busied himself separating a loop of diseased bowel from the abdominal wall.

'I did some training in Durham. You did well there getting that job. Scissors.'

The scrub nurse placed a pair of scissors in Mr Fox's open hand and they disappeared into the abdominal cavity shortly after. 'It shows how much confusion is going round that such a good job was still on offer in round two.'

Owen pulled harder on his retractor. He noticed a little bleeding around the edge of the newly-dissected tissue and placed the suction pipe in the pool so that Mr Fox's diathermy would be able to successfully cauterise the bleeding point.

'I want to go home, though. Durham is even further away than here. I am drifting northwards.'

'Ha. You drift where the job is. There is nothing wrong with drifting north.' He touched the diathermy pedal and a small plume of smoke arose from the inside of the open abdominal cavity before them, accompanied by a soft buzzing noise. 'What happened to Wales anyway?'

'Oh, I went to interview there but they never told me the result.'

'Bloody Welsh. Scissors.'

'I haven't seen my parents in a while. I'm glad I got this job, don't get me wrong, but...'

'Wales let you down, so why do you want to go there?'

'The land of my fathers.'

Mr Fox straightened, handing the scissors back to the scrub nurse. He looked directly at Owen and adjusted the retractor. 'The land of my fathers, and my fathers can keep it. Who said that?'

'Dylan Jones.'

'Clamp. Jones? Not Jones, Thomas. Dylan Thomas. Bowel clamp, quickly!'

The scrub nurse handed Mr Fox a bowel clamp while Owen placed a new retractor under a particularly slippery loop of bowel to hold it out of the way. He looked at the warm moist pinkness of the jejunal wall glistening under the hot theatre lights. Periodic peristaltic waves gently ran along the walls. How easy it would be to grab a handful of this fragile bowel and tear it out of the abdomen completely. He could do it before Mr Fox would have a chance to react. How gentle and fragile life was. Owen placed his gloved thumb against the bowel and felt warm life running past it, separated from him by only a third of a millimetre of latex.

'Don't touch the bowel,' Mr Fox said. 'It increases the chance of ileus post op.'

'Perhaps Durham won't be so bad. My parents could always visit.'

'Parents are overrated. I haven't seen mine for a year and my teenage son hasn't seen me for two weeks even though we live in the same house. Suture.'

Owen readjusted the suction tube to mop up some blood-stained serous fluid that was preventing Mr Fox from seeing the end of the bowel.

'Almost free. You want to do the ileostomy?'

'Thank you. Yes, I would.'

'Bit fat this girl. It'll be a challenge.'

'You'll be here so that's OK. I shall miss this place, you know.'

'Concentrate Owen, the bowel is slipping down again. Yes, I shall miss you too.'

As Owen readjusted his retractor he noted the pulse of the abdominal aorta, exposed and vulnerable now that the bowel was all to one side. If he slipped, the patient's operation would be transformed instantly into a battle of life and death. He could also be sacked. Sacking wouldn't be so stressful after all, Owen concluded. The stress over the job would be over and he'd be free. Everything else would fall to pieces, of course, but the release from pain would be worth it. Hope, he concluded, was more painful than the setbacks he was facing. On the other hand, perhaps Durham might be good for him. He would have to settle there, of course, and when he eventually got his numbered job on the ladder to consultancy it would probably be in that area. Perhaps he was destined never to go back home.

'The bowel is slipping, Owen.'

His mind returned to the here and now a quick adjustment of the retractor brought the bowel out of Mr Fox's surgical field.

'I should have applied here when you advised it; like Ahmed did.'

'Large swab.' Mr Fox pushed a large swab into the abdomen and straightened again. 'My back is killing me, I should sit down.'

As Mr Fox sat down, Owen's head began to ache again. He was conscious of having been consuming increasing doses of paracetamol since MTAS began, but the headaches kept getting worse. Medical school had taught him about the doctrine of learned helplessness, where a dog trapped in an electrified cage for long enough would eventually learn there was no escape and resign itself to a painful fate. Even when the electrification was then limited to half the cage, the dog would not bother to find a more comfortable place to sit as it had learned that it was not in control of its destiny. Neither was Owen. He would never get an offer from Wales and the sooner he resigned himself to this fate the sooner his recovery could begin.

Wales

The next day, just before clinic began, Owen opened his email and was surprised to find one from the lovely Ms Wales at the Welsh deanery. What manner of fresh hell is this now? Owen thought. 'We are delighted to offer you the post of Fixed Term Specialty Trainee Year 2 in Surgery,' it started.

'Shall I bring the first patient through, doctor?' the nurse asked.

'No. Not yet.' As he read on, the email invited Owen to call the Welsh deanery to secure the post, which if not accepted in the next forty-eight hours would be offered to someone else. What was he to do? The nurse led the first patient through the door and sat him down in the chair facing him.

'I said not yet. Why did you bring him through?' Owen conceded he would ordinarily have accepted the nurse's insubordination as a fact of life in the modern NHS, but with ninety-nine per cent of his cerebral activity devoted to the latest news his normal filtration systems were not working efficiently.

The patient looked nervous and glanced between doctor and nurse.

'The clinic is already late doctor,' the nurse said irritably.

'I have important work to do. Could you please sit outside for a moment?'

The patient shrugged and left the room while Owen reached for the phone. The nurse disappeared from view.

'Hello? Is that Ms Wales? This is Owen Morgan; I've just got your email.'

'Congratulations.' She did not sound sincere.

'Why could you not tell me I was getting close to the top of the list? I have accepted a job elsewhere now.'

'As I explained, Mr Morgan, I cannot give any kind of meaningful information over the phone. Now do you want the job or not?'

'I do want it, of course I do, but I am unsure if I can accept it now.'

'Shall I offer it to someone else then and strike you from the list?'

This was it. Crunch time. Perhaps he would think of this moment over and over in years to come and regret turning down his only opportunity to go home. His hands were tied, what could he do? He looked long and hard at the model of a plastic anus. The sphincter muscle was coloured yellow.

'Mr Morgan?'

'Yes. I will take the job.' What was he doing?

'Great.' She did not sound particularly pleased. 'I have a job in Glan Clwyd that is general surgery, do you want it?'

'Yes.' The rectal valves of Houston were coloured purple.

'You'll get the contract in the post. Congratulations again.'

As he replaced the receiver, the nurse returned with a heavy-set woman wearing mauve. Without any form of introduction, she stood over Owen and jabbed her right index finger at him while leaning precariously on the desk with her left hand. His immediate thought was that the centre of gravity of this mass before him was dangerously unstable and could topple over onto him at any minute. He pushed his chair back slightly.

'This is a busy clinic and I am told you are refusing to see patients. Is this true?'

'No.'

'We are already twenty minutes late. Are you going to tell the waiting room about the delay, doctor?'

'No.'

'Then what do you intend to do about it?'

'I have urgent business to sort out regarding my future.'

'Your future at this hospital is dependent…'

'Who are you anyway?'

'I am Consultant Nurse Vera Doughty.' Owen did not understand what a consultant nurse was and this failure resulted in him being unable to respond. After a short confusing and somewhat awkward delay, Consultant Nurse Very Doughty decided to proceed. 'Kindly start seeing patients.' With that she lost eye contact with Owen and fumbled a bit as she left the room.

The nurse grinned at Owen once the door had closed. 'Shall I call the first patient now, doctor?'

'No. Not yet.' Owen noticed the grin vanishing as he picked up the phone again to call Durham.

'Hello,' he said. 'This is Owen Morgan. I accepted a job at your hospital at the interview this week? I have to pull out I'm afraid.'

'Pull out?' the secretary said. 'I'm afraid you can't. We will report you to the General Medical Council if you do that.'

Owen hesitated. 'Really?'

'Oh yes.'

'Right then, bye.'

As he replaced the receiver, the nurse led the first patient through the door again. Owen looked at him blankly for a minute before the nurse walked forward.

'The first patient. Doctor.'

Suddenly he knew where he was again. 'Ah yes. Could you wait outside for a minute?'

Both patient and nurse were irritable by now and as the

patient left for the second time, Owen again reached for the phone.

'Hello, is that the GMC?'

'How can we help?'

'What do you normally do to people who accept a job then pull out shortly afterwards?'

'Is this you, doctor?'

'Very possibly. Do you strike them off or something hideous like that?'

'In this current climate all we'd do is send you a nasty letter, so no, nothing bad.'

'Nasty letter, eh?' He could cope with a nasty letter. 'Thanks a lot.'

Feeling happier, he called Durham back.

'You again?' The secretary clearly had not expected his call.

'Yes. I will be pulling out of the job. I have been given another job the interview for which I attended at the beginning of the year.'

'If you do that we will refer you to the GMC.'

'I am truly sorry for the trouble I have caused.'

'Well then. Do not bother applying for any jobs in the Durham region again as you will not get shortlisted. Good day.'

A smile broke over his face as the secretary hung up on him. He'd done it. He was going home at last. Admittedly Glan Clwyd was in north Wales and was possibly the hospital furthest from Neath that he could possibly work in and still be inside Wales, but it was an important step for him. He was going to be working in his native country for the first time. So happy was he, in fact, that when the nurse, Consultant Nurse Vera Doughty and Mr Fox came in through the door he beamed at them all brightly.

'Mr Fox. I've got the job in Wales. I'll be going home at last to work.'

'Good show,' Mr Fox said. Both nurses looked deflated.

'Shame you won't be working in Durham; good unit. I'll buy you lunch today to celebrate your departure. Ha ha!'

As they all trooped out Owen caught the eye of the mauve mass as she attempted a scowl.

'Kindly call the first patient in, will you nurse.'

The Royal Welsh Show

The next few days were truly glorious for Owen as the stress billowed out of his ears and he danced through the ward rounds and chatted animatedly with each patient in clinic. He noticed the flowers blooming in the hospital garden for the first time and heard the birds sing as they perched on the roof of the doctors' mess and defecated on his car. After work he'd scoop Padma into his arms and fuss over his children, who also seemed to catch his attention for the first time. He had a newborn son; when did that happen? Was he a different person altogether?

'We're going to the Royal Welsh Show,' he said to Padma on a Tuesday morning in the last week of July. Visiting the Royal Welsh had been a tradition in his youth although he had not gone in almost a decade. Now that the MTAS albatross had fallen from around his neck he had begun to think of himself as a proper father for perhaps the first time and determined to act like his own father as best he could. He would head this pilgrimage to the Royal Welsh like the father figure he wanted to be.

Padma had noticed this change in her husband and began to believe that he was indeed the successful surgeon she had always hoped and not the morose failure that she had begun to suspect. He was in charge this time and seemed so confident, so surgical. 'I'll make some sandwiches. Don't forget to call your new hospital to arrange the accommodation. The job is starting in only a week and you always leave things too late.'

'It'll be fine, my dearest honeybunch,' he said and kissed her on the lips. Honeybunch? He'd never used that word before and was unsure what it meant. Padma had smiled though, so he guessed it had worked.

Owen made the call as Padma loaded up the car with food and children. After locking the door he looked at the large 'for sale' sign on the garden wall. He smiled and shook his head and realised how much had changed in so little time. As he turned towards the car he saw how sweetly Padma smiled at him. Just then his mobile sprang into life.

'Hello there. You called us a few minutes ago to arrange accommodation?'

'Yes. Is everything OK?' He held up the phone and pointed to it in an exaggerated gesture to show Padma why he was not getting in the car.

'Well, we have no record of you coming to work here next week.'

He stopped pacing. 'No record? Have you spoken to Ms Wales at the deanery?'

'Yes. She told us to ask you to call her.'

After pressing the red button on his mobile Owen tapped Padma's window, which she wound down.

'Everything fine, baby?' she said.

'No. I need to make a phone call. Give me a minute. Don't come out of the car.'

Owen unlocked the front door again and sat down at the kitchen table as he dialled Ms Wales's number.

'I'm glad you called.'

'I was told to call by Glan Clwyd. They say there is no job there for me?'

'That's right.'

'What?' He had not expected this answer. Mess-ups with telling which hospitals were receiving which doctors, yes, but not this.

'It turns out that job was already given to someone else.'

'When were you thinking of telling me?'

'I was about to call you, actually.'

'But there is only a week to go.'

'Yes. I wanted to be in a position to offer you alternative choices of jobs.'

Owen relaxed. He might even end up nearer his parents. 'Right, OK. Which ones do you have?'

'Ear Nose and Throat in Carmarthen or Orthopaedics in Bridgend.'

'I want neither of those. I applied for general surgery.'

'And that is the job we don't have. It's very popular, general surgery.'

'But I was offered a job in general surgery in Durham! I turned it down because you offered me general surgery in Wales.'

'I offered you "surgery" in Wales. ENT and orthopaedics are both surgical specialties.'

Owen felt faint. His immediate options were not clear to him. 'I am on the way to the Royal Welsh with my family,' he ended up saying.

'Weather is meant to be bad there this afternoon.' She didn't add to this and neither could Owen think of anything to say.

'Which job do you want then?' she said after a long delay.

'Neither. I want general surgery in Glan Clwyd, as I was promised.'

'You were not promised. Look, why not start in one of the other jobs and see if general surgery becomes available as the year progresses? You could then swap over.'

'Is that likely to happen?' He knew it wasn't.

'I really can't tell.'

Padma reappeared at the door, an angry aura about her.

'Do you have any other surgical jobs?'

'No. The orthopaedic job is good.'

'I've done orthopaedics. I do not want to be an orthopod.'

'Owen,' Padma said. 'If you're not out in a minute I'm getting the kids out. Hang up.'

'This is important, Padma. Problem with the job.'

'One minute,' she said and slammed the door.

'Then can I put you down for ENT?'

'I've done that too.'

'Well, you aren't being terribly helpful, Mr Morgan. I'm offering you jobs and it seems you want neither one of them.'

The mistake was thinking he'd won. Why had he been so happy? The happiness might have tempted the gods to spoil it, like in ancient Greece, Owen concluded. Possibly the lack of prayer to the one true God, the God of Israel, had been to blame. He hadn't been to church in a while and perhaps He was angry. But then again God wasn't meant to do angry anymore, was He?

'Well, which job?'

It was too late to ask Durham for their job back. They'd spit in his face for even asking. They'd be right to do so, he concluded. How could a woman so inept and so piercingly unsympathetic be in charge of such an important project anyway? How did she get the job, this Ms Wales? Did she sleep with the dean?

'Mr Morgan, I am waiting.'

Owen clenched and unclenched his fists as tears of rage spilled down his cheeks. He had won, the victory had been his, and now it had been snatched away at the last minute. No words of insult directed at this hapless manager would make up for the personal harm she had done to him. Through the window he could see Padma unloading the car and unbuckling Rhys's seatbelt in fury as the sandwiches spilled onto the drive. There would be no going to the Royal Welsh now. Ah, but the weather was meant to be bad this afternoon anyway.

'Mr MORGAN!'

'Right, put me down for the ENT job. As soon as a position in general surgery becomes available, let me know.'

'If it does, I will. We'll find out as the year progresses.'

As she hung up, Owen resumed his angry crying and thumped the table in frustration.

'Yes, you do that. Show the children your violence,' Padma said as she crashed through the door. Perhaps he really was the hopeless failure after all.

CHAPTER 20

Home

'WAKE UP, BOYS, we're back.'

Rhys and Ifan were still both asleep on the back seat and probably the main reason that they had not woken was that Owen had not really raised his voice. In fact he had not wanted them to wake up. If they woke up it would be a lot of work suddenly and the serenity of the long drive alone with his thoughts, and Radio Four, would be shattered. He watched them sleeping, their gentle chests moving with each breath as they propped each other up limply in the back seat. He would get no sleep tonight if they did not wake up. He shook them gently.

Rhys opened his eyes sleepily and smiled. 'Did you get Monster Munch, daddy?'

The Monster Munch. He'd forgotten completely about the Monster Munch. Deciding to ignore this potentially bothersome question, he shook Ifan awake instead.

'Daddy,' he said. He looked about him very concerned. 'Where's mammy?'

'Mammy is in Malaysia,' his older brother explained. 'Daddy is looking after us and he will buy us Monster Munch.'

This must have been good news for Ifan as he hugged his father tightly and kissed him on the neck. Owen decided to give in and jumped back into the car for the short drive to Tesco.

'Be good in Tesco. No running around, OK?'

'OK, daddy,' Rhys said, still smiling.

When they reached Tesco, Owen threw a big bag of Monster Munch in the trolley and a few extra items for the next few days.

Perhaps being a single father wouldn't be so hard after all, he mused as he placed a large bottle of juice in the trolley beside a seated Ifan. 'Can I have the Monster Munch now?' he said.

'Wait till I've paid first, there's a good boy.' He ruffled his hair as he did so. It didn't feel natural somehow. Perhaps he was still a good father, just not the hair-ruffling kind of father that his own father was. As he examined a packet of frankfurters for a sell-by date, he decided that his own father wasn't the hair-ruffling type either. He tried ruffling Ifan's hair again. No, neither was he.

'Can we buy a new DVD daddy?' Rhys said.

'Perhaps tomorrow. We need bananas. Do you know where the bananas are?'

Rhys started pointing and guiding his father through the shop. Perhaps treating them like adults is best, he thought. Small adults. Rhys was clearly happy to show the way and possibly felt important doing so and Ifan had still not opened the packet of Monster Munch; a result on both counts.

Having successfully brought Rhys on board with his food-finding project, they now had everything they needed for at least five days of existence. Owen briefly considered getting eggs as well, but Rhys' attention was wavering and Ifan was eyeing the Monster Munch longingly and it looked like his will power could not hold out for much longer. Best to quit on a high, Owen thought, and wheeled his cargo to the till.

As the items were bleeped through by a cashier who seemed to be dreaming of something else, something better, Owen looked at his sons playing in the trolley once more. He might not be the best father in the world and he might not see enough of them, but he loved them deeply and could not bear to be without them. If he and Padma split up he'd be without them most of the week. How could they survive such trauma? How would he survive such trauma? It would be so much simpler if Padma disappeared. She'd always threatened to leave him and go home or to the Middle East to work. Why not let her go? He could cope. He was a single father now.

'Forty pounds fifty-seven pence. Do you have a Clubcard?'

Owen realised the cashier was looking at him in a totally unfocused manner. She was not accommodating. Either that meant she had an undiagnosed refractive error or she couldn't be bothered to contract her ciliary muscles to see him clearly. Perhaps he wasn't worth the effort after all. She was young and attractive and he had just returned from a long car journey and had two children in tow. He looked at her left hand; no ring. She was available, but not focused on him.

Retrieving his card from the machine with one hand and accepting his receipt from the cashier with the other he looked her straight in the eyes and said, 'Thank you.'

This time she focused her attention on him fully. It was not a refractive error after all. After a second's hesitation she forced a smile, though did not say anything. Owen suddenly realised he was unexpectedly emotionally exposed and looked to the ground as he pushed the trolley back to the car. He stopped to open two packets of Monster Munch for his sons and shook his head to himself as he completed the distance to the car. Was that why he was contemplating being a single father? For emotional support? For the excitement of a new partner? He knew it was most certainly not the second one as finding a partner was not something Owen found anything other than terrifying. Far better to stay an unattached single father. Less stress. Why leave one woman to burden yourself with another? Perhaps they were all the same anyway. He was basing this on a sample size of one, which he knew was scientifically unsound but was content to think bad things of people nevertheless. The base nature of human...

'Daddy, can we stay up late?'

Owen refocused his attention on the situation at hand. 'Yes, of course.' Why had he said that? He was exhausted and could do with the sleep.

'Yay!' his sons said in unison. Too late to backtrack now.

Bedtime

That evening the boys ran riot around the house as their father tried to work out how the microwave worked and attempted to make dinner for them. It turned out that the purchase of three ready-meals had been a wise decision as the first was destroyed in the attempt to heat it up. The box had told Owen to heat it for a total of six minutes but due to being more absent-minded than usual, Owen hit sixty minutes and busily prepared bread and butter while the microwave bellowed its vibrational energy into the Tesco meal for one and in increasing degrees the plastic covering as well. As he went into the living room to check the kids were watching the DVD and not destroying the place, Rhys asked his father what the yucky smell was.

'There is no yucky smell. Probably you need a shower, that's all.'

'Daddy there is a very yucky smell. Yuck!' Ifan said.

Owen smelled the air. There was indeed a yucky smell.

On re-entering the kitchen, the smell of burning plastic was thick in the air and his opening of the door had set off the fire alarm in the corridor. After the windows were opened and the microwave switched off, he assessed the black mass that sat in the middle of the glass plate. It seemed as though the plastic had merged with the food and become anthracitic in its appearance, if not consistency.

'I like the number eight,' Rhys said.

Owen held the plate over the sink and attempted to push the black mass off with a knife. It wouldn't budge. 'That's good. Why not five?'

Rhys pondered this intelligent question. 'Five is too fivey.'

Owen placed the whole plate in the sink, mass still attached, and reached for another plate to use instead. He could always deal with this when the children were in bed. 'Isn't eight too eighty?'

'You're right, daddy, it is. So I'm going to love five and eight just as much.'

'Great,' Owen said, reading the instructions on the second meal more closely.

'When is food, daddy? We aren't going to be eating the black blob, are we?'

'Yes, probably. Do you want it?'

Rhys made a bad face. 'Yuck,' he said, before brightening visibly. 'You can have it, daddy.' With that he ran off to watch more of the DVD.

Thank goodness for the hypnotising power of television, Owen said to himself as he reloaded the microwave and set it going again. The smell of plastic was still strong and he hoped it would not translate into bad-tasting food. His own meal had gone the way of the black blob so he reasoned he'd survive on the leftovers of Rhys and Ifan's meals.

When dinnertime arrived, Owen was disappointed that his prophecy about the smell was accurate and even transposing the eating of the meal from the kitchen to the living room, where the DVD was still playing, did not hide from the two young boys the contamination evident in their bangers and mash. A few mouthfuls were all they'd eat before Owen had to use a bit more stick and a lot less carrot to get them to eat as much as they could. Threats to turn off the DVD, to ban the television for a week and to make them do maths homework did succeed in making them both eat most of the food, although by the end Owen felt he was decidedly not in the same gang as his children anymore. With his children upstairs on the toilet, he cleared up what they did not finish and conceded that the lingering plastic smell did indeed ruin all enjoyment from the eating of the food. So this was a hiccup, that's all. Admittedly heating something up in a microwave was not cooking but those skills would come in time. He needed to practise, that's all. Even though he tried to persuade himself that he could be let off for this failure the earlier optimism was gone and two long weeks stretched into the future.

'Daddy, I'm finished,' Rhys said.

'I'm finished too.' It was Ifan this time.

The anxious father showered them both, brushed their teeth and told them a story about a monster who lived in the woods nearby and survived by eating children. As he was telling the story he seemed fixated on the different dietary requirements a monster would have and detailed the practicalities of living in an urban environment without being spotted, despite being thirty feet high and coloured red. Rhys and Ifan looked at their father horrified at the notion that a dangerous monster was so close by and needed to eat at least three children every night in order to fulfil its GDA. Owen did not recognise that their paying rapt attention was because of increasing fright rather than interest. Owen finished by detailing how children's bones were a good source of monster calcium and their eyes would be high in vitamin A, in all probability.

Prayer time came next. This was usually an event that Padma led, which Owen always thought ironic as she was a Hindu rather than a Christian, but the boys knew the words so well that their father's leadership was not really required.

'Can we have another story?' Rhys said. 'One that isn't scary?'

'A Power Rangers story?' Ifan helpfully added.

Owen told one more story and then put them to bed. Rhys fell asleep quickly but Ifan kept on asking detailed questions about the monster the existence of which he had been blissfully unaware of until a few minutes ago. How could his parents keep such important information away from him? His father obliged and finally Ifan, too, fell asleep. This was probably aided by the fact that Owen had fallen asleep on the floor next to his bed as well, such was the level of his tiredness.

Owen awoke with a start, having had a peculiar dream about a malnourished monster and after a moment's disorientation saw his son sleeping soundly in the bed. He smiled to himself as he pulled the blanket over him and made his way downstairs, stepping painfully on a Power Rangers action figure as he did so.

A Glass of Wine

The clock told Owen it was 10:30 p.m. He should call his mother about the on-call the next night, he decided.

After twenty rings, his mother answered. Her ring answer rate was increasing over time, Owen had worked out. He had even kept a chart but it seemed that this had got lost somewhere now.

'Sorry to bother you so late, mam. Owen it is.'

'What's the problem?'

'Padma's mother died last night unfortunately.' There was no response from his mother so he pressed on. 'She's had to go back to Malaysia and I'm alone with the kids at the moment. Can you babysit for me tomorrow night? I'm on call you see. Perhaps a sleepover with you in Neath?'

Moira exhaled loudly. 'Yes, of course. I haven't seen them in a while so it will be nice to catch up with them. Assuming they know who I am.'

'Of course they do. It'll be good for them to get to know more of you. How's the dog?'

'He died last week, I did tell you.'

'You did, sorry.'

'What time are you bringing them here?'

'Is seven-thirty alright?'

'I'll ring Glenda to call off the bingo and then seven-thirty should be fine.'

'Sorry.'

'Are you well?'

Owen paused. 'Yes, I'm well. See you tomorrow.'

After hanging up, Owen padded to the kitchen in his slippers to pour himself a glass of wine. He was pleased his mother had asked if he was well. He hadn't been well in a long time and although he'd tried his best to insulate his soul from the outside world as much as possible, it pleased him when attempts were made to uncloak him, even if these attempts were always rebuffed. The wine glugged into the glass and as it did so he felt saliva trickle into his mouth in anticipation. Like a big Welsh Pavlov's dog.

The second hand on the clock on the living room mantelpiece ticked on and on in its never-ending journey to nowhere and everywhere as Owen stared intently at it. The clock had been a gift from his parents to welcome them into their new Welsh home in Bridgend. They had been even more pleased than Owen when they all moved to Wales from the Midlands a few years before, though this could have been due to the fact that he was disappointed that his career hadn't quite worked out as planned. He had ended up doing a year of ENT without any transfer to general surgery being possible at all. In his heart he knew this was the way it would work out when he got that call the day of the Royal Welsh. Whatever had happened to that Ms Wales? Owen pondered as the second hand passed the number eight. The number eight, Rhys's favourite number.

Perhaps the lovely Ms Wales ruined many other people's lives too and then moved on to another job. Promoted probably, such was the logic of the NHS at the time of MTAS. The whole system was, of course, scrapped the next year, with training applications being broken up among the deaneries. By then the damage was done for doctors such as Owen though, caught in the middle and left with a substandard job. 'The Lost Tribe', the media called his type. Owen scowled at this thought. There had been many lost tribes over the years, groups of people falling between old and new and finding themselves nowhere. Then you could have an actual 'lost tribe', a tribe of people lost somewhere. This thought seemed to Owen more absurd the more he examined it. A group of people lost, yes, but a whole tribe? Where could such an event occur? He decided Amazonia was the most likely place that a tribe could get lost, though an attempt to define 'lost' in this context exposed to Owen the pointlessness of the process and he abandoned it shortly after to sit on the sofa and drink his wine.

He'd ended up with a good job as a trainee ophthalmologist, so why was he complaining? Owen snorted with derision at the process which had the following year led to him obtaining a much sought-after training post in eye surgery. At the same time people he knew that had always wanted to do ophthalmology had been shouldered aside to some other specialty. It made no sense. The system seemed back on track now but the Labour government's attempt to streamline medical training and produce more compliant consultants had caused confusion for years. After a year of doing his unwanted ENT job Owen applied, unsuccessfully, to join general surgery again but had been more than pleased to accept run-through training in eyes. On the other hand, he reasoned, he could strangle both Patricia Hewitt and Ms Wales to death with his bare hands given half a chance. He raised his glass to them both and took another sip.

It was such a shame the relationship between Padma, and by extension himself, and his parents had withered so much.

Not ended with an explosion but with a slow suffocation, really. What about the relationship between himself and Padma? Owen would be the first to admit that he did not understand the basics of human interaction and how to approach difficult situations so while he could see he'd gone badly wrong somewhere he was unable to locate where exactly. Perhaps there were many places. Perhaps it would be easier to count where he'd got it right. By the time of MTAS their relationship was in peril but under the weight of multiple blows hammered upon it by events, it pretty soon collapsed altogether. The move to Wales had not resulted in a renaissance, as Owen had hoped.

There was a noise from upstairs. Owen crept up the stairs to find a bleary-eyed Ifan standing on the landing clutching a teddy.

'I had a bad dream.'

'Oh dear. What about?'

'A monster was eating my bone.'

Perhaps the story had been too scary. 'Bones are high in calcium, remember, holding ninety-nine per cent of the body's calcium stores.'

Ifan gave his father a confused look as he was tucked back into bed. Owen kissed his son on the forehead and closed the door gently before resuming his place on the sofa and taking another tongue-chilling sip of fruity wine.

Things between him and Padma could hardly be worse now. If he was a braver man perhaps he would have divorced her. Or if he was a weaker man. She had not divorced him, despite the threats, and that was perhaps a bigger mystery than ever. He'd welcome divorce if she wanted it, as that would remove the decision from his hands. A surgeon who did not want to make decisions; how unusual. Or perhaps not so unusual, Owen thought. Perhaps he wasn't really meant to be a surgeon. He didn't get a job in his preferred specialty and hadn't taken to ophthalmology as easily as he'd have liked. Cataract surgery was the problem. It was scarier and more horrifying than he had imagined a twenty-minute day case local anaesthetic operation could ever be. Padma had not understood his suffering as he tried to learn the techniques; indeed how could she when he couldn't understand it himself? He remembered details from most eventful operations but none more vividly than the first operation where he dropped a nucleus, a few years ago now but it is one of the worst complications an ophthalmic surgeon can have. For a person who found change so difficult, more change had been thrust upon Owen than he ever considered survivable. But he had survived so there was hope in that at least, he surmised, before draining his glass.

CHAPTER 21

Cataract Surgery

No-ONE EVER FORGETS their first experience of driving a car. Owen's memory of his seventeenth birthday was dominated by the build-up and subsequent hideous disappointment of going for his first driving lesson with his father. He was studying A-levels at the time in the main science subjects and he naively assumed that if the basic scientific principles of operating a motor vehicle were known, then learning the practicalities would be a piece of cake.

'Stop, stop; STOP!' Idwal shouted. 'The starter motor will burn out if you keep the key turned for so long!' That day had not gone well. Having stalled thirteen times over the first hour he had begun to realise that driving was as much art as science and he was on the foot of a long learning curve that climbed depressingly on into the blackness of the future. To this day he still recalled with a shudder, if he forced himself, the feeling of helplessly being carried along the road in a ton of metal with only a rudimentary knowledge of how to guide the untamed beast that was propelling him along a road crowded with pedestrians, cyclists and other road users.

Though that indescribable feeling receded into his unconscious mind and lay quiet for years, it was unexpectedly pushed very much to the fore again when he started learning cataract surgery. Modern microsurgical cataract surgery, where the opacified natural lens of the eye is destroyed and extracted in a process termed phacoemulsification, has a notoriously long and difficult learning curve. Owen suspected this was the closest a surgeon would ever come to operating a one-man band.

During the operation the right hand holds the main instrument, the phacoemulsification probe; with the left controlling the vital second instrument, whose job is to break apart the cataract in a way that allows successful extraction. The left foot controls the microscope with movements forward and to the side affecting zoom and focus. The right foot is akin to the accelerator on a car. By moving the foot forward or back, the destructive power of the phacoemulsification probe is altered, and turning the foot right or left alters the amount of suction pulling fragments out of the eye. The progress of the operation is viewed by both eyes through the operating microscope – binocular vision being essential in judging the depth of the various structures. Lastly, the machine running the probe is tuned in such a way as to emit sounds of various tone and pitch dependent on how much power is being used, the degree of obstruction of the probe tip and the amount of suction being used.

Ophthalmic trainees are prepared in various ways before being let loose with all this technology on the eye of an unsuspecting patient. Owen had attended the compulsory basic microsurgical skills course run by the college in which trainees are taught the science behind the operation through lectures and tutorials. Vector forces are explained, as are the merits of the various settings on the phacoemulsification machine. All very straightforward, he thought to himself as he descended the stairs to the practical session in the basement, involving real instruments and plastic eyes. Having already seen real cataract surgery performed by experienced consultant colleagues, it all fitted together nicely. A harmony of man and machine in which the very latest technology was gently guided by the human operator using commonsense scientific principles with the aim of restoring sight to those afflicted by cataract. As easy as learning to ride a bike, or perhaps driving a car.

After attending the course, he spent several months learning easy steps in the operation – those that did not require much adjustment of focus or any use of the phacoemulsification probe – and his belief that he'd soon be as good a cataract surgeon as his seniors was utterly undiminished. Chomping at the bit for more action, the day finally came when he could use the probe for the first time and be a proper phaco surgeon.

Having inserted the probe into the eye, Owen gently touched the cataract and pushed the right pedal forward with his foot. 'No, no, no,' the consultant, Mr Gray, said. 'Push deeper but, hold on... that's too fast, slow down!' He hadn't expected the experience of using the pedal and probe to be so difficult. Judging how far to press or depress the pedal, interpreting the sounds and analysing the movement of the cataract through the microscope were all superficially simple things to do, but together the task seemed Himalayan. Coupled with all this he had always assumed his motor skills were smooth and well controlled, especially with his general surgical experience, but under the uncompromising magnified glare of the microscope – and beamed for all to see on a screen on the theatre wall – he was disappointed to note that his movements seemed jerky and tremulous.

His first attempt at phacoemulsification was brought to a swift conclusion when Mr Gray asked him to remove the probe, as he was worried Owen's experimental forays were stressing the zonules; the supporting ligaments of the crystalline lens. Owen did not know if he hid his crushing disappointment very well, but what he did remember most vividly was the return of that feeling of being powerless in the face of dangerous technology first experienced on his seventeenth birthday. Over time his skill improved, much the same way as he was eventually able to drive to school and back without ending up in the hedge.

It is said that advancing technology will at some point make the surgeon either redundant or at the very least reduce his role to that of a mere technician operating machinery to achieve their surgical aim. Owen disagreed. With expanding technological horizons, fine touch, eyesight and hearing are more important than ever to the surgeon, with an ability to assimilate all three to form a concerted plan of action the most precious skill of all. Owen wasted many hours of the night worrying if he had indeed got this ability.

Holby City

Padma was disappointed. Disappointed in her new life in Wales, disappointed that she was no longer the wife of a proper surgeon and disappointed that her husband had retreated so far into his shell that even eighteen months into the new job he did not seem to be finding his feet. He was certainly a loser now, she thought, but for how long had this been the case? Since starting ophthalmology? Since returning to Wales? It could not really be due to his parents' influence as he communicated even less with them now than he had when they lived in Wednesbury. Perhaps he had always been like this, but it was only now she was starting to realise it.

It was a Tuesday evening and Owen was sitting silently in the living room while Padma poured herself a glass of Jack Daniels, neat, and came to sit next to him.

'You're thinking about tomorrow, aren't you?' she said.

The next day was indeed Owen's theatre day and even though he knew this full well, indeed had been thinking about nothing else, he grimaced at the words as they were spoken. Somehow making it vocal made it more real, and this was not good. 'Yes,' he said. 'Please don't mention it again.' He was nervous a full twenty-four hours in advance and even though this weekly ritual had become embedded in his routine, as time went by it never seemed to get any easier. The feeling of euphoria he'd feel every Wednesday night that no complications had occurred would be matched only by the slide in his emotions as the week went by and a mental tally was taken of days left before the torture would begin again.

Padma looked at him with scorn. Cataract surgery was so much easier than proper general surgery in her eyes and yet he could not cope. It wasn't even an issue of life or death, she told herself and, frequently, Owen. She'd told him to calm down, not to worry, snap out of it; everything a wife was expected to say in these circumstances and now she was tired. It had been eighteen months. Eighteen months of torture for her as well, caused by her useless husband. She liked Tuesdays as it was *Holby City* night, where real doctors and nurses battled to save lives on a weekly basis, as many lives as could be saved in an hour of TV anyhow. As she switched on the television, she noted Owen's blank expression and threw a balled-up sock at him.

'If you're going to look like that, get out. This is the only enjoyment I have all week and I don't want you spoiling it.' Owen got up and left the room. Alone at last, she stretched her legs and placed them on her errant husband's chair. In front of her Mr Hope was battling to save the life of a young woman involved in a road traffic accident. She had developed some sort of cardiac problem and the ever heroic surgeon was busy stitching up her heart. There were some perilous moments, but Padma relaxed once it was clear that her hero had saved the day yet again. She felt a natural affinity towards surgery and was very sad that she no longer went to work herself.

She took a sip of her whisky and smiled at Joseph Burne, cardiothoracic registrar, as he explained to a baffled patient how a mitral valve replacement he was about to perform would save his life. He was so young and attractive and she would make such a good nurse at Holby City Hospital. She'd naturally do some sessions in Holby Care, the private wing, but would take time out to help Messrs Burne and Hope with their life-saving cardiothoracic work. Not so much Mr Griffin, the black general surgeon, as he had recently upset a patient needlessly and caused another's death.

Oh, the life she could have had but was denied her! She married a surgeon and was a top nurse herself, but she was unable to work due to the children and he was a failure and had moved to a different specialty. The time he had devoted to those surgical exams. How expensive and how futile all that turned out to be! He was also such a miser, not like a surgeon at all. He had no flash about him, did Owen. He refused to drive an expensive car and hated going out to public places. The suffering he had inflicted on her she could never forgive, of course. Would life have been different if she had stayed with David? How could she know? A Facebook search revealed he was married with children now, so that ship had well and truly sailed.

Padma froze as an intraoperative complication threatened to derail Mr Burne's valve replacement. The blood pressure was dropping. 'Find the bleed!' Padma told him. 'You can do it.' With that, he expertly clamped the offending vessel and the situation seemed to be normalising. Joseph had a flash car as well. She had made a big mistake, but it was a mistake she would have to endure for the present. Her pathetic husband wasn't in the room to witness surgical excellence at its best but seemed to have run away somewhere to panic about the list tomorrow. Did Joseph ever panic like that? Did Mr Hope? To be fair, they both did on separate occasions due to intense personal problems but Padma had already forgiven them for that.

How she envied Sister Morton, engaged to be married to her

hero. Padma had worked hard, crossed continents and made sacrifices. Why wasn't she driving around in flash cars and living the high life? Why wasn't she working? She was trapped in these four walls with two children and was of no use to anyone.

While she could not think of any obvious way out of this situation, she knew who was to blame for it and he was sitting at the kitchen table drinking a bottle of beer.

Owen held out his hand to see if it was shaking and was relieved to find it was not. The everlasting stress of Tuesday evenings took their toll on both of them but whereas the agony would end the next day for Padma when her husband left for work, for Owen it was only just getting started.

The Dropped Nucleus

The gap between waking and finding himself in Wednesday morning theatre was truly a test of Owen's resolve. The feeling of loss of control, of vulnerability and dread of the future were so powerful that Owen had considered engineering a car accident on several occasions just to skip theatre. He considered the fact that he never had, however, as proof that under the flaky unsure surface there was perhaps a solid core somewhere.

'Do you want to do the next one?' Mr Gray asked the turbulent ophthalmic trainee.

Owen put on a fake smile and managed to nod. This was it, he thought to himself. If only he could get through a few cataracts on this list he'd be fine till next week. He could relax for the next few days at least; just as soon as he'd climbed this mountain before him.

Owen adjusted the chair and the microscope and went to wash his hands. They were shaking as he was putting on his gloves so what hope had he got under the microscope? Everyone would see and he would be humiliated. If he could do a phacoemulsification in the dark that might afford him the anonymity he craved. He did not consider himself a very religious man, though he believed in the existence of the Almighty, and had started a ritual of prayer before each operation in a bid to secure its success. He would close his eyes and pray at the microscope, under his breath, before each operation. Quickly, so people would not notice, except of course God who would see and surely save him from disaster. He had also started to adopt other rituals as well, depending on the various correlations he had made between things he did on a day when there were no complications and things he had done when bad things had happened. As a result of these peculiar thought processes, Owen walked the long way into theatre on Wednesday mornings, never had breakfast and parked his car on the third storey of the hospital car park. The rituals would get adapted as time progressed and a recent run of good luck had convinced him that perhaps the tide would soon turn and he'd start relaxing into this kind of surgery, becoming a natural even, one day.

The patient was wheeled into theatre and the nurses went through their pre-operative checks as the surgeon, gowned and seated in his tall black chair, a foot at each pedal, increased his respiratory rate and felt his heart rate soar.

'All ready for you, Mr Morgan' the nurse said when they had finished. Perhaps she too was frightened of Owen's inability to progress and was worried about him doing the case. Too late now though, as he was in position and Mr Gray had left the room. No honourable way out now. No time left to think of an excuse or to invent a reason why the operation would be better done by the consultant.

'Thank you, nurse.' Owen accepted the iodinated swabs and began prepping and draping the patient. He adjusted the microscope and focused in on the eye. Thank goodness the pupil was well dilated at least, he thought.

'Knife.' The incisions were made and the anterior chamber filled with viscoelastic.

'Cystotome.' The instrument made a neat cut in the anterior capsule and a circular hole was crafted. So far so good.

The scrub nurse handed Owen the phacoemulsification probe and, with short blasts of ultrasonic power, a groove was fashioned in the cataract that would enable it to be cracked open and the pieces extracted. He would occasionally get into difficulties attempting to crack the cataract but on this occasion the crack went well and his heart rate started to fall and his breathing stabilised. He smiled at the scrub nurse under his surgical mask and the scrub nurse gave Owen a quick nod in recognition of this. Was this the light at the end of the tunnel? None of the theatre staff seemed uncomfortable or concerned.

The first quarter disappeared up the probe without incident and although there was some difficulty manipulating the second, it too eventually succumbed. Owen allowed himself a smile; perhaps he was going to get through the weekly traverses of Indian country without needing the cavalry. Alas this was not so, as when the probe was pointed toward the third quarter, the posterior capsule, the infinitesimally thin invisible layer that separates success from failure, fluttered forward and touched the probe tip. Naturally it didn't stand a chance against the ultrasonic power blasting through it and tore in half. The invisible became visible and the surgeon, preparing for victory, blinked twice on seeing the ugly rent through his microscope. He looked up, the staff hadn't realised as yet. Perhaps it was just a bad vision. Perhaps it would all go away if he had faith in God. Closing his eyes for a second and praying for a complete capsule on reopening, alas, did not work and the view instead was of a piece of cataract tumbling away into the vitreous at the back of the eye through the gaping hole he had just made.

The last quarter sat on the cliff edge right next to the torn capsule, mocking Owen. Should he attempt to get it before it too fell back? How would he do it without causing more damage? He was frozen in place, instruments as still as they had ever been, while his brain whirred away. It would not make any difference anyhow now, he told himself, whatever happened the patient would still need to go to Cardiff for the specialist to fish out what had already fallen. Like FDR during Pearl Harbour his difficult decision was made for him when the last quadrant spun and, like a slow-motion stunt crash, it too fell back into the jelly. The end.

Weak and tremulous he looked up at the scrub nurse. 'Could you call in Mr Gray, please?'

The nurse looked at the screen and turned around to her colleague. 'Call the consultant and tell him Owen's burst the bag.'

He removed the instruments and hung his head, avoiding eye contact with anyone lest he should dissolve into nothingness while his boss scrubbed up to tidy the situation as much as possible before the patient could be made safe for the journey to the University Hospital.

'You know how many times I've done that?' Mr Gray told Owen over a coffee when the list was finished.

Owen looked up at his ageing boss. Please let it be a hundred, a thousand, ten thousand times.

'Once in forty years. You've had yours now.' He supped his coffee and looked at his watch. 'So don't do it again.'

CHAPTER 22

Commiserations

THE DRIVE HOME that day was difficult for Owen. Everything was difficult. Every thought returned to that horrifying moment as the bag tore and a piece of cataract tumbled out of site into Davy Jones's locker. Normally he would be elated at the release the end of the list brought him but now there was only hopelessness and despair. The speed dial read only 50mph, the slowest he had ever gone on his journey home on the M4. Being alone with his thoughts was best now, he conceded, and he was certainly in no hurry to face Padma. Why had God not answered his prayer? Why had He allowed it to happen? He had prayed before the operation, parked in his lucky spot and touched the door to the canteen and yet it still had not resulted in success. Perhaps the Almighty was angry that he had put his faith in things other than Himself. Perhaps it was best not to pray before an operation. How would He feel then?

Owen considered that he was going through some kind of grief reaction, though his exact placement on the Kubler Ross model was not clear to him. These thoughts went round and around in his head until he parked up in his drive and turned the ignition off. Hopefully the patient would be alright, would see again. What did he think of him, the incompetent surgeon? What did the staff think of him? What did he think of himself?

'How did it go, hun?'

Owen had determined he should hide the information from Padma as he was more vulnerable than ever at that moment and any aggravation might cause him to fade into nothingness and become transparent. 'I dropped a nucleus today.'

Padma froze. 'I'm not sure what that means but it sounds like you messed up.'

Messed up. He felt his edges already starting to blur. He thought it best to escape before it was too late and made for the stairs. As he left the room, he heard Padma behind him. 'That's it' she said. 'Run away. You should have stuck with general surgery you…' Her voice faded as Owen passed through the house and for this he was grateful.

Rhys passed his father on the stairs and tugged his trousers as he passed. Owen stopped and looked at him.

'What's wrong, daddy?' Owen was touched that his son seemed genuinely concerned for him. He picked him up and kissed him on both cheeks.

'Daddy had a bad day at work.'

'Have I been naughty?'

'No, of course not.'

Rhys smiled. 'Ifan's been naughty. I saw him…'

'No, Ifan wasn't naughty either. If anything, daddy was naughty.'

Rhys looked confused. The thought obviously took too much effort to process and after a short pause he resumed his journey down the stairs and made no further comment. After he passed out of view, Owen completed his ascent and lay down on the landing floor. What would the patient look like when he came back to clinic in the morning? Would he be in pain? Would he be angry? If he was, what should he say? What if they stopped him from operating? He hadn't exactly been Mr Slick prior to this incident.

He must have been lying down for quite a while as when Padma arrived it was already time for the children's bath.

'Thanks for the help feeding the children,' Padma said. Owen made no comment but continued to lie on the floor looking at the ceiling.

'Why are you still in work clothes? Are you lazy as well as stupid? Change! If the boys touch you they'll get infected from all the diseased patients you treat at work.'

'They aren't all infectious. Most have glaucoma and things like that.'

'So it's fine to lie around all day?' She kicked him in the leg, which seemed to have the desired effect. As he struggled to his feet the world spun slightly; he had indeed been down for a while.

In the en-suite bathroom, a naked Owen stared blankly and without expression at himself in the mirror. Who was he now? What should he do? The answer was not immediately clear so he kept on staring. Having bathed and clothed the children all by herself, Padma entered the bathroom and surprisingly did not react unduly to seeing her husband standing frozen in front of the sink and in a state of undress. She sat on the toilet.

'Why can't you do it?' she said. Her tone was softer now. 'I hate to see you like this. Give it a good try and if you're not good enough, then do something else. Be a GP perhaps.'

Knowing Padma's opinion of general practitioners Owen tried to decide whether Padma was showing empathy or insulting him.

'I need to try and do it,' he said, more to himself than her. But he did not really know if he did.

'You'll blind half of south Wales if you give it too much time. You wasted enough time becoming a general surgeon and now you're wasting time again.'

He was, wasn't he? Standing naked in the bathroom for no obvious reason. 'I need an early night,' he said climbing into bed and leaving his wife sitting on the toilet. She made no attempt to follow him.

Sleep did not come easy, as expected, with recurring thoughts about the patient being in pain when they'd meet again in… Owen looked at the clock, it was 1 a.m. Seven-and-a-half hours. Seven-and-a-half hours between now and when he'd meet the patient again. He'd then have to make the embarrassing phone call to Cardiff and explain to the patient why he needed to go there. This process continued until Owen finally fell asleep around 4 a.m.

Padma slept in Rhys's room.

Eye Clinic

Where was the patient? It was eight-thirty, he was sitting at his desk in outpatients and the patient was not there. He was so tense he'd almost run away a few minutes before and each minute that the patient failed to present himself caused more and more of Owen's myocardium to infarct. Perhaps he had died in the night? Perhaps he was sat in his lawyer's office writing a formal complaint? Was it bad that he feared the latter more than the former?

A nurse appeared at the door. 'Your patient has arrived, the one from yesterday.'

'Thanks' he said. 'Uh… How is he?'

The nurse looked momentarily confused. 'He can't see and he's in pain.' She saw Owen's look of disappointment and felt sorry for him. 'Don't worry. He's still talking away though, so he can't be that bad.'

When the nurse had departed, Owen tentatively rose and slowly opened his door. The patient was in the waiting room telling everyone how horrible his experience of cataract surgery had been. 'Worse than my hip replacement!' he overheard him telling an elderly diabetic. This situation was worse than he could imagine. Closing his eyes, Owen felt the world starting to spin. Balance was seventy per cent vision so he opened his eyes and the sensation abated. There was nothing for it; he needed to get the patient out of the waiting room before he infected other patients with his dissatisfaction. Biting the bullet was the only thing he could do.

He opened the door wider and caught the patient's attention. 'Come through, please.' Even he noticed his voice was weak and unconfident.

Standing to one side and gesturing towards an empty chair, Owen's dismay mounted as a middle-aged woman busily pressed on in after him and sat down in his own seat. Relatives were never welcome although this could not ever be overtly expressed. She was probably a daughter and, knowing his luck, some kind of lawyer as well.

'I had a terrible night, doc. Pain and suffering like I have never had before.'

The female, without introducing herself, readily agreed. 'I have never seen him like this.' Knowing his luck she'd demand to know what went wrong.

'I demand to know what went wrong,' she said.

Owen tried to smile, remembering his communication skills training from many years ago in a London teaching hospital. Instead this produced a peculiar tension in the room as the patient and his guest spent a few seconds looking at a silent eye doctor attempt to force an awkward smile while leaning against a large plastic model of an eye that sat on top of the clinic table. The model slid off the desk and separated into its constituent parts after impact on the floor. The retina bounced on the solid floor and landed in the woman's handbag. Owen contemplated that this was possibly due to its concave shape. Having no place to sit now that his chair had been occupied, Owen asked his cerebral cortex what he should do and, finding no response, ended up attempting to smile again.

After a period of confused silence, the female started talking again. 'Well? Who are you anyway and what was your role in my father's treatment?' Ahh, so she was his daughter.

'I am Owen Morgan and I am an ophthalmologist.' He chastised himself for opening like this; this was not Alcoholics Anonymous. 'Firstly, I need to examine your father.'

She crossed her hands and glared at him. 'Carry on, then.'

'Would you mind, uh, moving from the chair?'

The daughter looked around the room. 'There is no other chair, where am I to sit?'

'I need that chair to examine your father. You can sit in the waiting room if you like.' Wishful thinking, that.

'I will stand in the corner.' As she made her way, she lost her balance after stepping on the plastic lens that was part of Owen's eye model, though she did not fall over.

Owen positioned the patient at the slit lamp and measured the pressure. 60mmHg; about triple the upper limit of normal. No wonder he was in pain. He sighed and wrote the number in the notes. Now for the clincher. If he looked in the back of the eye, was there a big piece of cataract swimming around? If there was, he'd have to humiliate himself by referring the patient to Cardiff, but if there was not then he'd be saved. He knew there would be, he'd seen the pieces fall during the operation, but for some reason Owen thought he'd be spared this if only he had faith they wouldn't be there. Perhaps things only existed if a person believed them to and if he, as the only witness to the dropped nucleus, was convinced it had not dropped, it was just about possible that it would be crystal clear.

Alas, this was not to be, as when he opened his eyes and looked into the fundus the cataract was there still, mocking him. What was he to do? What could he tell the patient? He needed a 'warning shot' first he supposed. Communication skills coming in handy there again.

'I'm afraid I have some bad news. The cataract has fallen into the back of the eye and you need to have it removed.'

'Will I be able to see again?' the patient said.

'Yes.'

'Can you take it out?'

'No. You need to get that done in Cardiff.'

The daughter leant forward. 'Who did it? Was it you?'

The game was up. Nowhere to hide. He had to come clean and admit what took place and his exact role in things.

'Your father is Mr Gray's patient and he himself completed the operation.' Why did he say that? To get out of trouble, that's why. Strictly speaking it was true, he was Mr Gray's patient and he had indeed finished the operation by cleaning up Owen's mess.

Even though this act of cowardice seemed to calm the situation, Owen found himself completely unable to look at either the patient or his daughter for the remainder of the consultation. Half an hour later, after numerous phone calls to colleagues at University Hospital, the patient was dispatched and he was free to get on with the rest of the clinic which by now was suffering a forty-five-minute delay.

Pathology

Morning clinic ran seamlessly into afternoon clinic with lunchtime squeezed out because of the delay. Nurses, of course, were duty bound to take every minute of allotted breaktime and the processing of the patients slowed during the nominal lunch hour due to the *Marie Celeste*-like nature of the clinic. Perhaps it would have been best if he had done pathology after all. No patients, no operating, no headaches. He'd have lunch every day, though he would reek of formalin and the satisfaction of seeing a patient get better would never be truly there. Not that there was much satisfaction with this current job as the good outcomes did not compensate for the bad. How many good outcomes would compensate for one bad? One? Ten? Perhaps even a hundred. In fact even trying to work out this ratio caused an artery on his right temple to pulsate in a manner that indicated the potential onset of a headache. Before switching the computer off at the end of clinic, Owen opened the histopathology specialty training recruitment website and briefly flirted with registering for the next recruitment round. It was the approach of a cleaner at the door ready to clean up after him that persuaded him to abandon this thought – rather than a more concrete action plan for the future.

By the time he'd finished for the day, he was exhausted, demoralised and although he was only too glad to arrive home initially, his first glance at a sulking Padma washing dishes at the sink reminded him that she had started a fight that was still in its infancy. He had lost his reserve of patience and sincerely hoped she would accept his truce.

'Look, Padma,' he said. 'I've had a terrible day…'

'Did you remember to get milk and bread?' She did not look at him as she said this but continued scrubbing a dirty saucepan noisily in the sink.

Owen could not remember being asked to get these items.

'No, I didn't tell you, but one look in the fridge should have told you we needed some. You've got the car all day so what do you expect me to do? Walk a few miles…'

'OK!' The volume of his own voice and the fact that he had not been privy to the fact that he was about to shout frightened Owen somewhat. He should try continuing in a calmer fashion, he thought, to divert attention from the shout. 'I'll go to Tesco now and get them.'

The look on Padma's face told him he had not been let off the hook. She stopped scrubbing the saucepan and slowly crossed the floor towards him. 'I stay at home all day, look after your children, wash…'

'OUR children.'

'Wash your clothes and then you come back from work and start shouting? What's wrong with you? Why do you not care for us at all in this house?'

'I've had a bad day. You know what happened yesterday.'

'Does that give you the right to shout? Do you want to set a bad example to your children?'

Owen could feel himself losing his focus and looked desperately around the shrinking kitchen for something to catch his attention. A knot formed somewhere in his chest and the injustice of the situation caused a laryngeal spasm of such intensity that he was at a total loss to vocalise his many and conflicting thoughts, which was no bad thing considering what they were. As he squeezed his facial muscles in a primordial bid to suppress some inner animal instinct, Padma pressed home her advantage.

'You fail your family by keeping us locked up in this house and then you fail your job by blinding people. You are such a failure and I don't know why I married you.' Owen felt increasing loss of control as his fists clenched and his gaze returned to his attacker in a calmer more detached way. He had little time left and if he didn't escape now he'd be done for. Using all his inner reserve Owen bolted for the kitchen door.

'Now you run away. Run, run, run!'

The door was unlocked and an over-exertional effort to swing the door open resulted in a loud crash as it collided with the fridge freezer. But he was free. He didn't look back as he bounded down the garden steps and dived into the car. A few minutes later, Owen was driving along the motorway, to where he did not know, with bitter tears flowing down his reddened cheeks. How could she be so unfair? Why would she say those things? Did she want him to lash out at her? If not, then she must have miscalculated that situation, Owen thought. Perhaps it would have been better to knock the bitch unconscious. A spasm of hatred caused him to punch the steering column with his right hand, resulting in a minor swerve across the road as the car logo detached itself from the steering wheel and the plastic underneath cracked.

The pain that followed a few seconds later caused the preceding thought to be overruled. It would have been truly terrible to do that. The children were watching television in the other room, they would have heard and he would never have seen them again. He held his bruised hand in front of him and gently flexed and extended his fingers. The pain was sharp and spasmodic. He wouldn't be able to operate now until the inflammation calmed down. Was it bad that this was his most pressing thought and not that he had narrowly avoided hitting his wife? Owen did not know.

After half an hour his mind cleared enough for him to ask himself where he was and where he was going. Evidently his default mode was to home back to his parents in Neath as he found himself only five minutes away. He might as well visit now that he was practically there.

CHAPTER 23

A Broken Heart

OWEN HADN'T INTENDED to pour out his heart to his parents when he had walked through their open front door. Indeed he'd resolved to keep the whole thing quiet and quite how he now found himself sat on their sofa with a cup of tea in one hand and a tissue in the other with his parents looking anxiously on, he did not know.

'I knew it the moment I first saw her,' Moira said. 'Bloody cold she was.'

Idwal did not say anything but simply stared at the floor with pain in his eyes.

'This was today, mam. It was fine before.'

'Fine indeed. You haven't visited us in months, you know. I thought it was all her and I was right. I said to you Idwal, didn't I?' Idwal said nothing, though Moira nodded with satisfaction as if he'd given her a supportive speech of some power and dignity. 'Didn't like our dog, didn't like our food, didn't like our house, didn't…'

'Mam. I'm sorry I haven't been able to visit. I should have done and it's my fault alone.'

'Nonsense. How could you with that witch at home, eh *bach*? No.' Moira took a sip of tea and replaced her mug determinedly on the coaster. 'You didn't stand up to her, that's what you did wrong. She walked all over you and you didn't hit back at all.'

'Truth be told, I came close to hitting back today, but in the wrong sense.'

'The right sense! She deserved it!'

Idwal looked at his wife. 'Hitting women is never right. Not for a man. I have never raised my hand against you.'

'You never had to with me I was so bloody good. No, I would have slapped her.'

'Moira!' The effort of this simple reprimand was clearly stretching Idwal's worried constitution as he slumped back in his chair immediately.

'OK, sorry, you are right. But our boy is suffering, Idwal, and we can do nothing about it.'

Owen could think of nothing to say, so he sipped his tea. In a way he was glad to get it off his chest and out in the open as, although nothing was resolved, he felt a great deal better for having shared his turmoil. He could hear the grandfather clock ticking away in the hallway and the room became quiet and tense. A blue and white rug made itself known on the living room floor. Owen could not recall this rug. It looked new. There was a brand new rug in the house and he had not been informed. Normally his mother would have taken it upon herself to bore him with every intimate detail of the rug selection and purchase, and the very fact that she had not was sudden evidence to him of how far he'd drifted out to sea. Perhaps telling them of his woes was one way of repairing his relationship with the old folks.

Moira became animated again. 'What about Rhys and Ifan? We haven't seen them for goodness knows how long and now we may never see them again!'

'You'll see them, don't worry.' Owen's voice did not contain much conviction.

'Hah. Remember your cousin Gwilym? His wife ran away with Williams the Meter and he's not seen his children since.'

'Gwilym was carrying on too, mam.'

'That's not the point. There were children involved and no one in this family has seen them since. Lovely they were. Two girls. Lucy, I think the youngest was called, but the eldest I can't remember now. See! I can't even remember their names and your Uncle Emyr is still distraught. Isn't he, Idwal? Distraught he is.' Idwal nodded.

'And your Auntie Betty, if she was alive the shock it would have killed her all over again. I never thought something like this would happen to a child of mine. I told Emyr I'd never let it but look at me now.'

There was a distinct pause in such a manner that someone else was expected to contribute although Owen could think of nothing to say, his mind being still occupied by the rug, and Idwal simply leant back in his chair with his eyes closed.

'I always supported your father. A more supportive wife he'd never have found than me. Imagine she wouldn't sleep here and went to a hotel. I should have known then. A bloody hotel. Not good enough this house, oh no. Why didn't you put her in line then, eh? You let it go on for too long. You're a doctor, you should know better.'

Owen could not see how being a doctor was any education for dealing with marital discord but the effort of challenging his mother seemed so substantial that keeping quiet was a better option.

'You'll sleep here tonight of course, I'll…'

'No, mam. I need to go home. I've got things I need for work there.'

'Idwal will get them, won't you?' Idwal lay quietly breathing in his chair with his eyes closed and neither confirmed nor denied this assertion. 'Yes, your father will get them.'

'I am not an abused wife, mam. This all seems the wrong way round somehow. I am glad I told you guys but I'm sure it'll all blow over given enough time.'

'Blow over! I've never liked Padma and mark my words, I will never let her forget what she did to my boy tonight.'

'But you must forget. Forgive and move on. I am already

starting to calm down now that I've told you and I am sure she's doing the same in Bridgend.'

'I don't care if the bitch calms down. She's always been a no good Indian and will always be one. There is no going back now! She needs to come and apologise for what she did and when she does I won't accept it. Why would I?'

Just as Owen started to regret telling his parents about his marital dispute and career problems, Idwal opened his eyes and leant forward, his face grey and perspiring. 'Moira,' he said. 'Call 999, dear. I think I'm having a heart attack.'

Glyceryl Trinitrate

The young doctor in accident and emergency closed the curtain behind him before he approached Idwal's bed. Although Moira and Owen were the only family members inside the cubicle, both sitting in hard plastic chairs next to the bed, a sizable Morgan contingent was accumulating in the busy waiting room as word of Idwal's misfortune spread around the south Wales bush telegraph. He hooked Idwal's chart on the end of the bed and scribbled some notes.

'Is the blood test back, doctor?' Moira said.

'Yes it is, madam.' Madam, Owen thought. Typical Indian doctor. 'I am afraid it does confirm that your husband Mr Morgan has suffered a myocardial infarction. It was nought point five.'

Owen leant over to his mother. 'Heart attack,' he said.

'He will be coming in to the hospital tonight to stay with us and the good cardiac doctors will be looking after him until he's better.'

'Is it serious?'

The doctor looked at the floor. 'We need to monitor him and keep an eye on him. His ECG shows he has had a small myocardial infarction in the past as well. Could you furnish me with the date of this first cardiac event?'

Moira squinted. 'What? Oh no, he's never had any myoparty attack at all, doctor. He had some pains in his chest on and off, that's all.'

Owen turned to his mother. 'Why didn't you tell me about this?'

'Oh, I did tell our doctor but he didn't want to worry you.'

'Your doctor, Dr Davies the GP? Everyone knows he's close to retiring and has forgotten practically everything by now. I am a doctor, why didn't you tell me?'

'Well you're not a heart doctor, are you? And he never had a problem with his eye.'

'I know more than Dr Davies. You might as well have asked the postman as ask him.'

'Yes, but he does know Idwal, and he's local.' Moira turned to the accident and emergency doctor who had been glancing nervously between mother and son during the previous exchange. 'I am sure a non-local like you would also have been good but he knew his history, did Dr Davies. I have no problems at all with people who are not local. Idwal could tell you that.'

The doctor was as confused as might have been expected by this comment and one look at the sleeping Idwal would have been confirmation that he was in no state to be backing up anybody's non-racist protestations. 'I need to start a GTN infusion to help his infarction lessen, madam.' Perhaps a direct response to Moira's confusing statement involved too much complicated mental arithmetic.

As he set up the infusion, Owen turned again to his mother. 'How long has this been going on for?'

'Only a year, if that. Don't worry now. Dr Davies started him on all kinds of tablets. We didn't ask you because it was best a proper doctor had a look.'

'Proper doctor?'

'Come on *bach*, you know what I mean. Someone who knows your father. Someone who does hearts. Of course, you are a proper doctor too. I'm very proud of you. We both are.'

Owen was not reassured. What should his role here be anyway? Was he expected to boss people in accident and emergency around because he himself was a doctor? He had certainly seen this happen before many times when he had been at the receiving end and it did keep him on his toes. The squeaky wheel getting the oil. Was his mother expecting him to do it? She didn't seem to be. Would his credentials as a 'proper doctor' be boosted if he did throw his weight around a little? Throwing his weight around was most definitely not in his nature, and after a short internal dialogue between good and evil he considered the forces of good had the upper hand and he remained quiet. The doctor setting up the infusion obviously knew he was a fellow professional as he had been party to the previous conversation. His setting up the infusion was almost complete and had been competently done. Owen frowned. If his only perception of him as a doctor was based on what his mother had said, then perhaps he looked down on Owen. Looked down on him for not knowing about his own father's heart condition and being kept in the dark by his mother. He was sneering at him, wasn't he? How dare a complete stranger look down on him.

'GTN,' Owen said. 'Glyceryl trinitrate.' Not exactly something inspiring or frightening to say at all. He was determined to act now though, to push home the fact that nobody should sneer at Owen when the chips were down.

'Yes, sir. All finished now,' the doctor said before removing his gloves. Time was running out for Owen; he needed to say something quick before he left to impress his mother.

'I need to see the ECG.' That was more like it. He hadn't had to read an ECG in years but it was the principle that counted.

The doctor wordlessly handed Owen his father's ECG. Lots of lines on pink paper; great. Perhaps nod a few times and say 'hmm' and he'd have pulled it off.

Owen nodded. 'Hmm,' he said before handing back the electrocardiograph.

'I'll check to see which ward he'll be going to and report back directly.'

'Yes, you do that,' Owen said and sat down as soon as the curtain was closed. Well that hadn't exactly gone to plan. He looked at his father and was shocked at how old he looked suddenly. Grey and old. What if he died?

A sudden and severe sharp pain in Owen's head forced him almost to his knees. Instead, he placed his head between his knees and swayed as the room turned and turned. This was his own fault. He had done this by telling his own dear father about Padma! Why had he done something so callous? He was at fault. He'd killed his own father.

'Are you alright, *bach*?'

Owen could barely hear his mother. This was not his fault, actually. This was Padma's fault. She had caused the situation and he had merely told his father and mother about it. Now this was perfectly natural and none of it was his fault. His anguish turned to anger and the head pain abated slightly. This was Padma's fault, it was clear to him now. She had killed his father, the vicious cow.

Righteous Anger

Padma sat at home crying as she attempted to watch an episode of *ER*. She had put the children to bed and it was now past midnight and Owen had still not come home. Why was he so mean to her? She did everything for him; iron his clothes, wash his underpants and look after his children in his house. She had given up her career to stay at home and was this how she was being repaid? He was not a proper surgeon; he had let her down and even now was trying to put the blame on her for his failed career. She hadn't said anything to him when he had come home all violent looking and angry. Why hadn't he called at least?

Owen, meanwhile, was driving home at 80mph along the M4, tears of rage and indignation boiling in his eyes. He'd been walked over all his life and he was done accepting it now. If Padma wanted a real man then he'd be a real man. Oh yes, she'd want the old man back anytime once she'd sampled what a real man would and wouldn't put up with.

As he parked his car, Owen could tell instantly by the soft white glow behind the curtains that his darling wife was still up watching television. No escape now, eh? Even as these thoughts ran through his brain, Owen could sense his anger draining away faster than he'd have liked. Earlier he was so angry he had to flee but now, with his father in hospital and possibly dying because of his errant wife, he had even more reason to be angry, indeed was actively encouraging himself, but found he was flagging. Entering the house, he could hear Padma crying to herself in the living room and the remaining anger inside Owen became detached and floated around behind him like a peculiar ghost, evaporating all the while.

'Hey,' was all he said when he opened the door. Hey? What the hell was that? Pathetic. Padma was right after all. No, even provoking himself like this was not working.

Padma removed a tissue from her eyes and looked away. 'Where have you been?' she asked the lamp. 'I've been worried sick. I thought you wouldn't come home.'

Owen, momentarily stunned at the fact that Padma was reacting in such an unexpected way, could think of nothing to say.

'I thought you'd left me. I don't want to be a single mother. Why did you leave like that?'

'My father had a heart attack.' His words were slow and deliberate. 'He's in hospital and he's not very well, possibly dying.' Why had he said that? He wasn't dying, at least not when he left anyway.

Padma looked at him and after some hesitation decided to hug him tightly. Owen held his arms out straight behind his wife. Should he hug her too? It didn't seem natural somehow, yet not doing so seemed churlish under the circumstances.

'I am so sorry,' she said, and it seemed to Owen as if she meant it.

'He's having a GTN infusion now but it looks like he had been having heart problems for some time.'

'I hope he'll recover. I really like your father.'

Best not to mention the fact that Padma had not seen him in almost a year and always complained about him whenever he came up in conversation. 'He liked you too.' Another lie.

'What was his troponin T?'

Troponin T. Oh yes, the blood tests the doctor was on about. 'Nought point five,' he said. What were the units anyway? This he had completely forgotten, his general medicine days were so long ago.

'Is he on a statin, an ACE inhibitor and a diuretic?'

'I really don't know.'

Padma pulled away. 'You didn't check? Did you speak to the doctor at all?'

'Yes, of course. They're admitting him under the cardiologists.'

'Did you tell them you're a doctor?'

'Of course.'

'I bet you didn't. You wanted to stay quiet and not say anything. I know you, Owen.'

What the hell was this now? 'He knew I was a doctor. I spoke with him. He knew because my mother mentioned it when he was there.' What a mistake. Why on earth had he volunteered that piece of information?

'I knew it.' Her smile turned into a sneer. 'Your own father and you won't stand up for him.'

'Of course I stood up for him. Wait now. Wait. This is unfair. You know it's unfair. Stop it.' The anger that earlier had deserted him was returning, right now when he didn't want it.

Luckily she listened this time. 'Sorry. You should have been more like a surgeon, though.'

'There was nothing surgical wrong with him. He didn't have an eye problem, at least.'

Perhaps it was because she had an open goal in front of her yet again she decided not to attack. It was too obvious and she had already made her point. 'The boys asked about you,' she said.

Owen brightened. 'Did they really?'

'No, but I thought if I said that they had it would cheer you up.'

'My father is ill in hospital, please don't be like yourself.' Owen stood up. This was her fault anyway and he had earlier decided not to tell her how guilty she should be for her terrible crime. Perhaps he had been too lenient on her.

'Go to bed,' she said. 'I'll be up shortly.'

As Owen climbed the stairs he told himself for the first time that when all this was over he'd make an appointment with a lawyer and start divorce proceedings against his wife. If he did not then there was a statistically significant chance that he would end up killing her some day.

CHAPTER 24

Colleen

Before starting clinic the next day Owen quickly called his mother to see how Idwal was doing. Apparently he was doing much better now that he'd been moved to the cardiac care unit, and although any news was unlikely to make Owen happy, his depression was lifted ever so slightly. He thought for the first time that he'd be able to see the clinic through without telling anyone of his troubles and ducking out.

'I saw you last time, Mr Morgan. My eye is a lot worse now.' Mrs Jones leant back slightly and allowed herself a look of satisfaction.

Owen had no idea who she was and ruffled through the disorganised notes trying to find his tell-tale scrawl. 'Are you sure it was me?' he said.

'Yes. You gave me new drops and I had to go back to the old ones because I nearly went blind.'

Owen grimaced. The angry elderly patient with nothing better to do than complain. Brilliant, he thought; and what was worse he could find no evidence he had actually seen her at any point in his life.

'I'm afraid the last entry is from August last year. When were you here last?'

Mrs Jones looked offended. 'Last month. Don't you remember me?'

He looked at the eighty-year-old sat before him, caked in make-up and wearing what appeared to be some sort of power suit. Perhaps she was the oldest practising lawyer in the world.

He was sure he'd have remembered somebody like her. After a further five minutes of scrabbling he finally found the last entry. She'd been seen by Dr Peter, the foundation year two doctor, who was not only thirty stone in weight and unable to tuck his shirt in his trousers over his whole circumference at any one time but was Indonesian as well. 'It was not me, but my colleague. Let's have a look at you anyhow.'

Mrs Jones looked put out. 'Well you look the same.' Owen looked at his belly; perhaps he needed to start dieting himself. He didn't look Indonesian though, so perhaps he should disregard this concern about him being overweight. As he finished Mrs Jones, he felt a vibration in his trouser pocket of the mobile variety and most of his thoughts from then until the end of the consultation were devoted to the possible disaster scenarios this new message might contain. Could it be Padma saying she was divorcing him and taking everything, or his mother to say that his neglected father had taken a turn for the worse? As soon the wobbly Mrs Jones had gone he fished his phone from his pocket.

A message from Colleen. How unexpected! How pleasant! Owen knew that Padma did not approve of his speaking to Colleen and he had subsequently neglected her friendship so much that they had not communicated a long time. Getting a text out of the blue like this from her felt vaguely immoral, dirty even. The more he thought of it the more he conceded that every contact with the outside world had started to feel dangerously problematic over the past few years. It had been far easier to pretend it did not exist than to try and form any meaningful relationship with it.

With trembling hands he opened the text message. 'I am doing a course in Cardiff and will be there tomorrow evening. Fancy a drink?' Without thinking through any of the practicalities and forgetting completely about the events of the previous evening, he replied in the affirmative. In fact, he'd replied so quickly he'd sent the message off with a few spelling mistakes and, strangely, this started to bother him as soon as the text had entered the ether.

The next patient was a Mrs Peacock. She too was dissatisfied. 'I am dissatisfied,' she said.

'Oh. Why is that?'

'I have waited thirty minutes. My Ivor has to see the GP at one you know.'

'Thirty minutes. That's quite quick for this clinic. The time is now only nine-thirty. How have you been doing? Still taking the drops OK'

'My appointment says 9 a.m. I want to be seen at 9 a.m.'

'There are six patients with 9 a.m. appointments. Drops OK?'

'Six. How awful. Terrible this place is. Truly terrible. And my glaucoma is playing up.'

'How so?' Owen was starting to switch off. Mrs Peacock wordlessly continued her rant as Owen's thoughts drifted back to Colleen and her text. Colleen with her shining, glowing auburn hair, running towards him with open arms, the sun glinting off strands of red as she bounces up and down. Bouncing up and down. Why did men have to reduce everything to sex in the end?

Mrs Peacock had stopped speaking. With no clue what she had said, he checked her pressures and examined her optic discs. Why was he so excited about Colleen? A spasm of pain hit him as his father's infarction elbowed itself into his conscious thoughts. 'What are you doing thinking of her when you should be thinking of me?' his father's image shouted at him.

'Everything is fine there. Keep on taking the drops, they're working great.' Mrs Peacock did not seem reassured by this and left in a huff. Having not thought about Colleen for a long time, Owen suddenly could think of little else.

The next patient was a Mr Gascoigne. Happily, this chap was so demented Owen did not have to force himself to engage in any meaningful conversation. As he pushed the tonometer against his watery eye and soothed him with gentle meaningless words he thought of lovely Colleen. Why had he never asked her out? Why had she never asked him out? After all it was all about equality in this day and age. This day and age. He was hardly an old man who remembered days any different to these ones, let alone ages.

'Your pressure is doing fine there. Well done.' Mr Gascoigne looked confused for a moment before he leant forward as if to whisper something in the young doctor's ear. Owen leant forward himself before the patient turned to look him in the eye. Owen sensed he was about to hear something unusually profound and his interest was piqued. Alas, nothing profound emerged from the broken man's mouth, just a stale breath of air passing between unbrushed teeth that expired right into the listener's mouth causing him to involuntarily gag for a few seconds. As he escorted him out of the door, a pleasing vibration was felt in his trouser pocket once again. What was Colleen wanting now? To say she'd always loved him and wanted to hug him and make him safe? As far-fetched as this seemed, it was at the forefront of his thoughts as Owen hurriedly fished around for the phone, having just dumped his patient unceremoniously into a hospital wheelchair and grunted at a nurse that he was now ready to leave.

Sadly the text was not from Colleen this time. It was his mother reminding him of his priorities. Her text informed him simply that his father had taken a turn for the worse. He'd visit him tonight. Obviously everything was going to be alright. How could it not be with Colleen coming to Cardiff?

The Family Doctor

Owen nervously surveyed the cardiac care unit waiting room, recognising various relatives who seemed to have congregated already from far and wide. As the only doctor in the family he knew that he'd be looked upon as the natural leader and didn't feel up to the task. He had never liked to lead, but was more than capable of helpful direction-giving from somewhere close to the back. Then again his mother hadn't put much stock in his opinion last night so perhaps everybody else felt the same and he'd be let off the hook. A pang of humiliation ran though him as he recalled his mother's comments. A voice in his head told him he needed to be assertive so that people would respect him for a change. Padma was right.

He strode confidently into the room as if he had just arrived and not been agonising at the door for five minutes. His burly younger cousin stood up and shook him warmly by the hand. 'Good to see you, Owen' his cousin Gareth said. 'Shame it's been so long.'

'Yes, it is,' Owen said a little more confidently than the situation required. He was revved up now and to let his confidence fail over something like this would invite disaster at an early stage. 'Have you seen my father yet?' My father. Yes, that was a nice touch, Owen thought. He had the biggest claim after all. He was nobody else's father, save Angharad's, and she wasn't here. He outranked just about everybody in the room.

'Been here all day, came as soon as I heard. Nobody knows what the hell's going on. Auntie Moira has been in there all day and nobody told her nothing, they didn't.'

While he tried to work out what the last sentence actually meant, his Uncle Theo approached him. 'Owen,' he said warmly. 'I have this lump in my right eye, had it for a few months. Been to see the GP about it…' His voice carried on while Owen inwardly grimaced. Would it be acceptable if he punched Uncle Theo in the face? Actually he was a head taller than him and although he was getting on, Owen had never been a fighter so would be humiliated anyway. Not that he'd ever consider doing it. He'd have to assert himself medically instead. Brain over brawn and all that. '…so do you think I should get it cut off?'

Uncle Theo pointed to an insignificant meibomian cyst over his right eyelid.

'That's an insignificant meibomian cyst that…'

'Wow, wow, Einstein.' Uncle Theo moved his hands dramatically as if he'd been overpowered by a complex explanation of string theory. 'Enough with the medical talk. What actually is it?'

'A cyst.' He was impatient now.

'Hey, hey, a cyst is it? Is that cancer?'

'Cancer? Good God, no.' Enough with the messing around. 'Have you seen dad? How is he?'

'Go and find out. Your mother's in there now talking to one of the doctors.' As Owen headed for the door Uncle Theo called after him. 'Should I rub ointment on it?'

Owen stopped. 'What?'

'Ointment. On my eye. Or should I get it cut off? Could be cancer.'

He had ten seconds at most to formulate an answer before his uncle would start advancing across the floor at him and he'd have to go through diplomatic protocol again, which would be time-consuming. He should not have stopped walking.

'No. Hot compresses twice a day and eighty-four per cent are better in ten days.' Someone had told him this before and although he doubted its validity, it worked most of the time and seemed to mollify his uncle for he gave him the thumbs-up sign and proceeded to tell Gareth about his upcoming inguinal hernia operation.

'They'll make a cut here, see, and fish out the bollock,' Owen overheard a fair distance down the corridor before he reached his father's door. Through the little window surrounded by flaking paint he could see his mother talking to a much taller female doctor as his Auntie Gwladys sat in the chair reading *Heat* magazine. He knocked and entered.

'This is my son Owen. He's a doctor.' Finally he had the maternal recognition he descrved.

The female doctor looked at him. She wasn't that tall really, on further inspection. Perhaps his mother had shrunk.

'Your father is doing well now. Chest pain eased and we're taking down the GTN infusion. He'll need an angioplasty before the end of the week but Dr Butler is away so we may have to wait a bit longer than usual. Urea a tad high but nephrology are happy his renal function is under control.'

Owen nodded as if he was used to hearing about his father's inner workings. Perhaps he should think of something to say to carry on the pretence that he was a doctor? He was a doctor, dammit.

'When will he be able to go home?' Great. The opportunity to impress with a medical question and he ends up asking a civilian question, the answer to which would invariably be, 'We don't know at this time'.

'We don't know at this time. It depends on what the angio throws up. He might need a cabbage at some point.'

'A cabbage?' Auntie Gwladys said, looking up from an article she had been reading about Halle Berry.

Owen smiled. His opportunity to shine had arrived. 'CABG, Auntie. Coronary artery bypass graft. It's just the lingo us doctors use.'

His auntie smiled and his mother seemed to beam with satisfaction as the female doctor whose name he did not know, looked obliquely at him.

'There has been some irreversible damage and the focus of what we're doing now is to prevent deterioration.'

'Yes. Like I say to people in the glaucoma clinic.' He'd gone a bit too far and needed to ramp it back a bit.

The female doctor looked awkward. 'Um, yes. I suppose. I'd better be getting on with seeing other people. Is there anything else?'

'No thanks,' Owen said. 'That will be all.' Even Auntie Gwladys recognised that he was beginning to sound a bit of a dick by now.

'Will you go and tell the family the news, *bach*?' his mother said. 'They're all in the waiting room. I didn't understand any of it, especially what she said before you came in.'

'I'll do it now,' he said with what he perceived as being authority. As he headed for the door, he spied his sleeping father in the bed, looking at least a hundred and fifty and with a collection of drool at the left hand corner of his mouth. He had never seen his father looking so vulnerable and the sudden sadness was so great that he did not concentrate on his footing, giving the catheter bag a big kick by accident and in the process of regaining balance collided noisily with the drip stand. Gwladys chuckled to herself as she turned the page to read about the woman from *Holby City* who had just had a baby.

The Insider

'Don't worry,' Owen told the waiting room, which was almost exclusively peopled with members of his own family. In fact the only person he did not recognise was an elderly lady who evidently had some form of facial paralysis dribbling through droopy lips as she too was trying to read an excerpt from an issue of *Heat* magazine. 'He's getting better. I have spoken with the doctor looking after him.'

A general hum of satisfaction emerged from the crowd. Somebody whistled. Who was that?

'When's he coming home?' Uncle Bryn said, replacing a three-year-old issue of *People's Friend* in the shabby magazine rack.

'It depends,' Owen said solemnly. 'He needs to have an angiogram first…'

'Hold on there, Marie Curie,' Uncle Theo said. 'What's that?'

Marie Curie? Why a female scientist? Owen was annoyed at this unwelcome issue that now seemed to derail his thought process at a time when he needed to be the Morgan family leader. What was his old uncle trying to say?

'An angiogram is when you put a dye in a vein and then take pictures of it going around the heart. It shows up blockages.'

'I'll pop in to see him tomorrow now that I know he's going to be OK,' Auntie Val said as she collected her things. It was obvious from the look of her handbag that a few of the more recent copies of celebrity-based magazines from the day room had found their way in there during the waiting process. Auntie Val saw Owen eyeing her bag. 'I pay my taxes,' she said.

'Well, I'll say hello to the old boy now,' Uncle Bryn said.

'It'll take him a while to get better, mind you, so be careful what you say to him. No sudden excitement.' He'd seen a doctor in a film say this once before.

'I wonder what set it off in the first place?' Uncle Bryn said. 'You were there, weren't you?'

All eyes suddenly turned on Owen and even Auntie Val stopped rearranging her handbag in a bid to hide the pilfered magazines to look at her nephew. He wasn't entirely sure what to say in the first instance but thought that were he to tell the truth he'd be blamed, as rightly he felt he should, for setting it all off. 'Yes,' was all he said in the end.

'A bloody good thing too,' Uncle Theo said. 'Imagine what would have happened if there hadn't been a fully qualified medical professional in the house. We wouldn't be here now I can tell you that, we'd be at the…'

'Shut up Theo,' Val said. 'Don't be insensitive.'

'Can you imagine Moira doing the old CPR? Cardiopulmonary resuscitation that is. See, I know stuff.'

'Did you do CPR on him?' Gareth said.

He hadn't. Hadn't needed to. What was he to do? Was it right to accept compliments for something that – if anything – he'd caused to occur in the first place? In fact, he hadn't even called the ambulance, his mother had. She'd made him tea while the ambulance was on its way.

'He didn't need much,' Owen said. 'Just a little bit.' How can you give a little bit of CPR? It was all or nothing really.

A collective gasp of admiration went round the room. Gareth hoisted himself to his feet and shook him by the hand warmly. 'Well done, cousin. I hope you'll be there for me when I cark it in sixty years' time.'

'Yeah, well, if he is he'll need a bloody front-end loader to get your heart going again, you lump,' Auntie Val said.

'He can do my eye lump if he wants,' Uncle Theo said. 'Or my hernia.'

'You wouldn't want an eye doctor doing your hernia you fool,' Uncle Bryn said.

'I'd trust him though. I've got this terrible rash on my back. Itchy as buggery. It goes right down under the…'

Thankfully Auntie Gwladys appeared at that point and spared any further description of the itchy rash from spoiling what was already a bad day. One look and her husband stopped his sentence dead.

'Time to go love.' She turned to Owen. 'We'll be back in the morning. Give my blessings to the kids. We have hardly seen them over the past year.'

'You're always welcome round.' Even he recognised the lack

of conviction. How could other people be welcome in his house when he was not himself? No one was ever welcomed into his house.

'Yeah, well, come round Neath way more often. I've got a lovely meringue at the moment.'

His phone vibrated again in his pocket and as he retrieved it, he waved distractedly at the departing couple. Uncle Bryn wandered over to Idwal's room to see if he'd be permitted in to say goodnight to his brother. Who could this text be from? Colleen hopefully. The text was from Padma. 'Where r u?' it read. 'Come home. How is dad?'

A shudder of dread ran through him as he deleted the message. 'I'm off too,' he told no one in particular, and wandered out of the room while a bored Gareth picked up a copy of *People's Friend* and was distressed to find that the cover story was about a middle-class, middle-aged woman falling in love with her childhood sweetheart after the death of her husband. He shuddered and placed it back on the shelf. Where were all the *Heat* magazines?

Moira entered the day room shortly after Owen had left and was rather distressed that her son had left without saying goodbye, especially under the circumstances.

'He's a busy man,' Val told her. 'He is a doctor, you know.'

'Yes, he is.'

'It's lucky he was in the house when it happened. Be grateful for that.'

Moira paused. 'Yes,' she said after some consideration.

'Owen says Idwal's going to be alright. Trust him. Remember how he fixed Theo's ingrown toenail? We're there for you if you need us, and Gwladys has a nice meringue on the go.'

'Thanks. I'll stay here for now though.'

CHAPTER 25

Cardiff Central

IT WAS HALF past seven the following evening and Owen was on the train hurtling east to meet the woman he'd decided he should have married instead of Padma. Should he have gone west to Swansea to see his father instead? The thought did pain him slightly but he reasoned that he'd see him the following day and his chance to meet Colleen should not be overlooked. Why had he developed such a fixation with her over the preceding twenty-four hours? He suspected it was some kind of survival mechanism, an escape, where his mind distracted him with dreams to avoid the crushing truth of reality, but these thoughts he disliked and tried to ignore as much as he could. Ahh, lovely Colleen.

How had Padma let him go on such a jaunt, jealous as she was about his comings and goings outside the house at the best of times? This was where Owen felt the deepest guilt, as he had used his father, his dear father, as an excuse to meet Colleen. Lied. Lied to her face. Perhaps Padma felt guilty for the way she had reacted. Perhaps there was another factor in play. Either way Owen was content not to look his gift horse in the mouth and instead savoured the meeting ahead. As he watched an Italian-looking man wrestle a suitcase to the top shelf of the luggage compartment on his carriage, the thought struck him that this was the Almighty's way of directing him towards a new life. To be free of the nightmare that was Padma and to give him an all new, fully functioning wife who would love him unconditionally.

Wasn't God against divorce though? Owen frowned. He was indeed. Then why was he directing him towards Colleen? Perhaps it was not a direction from God. Perhaps it was from the Devil. A test. Should he turn around and go back home? Too late now. He'd see her just this once and then see how things panned out. There, a compromise. Owen sat back in satisfaction now that he had solved his moral dilemma.

Cardiff Central station was the agreed meeting point and at eight he was standing next to the big clock. Where was she? When she'd arrive Owen imagined she'd throw her arms around him and kiss him passionately. He obviously had no reason to think this at all. They had never gone out and, for all he knew, she was married already. He was married already. These thoughts hurt his head so he decided to buy a bag of jelly babies from W H Smith.

As he emerged from the shop he saw her. She was standing below the clock, as promised, looking at her watch. He looked at her long hair. So it didn't exactly glow like he'd imagined, probably because the sun had gone down, but she still looked beautiful. Perfect, in fact. He turned his phone off lest Padma call and discover his liaison with his father was something altogether different.

'Hey,' he said and hugged her tightly.

After a moment of surprise, for Owen had approached her from the back and given her little time to realise who he was, she relented and hugged him back.

'Good to see you, mate,' she said.

He looked at her, holding her shoulders as he did so. He'd also seen this in a film and thought that it suited the moment. In fact he'd decided this as the train passed through Pontyclun. Colleen stepped back slightly.

'Let's catch up over that drink,' he said. 'I know of a nice place around the corner.' In fact he knew no places in Cardiff at all, especially drinking establishments, and had looked up suitable venues for their encounter on Google the previous night.

'The course finished late. Sorry about that. How are things anyway? You seem very happy.'

He was happy, though he felt he shouldn't be. 'I am. Are you happy?'

'I'll be a consultant soon. I've finished my training in paediatrics and in fact I'm here on an interview course.'

'Doesn't time fly? I can't remember when I saw you last.'

After reaching the pub, which as Google maps had assured Owen, was only a few hundred metres from the station, they ordered drinks and sat down at a small table.

'I always feel I should be drinking pints when I meet you,' Colleen said.

The whole class thing had always confused Owen though he was well aware of the fact that despite his medical degree he was nowhere near the top, or ever likely to get there. Perhaps it was genetic or perhaps, being Welsh, he was somehow exempt from it in some way. He was never sure if people were insulting him over the issue, though he decided to give Colleen the benefit of the doubt.

'It's been too long. I missed you. You were my closest friend in London and I hardly speak to you now.' Owen had planned much to say over the past day and was aware that his speech sounded a bit artificial.

Colleen took a sip of beer. 'Is everything alright?'

'Wonderful. Really it is. In fact… no, it's all terrible.' Owen left the script to one side and told Colleen the whole sorry story about his disintegrating marriage and father. She seemed to Owen to be genuinely concerned and as he told her of one particular altercation he'd had with Padma, she touched his hand. He looked down and although he could see her hand touching his, in sympathy in all probability he told himself, he was unable to form any more words and instead made peculiar facial gestures as he attempted to force words out against their will.

'I missed you too, mate. I did.'

Why mate all the time? How frustrating. With that she detached her hand to take another sip and the larynx was loosened again.

'I've told you my story, how about yours?' What he meant by this was 'are you available' and this was also part of the previously abandoned script.

To her credit she understood this and sighed. 'I'm seeing a Navy officer, just started to in fact. He's no big looker but I need to settle down.'

'The eggs aren't getting any younger, eh?' Bloody hell, Owen thought to himself. That was not in any script and did not sound good. He'd be scalped.

'You're right,' she said. 'You have children. I need children too, and a husband of course.'

'Do you remember when we told each other we'd marry if we failed to find partners by the age of thirty-five?'

'I can't remember that. But you got married.'

'I made it up actually, but it sounds like something we'd have said. We said a lot of crazy things back then.'

'We're not sixties rock legends out to grass, Owen.' She laughed. 'I'm sad you're in pain and I'm sad for your father…'

Owen felt suddenly that he was too exposed and vulnerable. Looking at his drink he decided to go back to the script. 'How was this course? Did you learn how to be a consultant after all?'

'It's a scary world out there as a consultant. The buck stops with you, that's the thing. I'm petrified. If only I could stay a registrar forever.'

'I know the feeling.' Owen did not know the feeling. 'What time do you have to be in tomorrow?'

'Eight. Owen, look. My sister was involved in an unhappy marriage and got divorced. She was much better afterwards.'

'Did she have kids?' What difference did this really make? It just seemed like the right thing to ask.

'One. A girl. She thought it would be better for her to grow up in a loving house with one parent than in a horrible house with two.'

Owen had no immediate answer to this, so Colleen continued. 'You are a good and kind man,' she said, 'and whatever happens I will be here to help you.' She touched his hand again, and as she smiled at him he could feel a loss of muscle power to his upper body approaching as every neurone in his skull was concentrating on the sweet touch that affected only a square inch of his left thenar eminence. 'After all, you are an old mate.'

Second Round

Feeling a bit peckish, Owen and Colleen removed themselves to a local restaurant, one that was not on Owen's secret list of Cardiff locations, to have some food.

'Let's have wine this time, be all middle-class about it,' Owen said.

Colleen seemed keen. 'Let's order a bottle,' she said.

Owen tried raising his hand to address the waiter but as usual nothing happened. He had always hated getting waiter attention as he felt that a non-response to his raised hand would cause such embarrassment that he would fall apart mentally. What if the waiter did not come; when would it be acceptable to take your hand down? When was it acceptable to use verbal commands? How could some people hail the waiter with a single twitch of an eyebrow? The end result was that Owen would always try and hail a waiter with one hand at glass level, which would not be seen, and he'd eventually be forced to stand up and seek him out in person.

'You still can't do that, can you?'

'No. I hate it. Padma hates it.'

'I think it's funny.' She got the waiter's attention and before long a lovely bottle of wine stood before them. Thankfully it was not the type of place where you had to taste the wine before accepting it. All wine tasted much the same to Owen and he hated the charade.

'I bet you're glad you don't have to do your tasting thing,' Colleen said. After initial annoyance at this comment, it dawned on Owen that she seemed to understand his mild social phobia and it would be easier to be grateful than to pretend he didn't have it.

'Tell me about your Navy man then.' Please let him be ugly, fat and ugly.

'He's not too pretty to be honest. A bit round around the waist but he loves me and that's important.' Owen secretly cheered inwardly that his prayers had been answered for once. Perhaps this was indeed another sign from above.

'Love is indeed everything. Do you love him?'

'I loved Nicholas and look where that got me.'

'Nicholas?'

'My last boyfriend. Why can't you men remember these details? I told you all about him at the time.'

'So you don't love him?'

Colleen thought about this as she sipped her wine, replacing the glass on the tablemat deliberately afterwards. 'I can grow to love him. It's the love of the man that's important. Women are flexible.'

Owen thought this comment so complicated and he was so happy in the company of Colleen, that he decided to leave its processing for another day and enjoy the moment. He was also slowly becoming intoxicated. An alarm bell rang somewhere in his head that Padma would surely detect alcohol on his breath when he returned home and know that something was up. This thought too was troubling and there being no easy way out now that the bottle was ordered, it was just best to figure it all out at a later date.

'You must be good at cataract surgery by now,' Colleen said.

Owen's daydream suddenly ended as the thought of operating cut through his thoughts like a sickle. 'It's coming along.'

'Good. How are the boys?'

Perhaps this was Colleen's script, Owen thought. 'Good also, yes. You should come and visit.'

'I don't think I'd be welcomed. Padma never liked me.'

'She did, of course she did.' Why he was defending her over this issue when he had been slating her for the past hour and a half was beyond him. It was true anyhow, she never liked Colleen.

'I guess I can tell you now what she said after you got married.'

'Go on.'

'I was standing outside the church door as she came out and she said, "It's too late for you now, but thanks for looking after him for me" before waltzing off down the path.'

'Really?' This was news to him. Had Padma seen what lay ahead, or indeed behind, years before he himself had? Was he seeing something now or was this a crazy dream, as a sixties rock legend might say? He remembered the time he became obsessed with walking Offa's Dyke; an obsession which began overnight and lasted all of three days. He never walked Offa's Dyke in the end, though he had the guidebook all ready for when the time came.

'Yes. She was quite rude. Alex was with me and he said it was rude too.'

'Alex. That's a blast from the past. What did you say back?'

'What could I say? It was your wedding day. Would you have been pleased if I'd have clocked her one outside the church?'

'Yes, actually. Preferably before going in, though. You could have shouted out when they ask for that "any objection" thing.'

'Why would I have done that?'

Why indeed. The evening ended forty-five minutes later, along with the wine, and a tipsy pair of doctors made their way back towards the station and their real lives. Owen was past caring about what Padma would think, such was his level of inebriation.

As they parted in the station, a taxi with its headlights on full power passed by on the road outside. The light glittered through Colleen's hair just as he had imagined it would before they met. This was a sign, he told himself. A sign of things to come. He should put some form of down-payment on the guidebook to show his commitment.

'Colleen,' he said. 'I have to say that I…'

'Mate,' she said. 'I'll look forward to seeing you again. You better go.' With that she turned and vanished into the night, her hair shining no more.

Signs

What constituted a sign? Owen considered that the glowing hair must be some form of divine encouragement, but then again Colleen had seemed less than interested. Was he interested himself anyway? Perhaps it really was just an escape. How could it work in practice? He had two children and was completely different to her. She was super sporty and he was a bit of a geek. Except that she did much better than him in every exam they ever did together at medical school. So she was generally better than him. Great.

He looked at his watch, eleven-thirty, and remembered his phone was still switched off. As he switched it on he cursed the time and started thinking of excuses for being so late. Excuses for being intoxicated were not forthcoming at the moment.

Three text messages had arrived, one from his mother, one from Padma and one from Colleen. Obviously he opened Colleen's message first. 'Had a lovely evening. Must do it again soon, mate.' Why 'mate' all the time? Under his breath he asked the Almighty for a sign. Then he opened Padma's message. 'Please come home. I am so sorry.' That was not the sign he'd wanted. Perhaps he was being directed back to his wife after all. Never argue with the signs. Was she really sorry, though, for what she'd done, was she? He then opened his mother's message. 'WHY PHONE OFF. CALL ME NOW.' Why did people of a certain age only text in capital letters? He'd have to show her the correct way to text when he went round to see his father tomorrow, his good deed for the day.

He dialled his mother's mobile; no answer. Then he tried the house; again, no answer. How typical of his mother, Owen thought. She'd always be unavailable when he tried to call. Then again he'd been unavailable too a few hours ago.

After a brief doze, he awoke to find himself in Bridgend station and only just managed to get off the train before it started moving again on its inevitable journey to Fishguard. There was a missed call from his mother so he tried dialling again.

'Owen, where have you been, *bach*?' She sounded concerned.

'I went to see a friend. What's wrong?'

'Your father's not been well today. He died.'

Owen stopped walking and held the phone as he looked at a train timetable. He wanted to say something but failed.

'He had another heart attack the doctors said.' She started crying. 'He never spoke at all. He never spoke since, never.'

Grammatical breakdown was always a bad sign for his mother.

'I… I… I'll come to the hospital.'

'It's too late, *bach*. Too late. He died an hour ago.'

There were only two direct train services to Fishguard a day, Owen noted. 'An hour ago. What should I do?'

'There is nothing you can do, is there? Nothing anyone can do.'

Oh God. He'd told his family he was going to be alright. He'd made everybody's life all the worse by pretending to be a bigwig. 'Were you there when he died?'

'We were all here. We'd been here all day then the machine started bleeping. They tried, Owen, they tried to help him. They did allsorts but they failed. Another heart attack it was, that's what they said.'

'Was Angharad there?'

'She was here. You were the only one.'

'Did Padma come?'

'What? Don't mess around at a time like this.' He listened to his mother crying at the other end of the phone. Only two services to Fishguard, he thought. That seemed a bit odd. No going out for the night if you lived there, unless you wanted to be partying for twelve hours.

'I'm sorry.'

The crying continued yet she did not hang up the phone. What was he to do? His strength failed him and he sat down on the pavement listening to the crying. Perhaps the only reason the train went to Fishguard at all was because of the ferry.

'I'll come round to see you.'

The crying continued. There would be no more Idwal for him to visit. No more jokes and audible bodily functions. No more road directions whether he wanted them or not.

'Mam. I'm coming to the hospital. You stay there.' After

he hung up he looked at the pavement. How could he go to the hospital? He could not drive now that he had consumed alcohol and the next train was in… He got up and examined the timetable. The letters were blurry through his own tears and he could not understand the writing. Too long. The only option was to either ask Padma to drive, or take a taxi.

The taxi driver sensed something terrible had recently happened to his passenger and decided to keep quiet on the journey to Morriston Hospital. Owen looked out of the window as memories of his father returned to taunt him. He could see his father teaching him how to ride a bike as a child, accidentally exploding the new television that Christmas when he was seven and showing him how to play rugby. He never had been any good at it, even then.

Secretions blocked up his nose due to the increased lacrimal duct flow and he felt the need to blow his nose as the taxi crossed the Briton Ferry bridge. They'd taken a walk once to see this bridge being built. A miracle of engineering, his father had called it. Why was he in Cardiff? Why had he become obsessed with Colleen all of a sudden? He'd wanted a sign and now he'd been given a bloody big huge one. His father had died because of him and he'd missed his final moments for no good reason at all. What was most painful of all was the fact that he'd neglected him for many months, years even, before he'd died. It was too late now; such was the cost of asking for signs.

CHAPTER 26

Llef

FUNERALS ARE TERRIBLE things, his father had told him on more than one occasion. Designed to make everybody cry for no reason. Best to just blow the body to bits on an island somewhere where no one sees. Though he didn't quite agree with his conclusion, Owen agreed that funerals were horrible, horrible events. Especially Welsh funerals.

The service was held at the family church in Neath. It was called the family church although the only time any family ever visited it was when somebody died, or, less commonly, somebody got married. Hatch, match and dispatch. Though there was not much hatching going on either.

Owen sat near the front of the church alongside his mother and Angharad, his father's body lying in the sealed coffin around two-and-a-third metres in front of them. He'd guessed two-and-a-third metres, as he'd counted the number of wooden blocks between the wheel nearest them and his own foot and multiplied the length of one block by the total number. Once upon a time he'd have been praised for a pointless act of mathematics like this. His mother wept silently beside him. Padma was back at the house with the boys. A funeral was no place for children, he had told her, but in reality there was nothing more unpalatable than thinking of Padma being reintroduced to the family at this most sensitive of times.

'Fancy Padma didn't come,' his mother seemed to tell the damp tissue she was holding in front of her.

'I told her not to, mam,' Owen said. 'I'm sorry for the whole thing. I really am.' He could feel his own voice breaking so thought it best to stop talking lest he upset his mother further.

'It's not your fault. He was just so young, that's all. Not even retired. What am I going to do for the rest of my life?'

Angharad leant over. 'I think it's about to start. The priest's arrived.'

The family priest, whom many in the family had never met but felt a form of unspoken affection for, started the funeral mass and although Owen found it impossible to listen to most of the words he was just about able to hold back his tears. He had caused his own father's death and, were it not for him, he'd still be alive now. If only he had listened. If only he had cared. He felt he'd been so wrapped up in his own business that he did not see what he was possibly put on the earth to see; his father's suffering. Perhaps it is human nature to absolve oneself of responsibility where possible, and in increasing bursts of inner anger, Owen began squeezing the life out of the family copy of the New Testament that his mother had handed to him at the start of the service. He could see now that the fault for all this in fact lay completely with his wife. She had done this. Broken his heart like this by stressing him at each and every opportunity. His deceased father had even told him it would have been right to hit her for being so mean. He clenched the Bible so hard at this thought that he only relaxed when he remembered that in fact he'd said no man would ever do such a thing. His hands had turned white with the force of the squeeze and the New Testament appeared permanently mis-shapen now. His gentle father had given his life to keeping Owen sin-free. Was he sin-free though? He'd killed his own father. What was that called? Patricide? He wasn't sure, but patricide sounded right, and if it wasn't then it fitted anyway.

By the time Owen had extracted himself from his thoughts, the priest had already finished most of the service. Even though he had not been to church in a long time, the rituals were so ingrained in his cerebellum that he could perform them without active mental participation. Was that good or very bad? This thought set up a new chain of thoughts that continued until the priest completed the service and asked the bearers to step forward for the committal of the body to the ground. His mother nudged him in the ribs and he, his cousin and various uncles stood up to bear their relative on his final earthly journey. It was a journey of sixty-one steps from church to grave. Owen knew, as he had counted every one.

Owen and assorted other wheezy overweight Welshmen lowered Idwal to his final resting place amid the frantic instructions of the funeral director who was worrying that a general lack of co-ordination in the lowering process might cause a sudden slippage that would damage the casket and lead to further trouble. 'Like a slippery slope,' the funeral director had said. Just like cataract surgery going wrong, Owen thought.

After the lowering was complete and the final prayers undertaken the choir sang the old Welsh hymn *Llef*. Very few people present knew enough Welsh to understand the words but the tune was such that those people who had prided themselves on retaining their composure thus far were broken down and began to sob. Yes, Owen thought, his father had been right all along. The purpose of the funeral is to upset everyone as much as possible and if the service itself does not succeed then underhand tactics like *Llef* are used.

He looked around at his relatives. They were all blubbering, man and woman, young and old alike, as the beautiful unknowable words of the song echoed around the graveside. Perhaps the fact that the words were unknown made them all the more powerful, Owen mused, as he himself finally broke down completely and lost what little composure he had retained.

'This was the choir what sang at your wedding,' his mother

whispered at him after the song reached its tearful conclusion. 'Good, aren't they?'

The Lamb and Flag

After the proceedings came to an end Uncle Theo stood up and told everyone that there was food laid out at the Lamb in Bryncoch. Idwal and Owen alike had never understood why there would be a feast after every funeral. It didn't seem right somehow.

'Can you give a lift to Theo and the Joneses?' his mother asked him outside the church.

Dammit, he thought. 'Yes. No problem, mam.' He watched his mother, already looking fifteen years older that she had two weeks before, negotiating her way into the main mourners' car with Angharad and Auntie Betty Glynneath. Why was he not invited into the mourners' car? He was mourning too.

'Hey, Owen,' Uncle Theo said as he sat in his passenger seat. The seat usually carried Padma who was small and slight, unlike the red-faced overweight Uncle Theo, and so he was distracted for a minute or more carrying out vital adjustments to the infrastructure so that it could carry him without causing major blood vessels to kink or his back muscles to be put under undue stress. Most of these adjustments were at the expense of Mrs Jones Station Road who had the seat unceremoniously rammed right up against her not-insignificant frame while her own husband and teenage son struggled to occupy the back seat next to her without herniating through a window or into the front seat. Owen considered that the car had never held so much weight before and on the way to the Lamb was slightly concerned by a new dragging noise that was becoming audible as the journey progressed. Knowing nothing about engines, Owen was worried that some vital part was engaged with the road and a small bump might end up with burning fuel spraying all over the occupants of the car, himself included.

The journey to the 'family pub', though not long, seemed like an eternity as Uncle Theo regaled everyone with tales of the bloody stool he had passed that morning as he went to the toilet. Nobody else was permitted to contribute to the conversation and Mr Jones Station Road's one attempt to add some flavour by recounting the time he had a twisted bollock repaired at the general hospital was shot down in flames by Uncle Theo before he had even got properly going.

'We're here,' Owen said as the black and white pub rolled into view. He had no idea why people called it the family pub. Nobody in the family ever went there, except on the occasional Sunday for food, since the older, more alcoholic generation had passed on. Everybody had been more alcoholic in previous days, Owen mused, as he entered the pub passing various dusty horse tack as he did so.

'Sorry to hear about Idwal,' Dai Davies the proprietor said to Moira, who was sat down on the end of a large table drinking some water from a glass.

'Thanks, Dai *bach*. Sudden it was.'

'Aye,' he said. 'Funny how death strikes so quick in some people but takes years to whittle down others. Personally I'd rather go the way of Idwal, mind you.'

'You're right there,' Uncle Bryn said. 'He never saw it coming. Theo here dies each day.'

'I do and all,' Theo said, and began recounting the story of the bloody stool again. Owen made his way over to a small pile of egg sandwiches. His grandmother had been good at making egg sandwiches in her day and they used to go on picnics in the Dulais Valley when he was a child. The warm memory must have caused some form of hypotension to develop so Owen found he had to sit down quickly to avoid collapse. He found himself next to Mr Jones Station Road, who was busy working on an éclair.

'Sorry about your dad, Owen. I wanted to tell you in the car but I never got a chance.'

'That's OK.'

'I hear you were there at the first. Did some CPR or whatever it's called.'

Owen sighed. For him to know about that little white lie, it would have had to have passed through at least six people. What did his mother think? If he were in her shoes he'd be angry as hell. 'Just a bit,' he said. How can someone do 'a bit' of CPR anyway?

'Sorry it didn't work. Apparently most CPR doesn't work. All a load of crap, Dai the pub says.' Owen looked at Mr Jones who must have realised the inappropriateness of his comment as he made a few choking noises and waved his hand apologetically as a piece of éclair that had entered his windpipe was redirected. Owen grasped the opportunity to escape and made his way towards the bar.

'Sorry about the old man,' Dai said.

'Thanks. How's Yvette?'

'She's fine. Touch of the old swine flu, you know.' Owen raised his eyebrow but Dai did not elaborate. 'I knew your father when he was six, you know.'

'You went to school with him, didn't you?'

'Well yes, that's how I knew him. Fine man. Very proud of you.'

'No, Dai, no, he wasn't...'

'He WAS. He told me so, right after you graduated from medical school. Here, have a pint.'

'No thanks, I'm driving.'

'Damn it, nobody drinks nowadays. I'll be ruined.'

'You mean it wasn't offered on the house?' Owen was quite

surprised he'd said 'on the house,' having never said it before. Perhaps he was more a man of the people than he had let himself believe.

'I've got a business to run, son,' he said as he turned to clean some glasses.

'Tell Yvette to get well soon,' Owen said as he turned back to the table. His mother was talking to various aunties while Angharad seemed to have been lumbered with Uncle Theo, and though they were too far away for Owen to make out any conversation, by the look of disgust on his sister's face he surmised it was about another of his uncle's ailments. Perhaps he had so many diseases that they cancelled each other out in some way, Owen thought. More likely he had no diseases in the first place; that's what his father had always said.

There must have been about fifty people in the room. His father would have been proud. He doubted Dai the pub had had fifty people in there over the whole of the past month.

'I'm sorry, mam,' he said as he sat down next to his mother and loaded his plate with a slice of quiche.

'I know, *bach*,' she said. 'He was a good man, very proud of you and your sister.'

Owen sighed. 'I don't know why,' he said more to himself than his mother. A large lump of quiche missed his mouth and landed on the flood with a plop. From the corner of his eye he saw that Dai had seen and was shaking his head in a melancholic way.

His mother looked at him. 'Don't start with that now. Feeling sorry and all. I'll be alone for the rest of my life, I'm the one that should be feeling sorry.' She started crying into her plate due to the lack of tissues and a few cocktail sausages rolled onto the floor, one of them getting immediately squashed by the unseeing boot of his cousin Gareth. Owen heard a groan from the direction of the bar.

Owen found a tissue in one of his pockets and passed it to his mother. 'You'll always have us,' he said. 'We'll always be there. Just call if you need something.'

His mother looked at him but did not reply.

The Painting

After another hour-and-a-half, the wake petered to an end and as Angharad helped their mother home, Owen made his way back to Bridgend. Since his father's death there seemed to have been a form of ceasefire in the house and although the relationship between Owen and his wife was certainly not a happy one, it could have been a lot worse as well. While approaching the junction for Pyle a bleeping in his pocket informed him a message had arrived. All excitement that it could be Colleen evaporated after his father's passing, and he had thought about her little. All the same, when he saw that the text was from her he did cheer up more than a person would be expected to do under the circumstances. So much so in fact, that he almost rear-ended an Eddie Stobart as he read it. 'Sorry to hear about your father. Give me a call when you're free,' it said. Should he ignore the text or actually call? What did it mean?

There were no two ways about it, Owen told himself aloud as he approached the Bridgend slip road. He had asked for a sign and that sign had told him to stay away from Colleen. Perhaps there was a future with Padma after all. She'd been relatively nice over the past few days and what with the kids and the house it was just too much of a headache to think about a divorce. His brain might split apart like a melon under the stress. As he negotiated the McArthur Glen roundabout, a realisation hit Owen that caused him to slow considerably and dampen his already flat mood yet further. Colleen did not want him. She had someone else. It was never his decision in the first place.

Why was he even thinking about this again on the day of his father's funeral anyway?

The door to the house was locked; Padma had obviously gone to the park with the boys. As he climbed the stairs to undress, he caught sight of a painting of the family church stored on its side in his office. It had been a gift from his father many years ago. In fact, if he recalled correctly, he had even commissioned someone to do it for him as a present. It had never been hung in the house, mostly as Padma disapproved of pictures containing gravestones being on public display. His father had asked a few times afterwards where the painting was hung but had stopped after a few months. This sad thought caused Owen to fall to his knees and he wept bitterly as he held the painting, hugging it hard to his chest and occasionally thumping the floor. The painting needed to be hung, and that was that.

Still in his funeral suit, Owen dug out some nails and a hammer and proceeded to scout the house for the best location for his recently rediscovered prize painting. Where better than over the fireplace itself? As he drove the nail home, a voice inside him tried to reason that Padma would be unimpressed and such an act would only inflame the situation and cause him further problems. Besides, his father would never see the painting hanging now, would he? The voice of dissent was quickly tied up and thrown into a cerebral cupboard, and with one almighty strike of anger, Owen hit the nail so hard it embedded itself in the plaster. With a groan Owen realised it had gone too far in and the attempt to bring the nail back a notch to facilitate picture hanging, though futile, caused him to calm down slightly.

He stepped back to assess the wall. There was an embedded nail in the plasterwork and a depressed hollow where the hammer head had last struck. Around the nail head itself there were some unsightly scratch marks that were proof of his attempts to pull it back. Whatever happened now he needed the painting up to cover the defacement of the wall.

With far more control and a lot less crying, Owen drove a new nail into the wall an inch above the old one and hung his picture proudly upon it. By this time he had calmed enough to understand that Padma would be annoyed at this new painting on the wall and began to feel slightly nervous about her reaction to it. Would she see it as an act of war or would she understand under the circumstances? He didn't have long to find out as, moments after he'd started to realise what he'd done, he heard the front gate squeak and the chatter of tiny voices that told him Padma and the boys were back from the park.

CHAPTER 27

Padma

'WE JUST WENT out,' she said. 'How was the funeral?' Owen looked at her, the hammer in one hand and an extra nail in the other. It would obviously be too late to hide the evidence now.

'Emotional,' he said. Perhaps he'd get away with it; nothing like hiding things in plain sight and all that.

'Hello, daddy! Why do you have a hammer?' Rhys said.

'Can I have the nail, please, please, please?' his brother added.

No hiding now, Owen thought.

'What have you been doing?'

'I put the picture up. The one from my father.' It was his house too, he should be angry not afraid. What was he, a man or a mouse?

Padma pushed past him into the sitting room and screamed. Rhys and Ifan, who had been pulling at their father's arms begging for the tools so they could do some hammering of their own, immediately froze.

'Why scream? It's a good picture. My father's picture. It was a present from him, remember?'

'I do remember. Why did you put it up?' She jabbed him hard in the chest with a bony Asian finger. Owen stepped back.

'Can I have the nail, daddy?' Ifan said.

'It's because it's your house, isn't it? You think that because it's your house you can do anything you want? It's my house more than yours.'

Though he took issue with this, Owen knew that now was not the time for correcting misconceptions. He felt raw and Padma's attack was more violent and damaging than even he had expected, for he had come to expect violent and damaging attacks from her.

'It's the day of my father's funeral. Come on, please.'

'Can I have the nail, daddy. Please?'

'You think you can keep me cooped up here don't you? Like a slave.'

Owen most certainly did not think of Padma as a slave. She was much too unruly and wouldn't be a good slave at all. 'Please. If it's that much of an issue I'll take it down.'

'Yes, you will. You're going to suffer for putting that up, let me tell you that. An ugly painting like that.'

Owen's nervousness started to turn to anger but all seemed manageable at this point.

'GIVE ME THE NAIL, DADDY!'

Owen, much more responsive to orders than requests, his mind cooking with stress, handed Ifan the nail.

'Wow. Thank you.'

'You're welcome,' Owen said.

Padma marched into the kitchen, returning with a small blue stool. She proceeded to stand on it and reached up to unhook the painting from its new prominent location.

'Can I have the hammer too?'

No reply was forthcoming, as a second later Padma let out a second scream when she saw the dent in the wall underneath. Some primal reflex led to Ifan and Rhys simultaneously bursting into tears. Padma stepped back slightly on the stool, perhaps as a response to her revulsion at the desecration of the sanctity of the wall. The stool being a small stool, her centre of gravity soon passed beyond its base and in a bid to steady herself she let go of both her handbag and the painting.

As if in slow motion, Owen saw the painting descend to the ground, the church where his father had so recently been committed to the ground rotating slowly in the still sitting room air. Voices were distorted and Padma's scream in particular was unintelligible but as the edge of the painting hit the grate, the peculiar visual effect disappeared and the normal rules of physics seemed to apply once more. Glass shattered everywhere and rained down over Rhys, with the broken wood of the frame tearing a large hole in the painting underneath.

Such was the completeness of this disaster in Owen's eyes that his hands went limp and the hammer he had been holding fell to the floor.

'Wow,' Ifan said, as he picked it up.

Padma regained her balance. 'Nobody move, there's glass everywhere.' Ifan ignored this advice and carried the hammer and nail into the kitchen, stepping over broken glass as he went. Rhys brushed glass off himself while Owen stooped to pick up the mangled painting.

'I lost balance. I didn't mean for that to happen.' Owen knew it was an accident but his peripheral vision was contracting fast as he picked up the ruined picture gently from the floor and his world shrank to the few square inches of air separating him from the sacred church. It was no accident, he told himself, though he knew that it was. His dear dead father's gift, ruined by her, just like everything else. Bitter tears flooded his eyes and though he tried his best to stop he seemed to have no control over his own body at all.

'It was your fault for putting it up,' she said. The tightness in his chest increased and his fists hardened.

'We'll need to throw it all away now. It's damaged.'

'We will NOT be throwing it away,' Owen said as his gaze remained fixed on the torn paper in his hands.

'It was an ugly painting anyway.'

Owen stood and faced his wife. 'I'll get it repaired.'

'No. Get a dustpan for the glass. The problem is you're not responsible.'

'I am.' Owen closed his eyes.

'Mammy!' the cry came from the kitchen. 'Help!'

Padma and Owen ran to the kitchen to find Ifan had managed to hammer the nail through his own shoe into the floor and was now unable to remove it. Half a dozen holes in the surrounding wood were evidence of previous nail-hammering attempts.

Padma turned to Owen again, her anger returned. 'Responsible! Responsible! You gave a hammer and nail to a young child. You're a useless husband and a useless father.' And it was then that Owen hit her.

Bridgend Station

He was still in his funeral suit when Owen found himself on one of the benches at the station holding his head in his hands and swaying slowly back and forth. There was nobody standing nearby, but quite a number of passengers gathered at the far end of the platform in one group. One or two of them eyed him suspiciously, so perhaps they assumed he was drunk. He felt drunk, though he had taken no alcohol.

His memory of the previous few minutes was not as clear as he would have liked, disfigured as it was by emotion. What he did remember was so hideous that he'd rather not remember it at all. Mostly just screaming children, screaming Padma nursing her cheek and him running for the door and ultimately, for no good reason, to the station.

Immediately before the event, he had felt something inside him wasn't quite balanced. Perhaps he should have run away then. It was all too late now, he told himself as the five-thirty service to Swansea came and went. How on earth could he solve this problem? He couldn't ask his mother, obviously. The shock would kill her, though Owen did have some memory that it was she who had urged him to do what he had just done. Or was it his father? He did not know and was not in the mood for racking his brains as it did not change management, as he'd say concerning his patients. He had nowhere else to go and besides, what about his work? He had clinics the next day and a theatre list the day after. Perhaps he could stay in the hospital accommodation while it all cooled down.

Owen shakily got to his feet and pushed a pound coin into the vending machine next to his bench in order to extract a bottle of Coke Zero. After a few failed pushes of the big button, he realised he needed another ten pence and fed this too into the machine which then released the hostage. He remembered when a can of coke was thirty pence. It was at the summer camp in Llangrannog that he'd purchased his first ever carbonated drink. He was an old man and pretty soon he'd be talking about 'his day' like his father used to. His father. A fresh trickle of tears down his right cheek reminded him that he must look appalling and set off for the station toilets in order to freshen up a bit. This involved moving past a group of passengers who eyed him cautiously; so much so that he was forced to focus on the floor as he walked past lest he catch anybody's eye. He was unsure what would happen if he did, though he did know that it would be bad in some way.

Finally he reached the toilets and pushed against the chipped green door. It wouldn't budge. He tried again with the same result. Great, he thought. They probably kept it locked now to keep out all the gays that used to meet there on a regular basis. Owen hadn't seen any gays there, of course, though he had been inside the toilet a number of times in the past and seen the multitude of cock-based invitations scratched onto the cubicle walls, as well as the holes created between the stalls that the station maintenance team seemed to have given up repairing. Now the gays were ruining his life by preventing his access to the toilets. The gays, indeed. He had even begun to sound like his father. Homosexuals, perhaps he should have said, or men who have sex with men. Or just gays. But not 'the' gays. That made it sound weird somehow.

Why did he need the toilet anyway? He had no need to pee. Suddenly the memory of the punch and the reason for his being at the station returned and yet more tears escaped.

'You OK, mate?' a station guard said.

Owen could see he was there, that he had white hair and possibly a moustache, but was too embarrassed to look at him directly. The image of the man was projected on his peripheral retina only, where the rods and cones were lowest in their spatial distribution, thus rendering the image too blurry to be made out in detail, Owen told himself. Like macular degeneration.

'Been to a funeral?' The man was still there. There was nothing he could say to the man, especially considering he was unable to look at him, and he was now clearly unable to stay on the platform either. There was nothing for it, he had to leave.

'Fine thanks,' he said under his breath before jogging out through the station lobby, his eyes fixed on the floor all the while.

Where could he go to now? Owen weighed up the pros and cons of all the options before him, which calmed him somewhat, though before reaching any satisfactory conclusion he found himself opening his own front door and entering the hallway. What the hell was he doing now? Was he out of his mind? Perhaps it was some kind of autopilot, Owen surmised, as he stood frozen in the doorway.

Before he could make up his mind what to do next, Padma appeared from the kitchen door and threw her arms around him.

The Treaty of Lausanne

'What do you think we should do?' Padma said in a trembling voice. Owen had no idea. As she awaited his response he saw two anxious faces looking at him around the door frame. As soon as he made eye contact with them they fled. Great, he thought. His own children were frightened of him.

'Divorce, I guess.'

Padma looked concerned.

'Don't worry,' Owen said. 'You can keep on living here and we'll sort something out with the children.' He suddenly realised she was hugging him and was increasingly confused by this. What was the protocol in these circumstances; should he call the police or turn himself in? How does someone turn themselves in anyway?

'You hit me. I never thought you would. I never thought you had it in you.'

'Neither did I.' He knew he did.

'You didn't hurt me much. Mostly you missed.'

Owen looked at Padma's face and could find no evidence of any abrasion, swelling or bruising. It didn't even seem painful to the touch. Come to think of it he didn't think he had his eyes open when he hit out at his wife earlier, or at least if he had he was looking in another direction completely.

'Perhaps I hit you somewhere else?'

'No you didn't. I didn't think you'd do it at all.'

'I am so sorry. You don't know how sorry. It's a terrible thing and it will never happen again. Never.'

Padma pulled away.

'Which is why we need a divorce.' Why did he say that? It was true, he guessed, but it was very unlike him to have a plan in such circumstances.

Padma hugged her husband again. 'Don't divorce me. Please don't.'

'I hit you. It is unforgivable to hit a woman.'

'You didn't mean it, I know you didn't.' Owen recalled an episode of *Frost* he had once seen, possibly the only episode he had ever seen, in which a bullied wife made repeated excuses for her controlling violent husband. Was he a monster? What did a monster look like? Him, he supposed. The banality of evil. This phrase was dredged up from somewhere in his mind though he was too tired to even begin to work out who said it and about whom.

'I don't think we're right together. We haven't been for a long time. I'll find a lawyer for myself and I suggest you do so too.' Where was all this coming from? He had no plan and Padma was as surprised as he was that he seemed to have it all figured out. She sat down in one of the sitting room chairs and began to weep herself.

Owen looked at her and then at the children staring at him from behind the kitchen breakfast bar. They ducked immediately, so he walked over to them.

'Hey,' he said.

'You hit mammy, you nasty daddy,' Ifan said, and threatened his father with a plastic screwdriver from his toy tool kit.

'I know. That was wrong and I should not have done that.' Owen felt ashamed. His own father, God rest his soul, had warned him against this very thing. He was nothing like his father. He was a tired wife-beating fool.

'Why did mammy break your picture?' Rhys said.

'It was an accident. Accidents happen. Remember the time Ifan nailed the floor today?' Ifan looked sheepish. The three boys in unison felt the dimpled, broken wood with their fingers and Owen marvelled how a boy so young could be strong enough to cause such damage.

'Sorry about the nail,' Ifan said, and his face contorted so dramatically that Owen knew he was about to start crying with a vengeance. He held him tight and kissed him on the head.

'Can we forget the whole thing and move on?' Owen said, feeling guilty for asking children to keep the secrets of adults for their own benefits.

'Sorry about the nail,' Ifan said again.

Owen laughed. 'Forget about the nail. We'll forget everything. Let's have a happy day today.'

'Let's go to the sea,' Rhys said.

'Let us stay here and hug,' Owen replied. 'Let me speak with mammy because I think she's upset.'

Owen got up and made his way back to the sitting room. He couldn't quite explain why he felt more in control now than he had ever had, but felt strong guilt for it all the same. Padma was still on the edge of the sofa crying into a handkerchief. Owen sat down on the floor next to her.

'You OK?'

'I don't want to be a single mother. I don't want the children to grow up without their father. I want you around. I like being Mrs Morgan.'

'You know it's for the best.' Padma's crying intensified as he said this. Owen recognised that he was in no real position to judge whether a divorce really was the best way forward, today of all days, but felt pressed to continue. Was it sadism? Was it realism? He certainly did not want to stay married to her; in fact had not wanted to be married to her for a long time.

'What about the children? My poor innocent children?'

Owen considered he had never known his wife's mind, but a realisation was starting to dawn on him. She had threatened divorce many times and had treated him badly on occasion but until now Owen had never shown his hand emotionally, just used each new development as an adjustment to some inner mathematical algorithm that was tasked with producing a plan of action but never came to any definitive conclusions.

'They saw a terrible thing today, Padma. Terrible. Something they should never have seen. Ifan almost attacked me with a screwdriver because of it.'

Padma laughed through her tears. The laugh was short-lived however and she was back to her blubbering in no time. 'I want to stay married to you, I want to work something out. We can do it, I know we can.'

There is nothing more peculiar than people, Owen told himself. Sometimes, in order to make peace an enemy has to know your strength. Perhaps his concessions over the years had led to this. Perhaps it could work after all. It would certainly be a lot less hassle, he thought.

CHAPTER 28

Moira

L ATER THAT EVENING Owen called round at the family home in Neath, still a little disconnected due to the day's events.

'How are you, mam?'

'Do you want some tea?'

'Go on then, thanks. Everyone gone then?'

'Angharad left an hour ago. She waited for you, thinking you'd come, but you never did.'

'I had things to do at home.' Like punch his wife.

'I understand. You're a busy man. You only have one sister, though, and it would be nice if you got on more.'

'I'll call her.'

'There's a good boy. You know it still hasn't sunk in. Look over there.' His mother pointed at a perfectly-made dinner wrapped in cellophane on the kitchen worktop. 'I made it for your father by accident. I've been doing it all week. I forget that he's not coming home so rather than throw the food out I wrap it up. I don't know why.' She leant both hands against the table and closed her eyes, as if trying to stifle tears. She appeared to be winning. Owen, realising he should be doing something emotional, stood up and walked over to his mother. Now what? Should he hug her or pat her on the back? They had never been a Mediterranean-style hugging, kissing family so hugging seemed alien and a pat on the back just seemed weird. Instead Owen stood next to his mother, his arms dangling uselessly by his side.

After a minute she regained her composure. 'Kettle's boiled,' she said.

'How much did Dai charge for the Lamb and Flag?'

'Not much. He's good, our Dai. Apparently he's related in some way to Uncle Theo so we consider him family.'

'Got a bit of an opinion on everything though, hasn't he?'

His mother sipped her tea. 'Yes, he has.' Talk of Dai, or indeed any other character, would normally incite a colourful conversation on everybody's failings or relative merits but not tonight. Owen realised it was silly to continue to pretend it was all normal.

'I've been crying too, mam. I felt I...' Confessing his true feelings was still beyond Owen, he realised, and so decided to retreat a bit to sturdier ground. 'If you need anything, just call. I'll be here whenever you need me.'

'You're busy,' she told the teacup. 'You're both busy. I understand.'

It was true, Owen confessed. He felt very guilty in fact, though the feeling was so nebulous that rather than dealing with specific points he thought it best to let it settle like dust over everything. 'Just call, mam.'

Suddenly she brightened. 'Do you want the dinner?'

'Yes. There is nothing I'd like more.' He did not want the dinner.

As he forced himself to eat the large dinner, he considered that this sort of diet must have been a contributory factor in his father's myocardial infarction. That and his son, of course. As he ate silently, his mother busied about the kitchen wiping surfaces that were already clean and rearranging cupboards and shelves that looked well-organised and tidy as they were. Perhaps it was predetermined, Owen mused. Perhaps it would have happened anyway. God had not saved him, though perhaps he was in a better place right now and was luckier for it. Death was always said to be harder on those left behind, but how could such a statement ever be scientifically validated when no data from beyond the grave could ever be collected? Still, if a test could be devised it would secure a paper in the Christmas BMJ at least.

What if life was predetermined? That he would have married Padma, that his father would have died and he would have had such trouble with his career despite his best efforts? Perhaps he had not invested his best efforts after all? He got into medical school despite the odds. Was that due to divine intervention or the result of hard work? Divine intervention. Was there such a thing? He'd prayed over cataracts and prayed over his father but nothing had come to any good.

The meat was a bit tough but a mother's cooking always has a peculiar taste that sets it apart from all other cooking in some indescribable way. His mother had always looked after him well but he had let her down at every opportunity. No more, he told himself. From now on he'd be there for her. His new, and odd, stability pact with Padma would see to it that he had enough freedom to help with such things.

As Owen harpooned a piece of broccoli with his fork, his thoughts returned once more to predestination. He had once dated an Islamic girl in medical school who had informed him quite confidently that everything in the world had already been planned, so to try and change things would be utterly pointless. When they broke up he asked her if that too had been determined and with utter conviction she replied that it must have been, as it had just happened. What about the value of work? If your path was determined, why try at all? Because the amount you tried had also been predetermined, was the answer. This did not sit well with Owen as he was frightened of being out of control, of being unable to make his own decisions.

He asked his mother for a piece of bread to mop up the remaining gravy on the plate. Although this had been a tradition in his family, Owen knew that this was a working-class indicator and so he always asked for bread with the pride of a man with a chip on his shoulder. It didn't count with his mother of course, as she had always given out pieces of bread after a gravy-based meal.

It dawned on Owen that he'd been the perfect example of the compliant Islamic man that had scared him so much a decade earlier. He could not think of a single decision he'd taken, ever, that had altered the course of his future. Not one. He'd almost taken a decision earlier to divorce Padma but that seemed to have been scotched now. At the time though, it seemed as if the decision was being made elsewhere and he was merely a puppet. Perhaps Islam was the way forward for him; that would certainly be a way of upsetting his mother as much as he possibly could in a single human lifetime.

Decision

On the way home in the car, Owen remembered the text he had received from Colleen. He'd thought about her many times but had not actually called her back at all. If he didn't do it now he'd forget and it would be like history repeating itself all over again. He pulled over and called her.

'Owen,' she said. 'I thought you'd started to ignore me again.'

'Nonsense,' he said. So she had been offended all those years ago, after all. 'I've had a pretty bad time since I last spoke to you, to be honest.' He told her the whole story in the following forty-five minutes, the death of his father and even the domestic incident despite being very embarrassed about this and not intending to tell her at all. She listened patiently, so patiently in fact that when Owen stopped occasionally to formulate his thoughts she would not interject and on more than one occasion he thought she'd hung up on him. He wouldn't blame her if she had, of course.

'Sounds awful,' she said. 'I am sorry to hear that. Really.'

'Thanks.' Owen was conscious of the fact that she hadn't said 'mate' as she usually did. 'I think in all probability divorce is the only answer here. You were right in Cardiff.' Hesitatingly he began to tell Colleen his new theory about human volition. Padma would never have tolerated such abstract thought about issues of no real relevance and he was unsure if Colleen would think him even more bizarre than she might already do if he mentioned it. Oddly she did not seem to hold against him the sins he had committed and he felt better for talking to her.

'When are you next down in Wales on a course?'

'There is no course in Wales again.'

'Oh.'

'But I could come down if you wanted me to.'

Owen was never really a man who picked up on subtleties but he felt a door opening somewhere, although he was unsure where.

'Well. Do you want me to come and visit? We could go for a pint again. I'm good at cheering people up, you know.'

'I imagine you are. You know he died when I saw you last time.'

'So I'm a harbinger of death, am I?'

'No.' Oh great; he'd upset her needlessly now. 'I just feel guilty for having enjoyed the time with you instead of being with him.'

'Apparently Gandhi felt similarly guilty for making love to his wife while, unknown to him, his mother lay dying upstairs.'

Owen melted. How lovely to hear such a comment from the lips of a woman. This misogynistic thought shocked him and for a brief moment he considered whether he had a Professor Higgins complex.

She was not finished though. 'It was because of that incident that he became such a firm believer in sexual abstinence and control.' This was the kind of conversation he could have with himself, he thought. No need to anguish over the correct things to say or do.

'I love you,' he said without really processing the information. Bloody hell, what had he just said? He was lulled into a false sense of security and had now caused a big problem for himself. She'd hang up and he'd lose his only good friend.

'Uh, to be truthful, if I'm being honest…' she said. What was this? She hadn't hung up. 'I've always liked you too.'

Owen was unable to formulate an answer as his brain had stalled.

'I'm sure you knew that, though. Ever since medical school.'

'No. I knew nothing of this,' Owen said in a hesitating, stammering voice. Even though he had dreamed of this moment countless times over the past few days, the transition from dream to unexpected reality was an extremely stressful one. He was now being tested in a completely new way and new things were stressful for Owen.

'I asked you out to the medical school dance, we had endless coffees and meals when we were house officers and we got drunk together so many times I cannot remember.'

'You were always going out with other people though.' Yes, what about that, eh?

'Only because you never asked me out. I thought I'd made it clear to you.'

'Oh no. But now you have your Navy guy.'

'And you have a wife and two children.'

Neither Owen nor Colleen could think of anything to say at this point. Owen checked his phone; he'd been on the phone now for the past hour and five minutes and the red 'low battery' light had begun to flash.

'My low battery light has begun to flash,' he said.

'Mine's been flashing for the past ten minutes.' Even their phones were in harmony.

'I really want to see you, Colleen. I made a huge error in not recognising obvious things. I think I…'

'Listen. Before my battery conks out.' She said 'conks', Owen thought, how sweet. 'I am here for you, as a friend, as a… Well, I'll leave it up to you. You make a decision about what you want and then we'll meet up. If you decide you don't… Well if you don't… Then that's OK with me too.'

'Goodnight, Colleen.' It sounded formal as soon as he'd said it but he felt awkward saying anything else. Did the fact that he and his old friend had opened up in such a way mean that he should have said something more emotional, more passionate? Perhaps she knew he was not a passionate man and did not expect such a response.

'Goodnight, Owen.' The phone clicked, indicating she had hung up and Owen then restarted the engine and continued homeward.

Evidently not, he concluded, which was just fine by him.

The Homecoming

Owen's head spun as he drove, spun so much in fact that he was grateful it was past midnight and there was no traffic on the road for he would surely have struck a vehicle if it had been earlier. Past midnight! How could time have gone so fast? Then again it hadn't, Owen thought, as the earlier domestic punch-up seemed so long ago that it was in a different century, the funeral a different millennium. Hang on, if it was past midnight and so many things had taken place why had Padma not called? Was she frightened to? Did she not care? Perhaps she'd be angry that he'd been out with his mother, and Colleen in a way, so late? What about their new peace treaty, though?

Half an hour later he pulled into their drive and by the glow of the sitting room window he knew Padma was still awake. He sat in the car for a further ten minutes looking at the glow in the window. Had she somehow become aware of the conversation he'd just had with Colleen? Although the idea seemed crazy, his mind had been fried by this point and he was not entirely sure what was mirage and what was sand. He had begun to doubt whether the conversation with Colleen had happened already. Could he call her to confirm? Owen doubted she would appreciate that either way.

He unlocked the door and dutifully placed his shoes in the cloakroom and hung his coat on his dedicated hook; just like Padma had always implored him to. This was possibly the only time he'd remembered to perform this task although its completion on this occasion proved unusually satisfying. Padma was asleep on the sofa, the Tiffany lamp next to her illuminating her small vulnerable body, curled up in the foetal position. Owen sighed. How could someone so vulnerable be responsible for so many problems? Was it really all her fault? He now had a way out, courtesy of Colleen, but how would Padma cope with it? How would his two children cope? How would he cope? That Tiffany lamp had cost almost £900, he suddenly remembered. Nine hundred pounds; what a waste. That would have paid for a month-and-a-half of mortgage payments.

'Padma,' Owen said as he shook her. 'It's night time. You need to be in bed. Come on.'

Padma slowly opened her eyes and looked at him, confused for a moment.

'It's 1am. Come on. Let's go to bed.'

'I thought you wouldn't come back,' she said.

What was clear a moment ago regarding his future was now

murky once more. Various decisions and outcomes jostled against each other until the path ahead was obscured with foliage, just like it usually was. Perhaps the clarity he had experienced earlier had itself been an illusion.

'I did.' He helped Padma upstairs to bed and switched the bed-warmer on for her. As he lay down on his half of the bed, he ruminated about how it would be if this were the last time he'd have this experience. Owen told himself that even though Padma seemed alone and vulnerable now, this was probably because she was sleeping. Things wouldn't really change, would they? He logically concluded they would not. Logically speaking, he'd be better off with Colleen and he might even be happy. His children? His children. The thought was too painful for him to process. Either way, the outcome would not be great.

Padma started to twitch next to him. Her gentle brown skin wrinkled in the soft light of the bedside lamp and her long black hair framed her face perfectly. Perhaps he was wrong about her. She was so beautiful, always had been. How much control did a person truly have over their destiny anyway? Was it all really predetermined? Was it written that he'd always stay married to Padma forever more? Could he alter his destiny? That study with the MRI machine had indicated that we became aware of our decisions only after the subconscious had already made them. The illusion of choice, perhaps.

Padma stirred again. 'Turn the fucking light off,' she said, before turning over. Owen complied. If he truly did have control he would divorce her and marry Colleen. His mind was made up now, truly and utterly. The fog cleared once again and he could see an alternate life unfold before him, just as he had before. How did one divorce? He'd have to look it up on Google in the morning. Yes, nothing could possibly happen that could change his mind now, he thought. Just a few words had made him see sense. Yes, he would not take the easy path; he'd forge a new path for himself and make positive decisions that would bring about a better future. The details he would work out later. Owen determined to prove his old Islamic girlfriend wrong. Perhaps he'd send her a text once it was all over, just to prove a point.

CHAPTER 29

The phone call

THE NEXT MORNING Owen was awoken by Ifan poking him repeatedly in the eye. It took him a few moments to orientate himself, he was so tired from the previous day's events dropping Padma at Heathrow.

'I wee-wee'd in the bed,' he said sheepishly. Normally Padma would sort this kind of problem out but in her absence Owen stood up and made his way to his son's bedroom. The bed did indeed have a large damp patch on it and the bedclothes were sodden. Great.

'Don't worry, my baby,' he said, picking Ifan up and hugging him tight. A feeling of cold dampness made itself known on his abdomen and he looked down in time to see that the urine, after affecting every visible external surface was now affecting his own. He'd have to launder a whole big pile of clothing now. What a great start to his time as a single father, he thought.

'Don't worry, we'll just change your trousers then we'll go downstairs and have breakfast.' This horror could wait. 'Let's wake Rhys up.'

Rhys was already awake when they entered his room, colouring in a large picture of Wall-E from his prized colouring book. 'Look at this daddy,' he said, proudly holding up the almost completed picture of a green Wall-E. 'I made him green.'

Owen laughed. 'So I see. Let's go downstairs and have breakfast.'

'Yay,' he said, and his two boys bounced past him and half-tumbled downstairs before their father had even reached the bedroom door. While they were busily concerned with trying to turn the kitchen television on so they could watch CBeebies while they ate their Coco Pops and toast, a treat denied them by their mother, Owen padded to the bathroom to try and wash some of the sleep out of his eyes. He looked even more scruffy than usual in the bathroom mirror. How could he look after two boys until Padma returned from Malaysia? He looked like a tramp, hair all untidy and skin pasty and white. Owen scratched his head. Perhaps a tramp didn't have pasty white skin on account of all the outdoor living. Either way though, he didn't look like what other people considered a responsible adult was meant to look, not at the moment anyway.

'Daddy, we're hungry,' Rhys shouted from the kitchen. Owen decided to forego brushing teeth, shaving and other niceties and descended the stairs to fix breakfast for his boys.

'All ready for Coco Pops?' he said on entering the kitchen. He saw that his boys had failed to figure out how the television worked properly as although they had managed to switch it on it was beaming out what appeared to be the *Eastenders* omnibus to two disappointed young Welshmen. Owen chuckled to himself as he switched over to CBeebies and watched his children's expression immediately transform to a smile. A cartoon sheep was teaching a whole classroom of sheep to count. The main teacher sheep appeared to have long red hair. He wondered how Colleen was getting on. He hadn't spoken with her for a long time now. She'd tried to call a few weeks ago but he'd been too busy to take the call. He'd intended to call her back but kept on forgetting. By the time he'd remembered he reckoned too much time had passed and it would have caused unnecessary awkwardness. Always a good plan to avoid awkwardness. If he didn't have to think about it perhaps it wouldn't hurt so much.

Owen placed two bowls on the worktop and filled them with

Coco Pops, then opened the fridge to retrieve some milk. No milk. 'Sorry boys. No Coco Pops this morning.'

'Daddy,' Rhys said. 'I want Coco Pops.'

'Me too,' Ifan said.

'I'll tell you what. How about some nice toast and honey instead and then we'll go back to Tesco later to get milk?'

The boys said nothing as they watched the sheep playing in the schoolyard. One of the sheep was mischievously attempting to open the school gate. Ifan gasped as he succeeded; all the other sheep were now running away from the school and the red-headed teacher sheep was ineffectually trying to round them up again.

There was no bread either. Before Owen had enough time to process this information, the phone rang. It was Padma.

'You've arrived safely. Great.'

'How is everything, how are the boys?'

'Oh they're all fine here. Ifan did a wee-wee in the night unfortunately, so I guess I have a lot of work ahead.'

Padma remained quiet for a few seconds; enough to unsettle him. 'Are the boys watching television in the kitchen?' she said, and she did not sound pleased. Before Owen could think of something to say in his defence Padma went on. 'You didn't get bread and milk like I told you to, did you?'

'Well… I'll… don't worry now…'

'You idiot. You absolute idiot. Ifan wet the bed, you didn't get the breakfast things and you're watching television in the morning. Why do you always do the wrong thing, Owen, eh? Always. You never do anything right, do you?' And for once, Owen agreed with her.

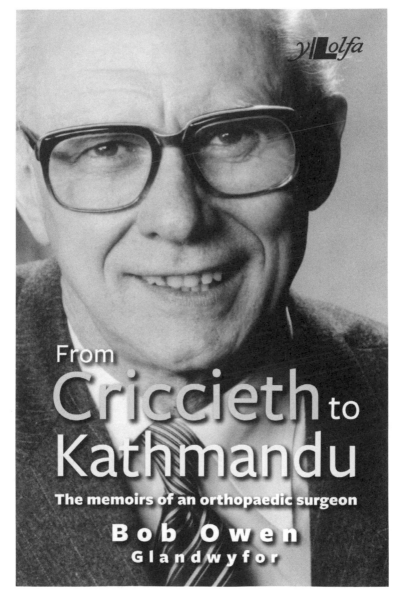

From
Criccieth to
Kathmandu
The memoirs of an orthopaedic surgeon
B o b   O w e n
G l a n d w y f o r

£6.95